The Queen's Avenger

Anna Legat

Copyright © Anna Legat 2024.

The right of Anna Legat to be identified as the author of this work has been asserted by her in accordance with the Copyright, Designs and Patents Act, 1988.

First published in 2024 by Sharpe Books.

Dramatis Personae
(Historical figures featuring in Ninian's confessions, in order of appearance)

Mary
: (born 8/12/1542) Mary Stewart, Queen of Scots. Mother of King James VI of Scotland/ James I of England. A devout Catholic. Married to Francis II, King of France (1558-60). Married to Henry Darnley (1565-67) and on his death, to James Hepburn, the Earl of Bothwell. Accused of complicity in Darnley's murder. From 1568 held prisoner by Elizabeth I until her execution in 1587.

Ninian Winzet
: (born 1519) Mary's secretary and covert confessor. Provost of the Collegiate Church of St Michael, Linlithgow. Theologian and champion of Catholicism in Scotland. Ardent opponent of John Knox. Queen Mary's loyal supporter and a member of her embassy to Elizabeth I.

    From 1577, Abbott of the Benedictine Monastery of St James, Ratisbon ("the Scottish Monastery") until his death in 1592.

Moray
: (born 1531) James Stewart, the 1st Earl of Moray (since 1562). The illegitimate son of James V. Mary's half-brother. A Protestant and one of the Lords of the Congregation. Mary's mentor on her return to Scotland, he later rebelled against her and forced her abdication. Regent of Scotland during James VI's minority. Assassinated in 1570.

Darnley	(born 7/12/1545) Henry Stuart, son of the 4th Earl of Lennox, with a strong dynastic claim to the English throne. A Catholic. Queen Mary's husband until his assassination at Kirk o'Field in 1567.
Bothwell	(born 1535) James Hepburn, the Earl of Bothwell. A Protestant. Mary's general recalled to Scotland to suppress Moray's rebellion. Accused of murdering Darnley in order to marry Queen Mary. Fled Scotland after her surrender to the Lords at Carberry Hill. Died insane in captivity (1578).
Morton	(born 1516) James Douglas, the 4th Earl of Morton. A Protestant and one of the Lords of the Congregation. Mary's zealous accuser. A leading player in the assassination of Rizzio. Regent of Scotland after Moray's death. Executed in 1581 for his part in the murder of Darnley.
Ruthven	(born 1520) Lord Patrick Ruthven. A Protestant and one of the Lords of the Congregation, although Darnley's supporter. A leading player in the assassination of Rizzio. Died in exile in Newcastle-upon-Tyne in 1566, raving about visions of spirits come to get him.
Maitland	(born 1525) Sir William of Lethington. A Protestant. Mary's Secretary of State. Involved in the conspiracy to assassinate Rizzio, he took Moray's side against the Queen. As a proponent of Scotland's union with England, he later tried to have

	Mary exonerated and restored to the Scottish throne. He died by his own hand, taking poison, to escape execution by Morton (1573).
Rizzio	(born 1533) David Rizzio. A Catholic. An Italian musician and courtier who became Mary's Private Secretary in 1564. Murdered by the Lords acting in concert with Darnley.
Leslie	(born 1527) John Leslie, Bishop of Ross. A Catholic. Mary's adviser and ardent supporter, he led her embassy, defending her cause in York. Implicated in conspiracies to put Mary on the English throne, he fled to France.
Cardinal de Lorraine	(born 1524) Charles de Lorraine, Duke of Chevreuse, France. A Catholic. Member of the influential de Guise family who led the persecution of Huguenots. Mary's uncle and her mentor.
Duc de Guise	(born 1550) Henry I of Lorraine, Prince of Joinville. An ardent Catholic, he led the persecution of Huguenots. Mary's uncle on her mother's side.
Balfour	(born 1525) Sir James Balfour, Lord Pittendreich. Member of Mary's Privy Council. Opposed to her marriage to Darnley, he was implicated in Darnley's assassination at Kirk o'Field, a house owned by Balfour's brother, Robert.

Sir William Douglas	(born 1540) the 6th Earl of Morton; Moray's half-brother by his mother Margaret Erskine who was James V's mistress. Mary was kept prisoner at his castle at Lochleven prior to escaping to England.
Willy Douglas	An orphan and cousin of Sir William, he lived at Lochleven and helped organise Mary's escape.
George Douglas	(born 1544) brother of Sir William Douglas. He organised Mary's escape from Lochleven.
Kirkcaldy	(born c. 1520) Sir William Kirkcaldy of Grange. He persuaded Mary to surrender to the Lords at Carberry Hill. Later appointed Lord High Admiral of Scotland.
Lindsay	(born 1521) Patrick Lindsay, the 6th Lord Lindsay of the Byres. Confederate Lord. He forced Mary to abdicate at Lochleven in favour of her son, James VI.
Robert Stewart	(born 1533) 1st Earl of Orkney. An illegitimate son of James V; Mary's half-brother and her supporter.
John Hamilton	(born 1512) Archbishop of St Andrew's and the last primate of the Catholic Church in Scotland. Mary's supporter implicated in the assassination of Moray.
James Bothwellgaugh	John Hamilton's nephew. He assassinated Moray at Linlithgow in 1570.

Herries	(born 1512) John Maxwell, 4th Baron Herries. A Catholic and Mary's staunch adherent.
Norfolk	(born 1536) Thomas Howard, 4th Duke of Norfolk. A Protestant and Queen Elizabeth's second cousin; one of her Commissioners at York where Mary's case was heard. He colluded with Maitland to become Mary's fourth husband. Executed for his involvement in the Ridolfi Plot to free Mary.
Sadler	(born 1507) Sir Ralph Sadler. Member of Elizabeth's Privy Council and one of her Commissioners at the York Conference.

THE QUEEN'S AVENGER

PART 1

29th September 1592, Ratisbon, Bavaria

Brother Gunther's attention was straying. He forced his gaze up to the apsis to seek inspiration for his night prayer, but none came. The scene of the Crucifixion at the high altar – the Lord's earthly form prostrate on the Cross, his spirit departed – served only to remind Gunther of the passing of Abbot Ninian. His thoughts drifted further to the scrolls hidden behind the wall panel in his scriptorium. Gunther was eager to get back to them.

He had uncovered them accidentally after Mass this morning. He had been assigned the task of cleaning the late Abbot's chambers by Father Archibald who was to succeed Ninian. The office was yet to be conferred upon him by His Holiness in Rome, but that was a mere formality. Father Archibald was desirous to take residence in the elevated tower apartment as soon as possible.

Never before had Gunther been granted access to the Abbot's lodgings. He had found his bedchamber basic in comforts, befitting the Benedictine vow of poverty and abstention: a simple bed, an enamel washbasin, a prie-dieu with a cushion to kneel upon in prayer and a wood carving of Holy Mary, her robes painted pale blue, trimmed with gold. A scourge whip with nails set in leather straps lay beside a lantern and a Holy Book on a small sideboard. A Cross of rosewood hung dominant above the door.

Abbot Ninian had been an avid advocate of asceticism. In his teachings, he would often warn the brothers against material and carnal temptations. It appeared he had lived by what he had preached.

The late Abbot's scriptorium however painted a very different picture of his character. Gunther would have no words to describe the pandemonium he had walked into as he stepped over the threshold of the airless chamber, small as it already were, and made even smaller by the accumulation of clutter. The desk, central to the room, was grunting under the weight of heavy volumes, parchments, quills broken and spent, papers crumpled by a frustrated hand, discarded and forgotten, inkwells with the tar of dry ink hardened inside, a knife for sharpening quills, a double candlestick caked in yellow beeswax, two oil lamps, one chipped, with a missing handle, the other new, its belly glistening. The walls were draped with pine shelves heaving under the weight they carried, darkened with age, cramped with books written principally in Latin, but also a few in German, French and Italian, as well as copious pamphlets and ledgers, some bound in leather, some in wood. The smell in the scriptorium was that of mould and decay, and something sour that Brother Gunther associated with death.

He had cleared the desk and scrubbed it, spots of hard-set wax peeling off the surface like old skin from a snake. He had refilled the inkwells and sealed them with stoppers. He had gone about washing the wood-panelled walls and wiping layers of dust from the skirting boards when his eyes became drawn to an ill-fitting panel. Curiously, it was covered with many inky fingerprints. Gunther attacked the stains with vigour and pressed hard to remove them when the panel gave a dry click and sprung open. Behind it, was a small vault packed with scrolls.

Gunther pulled them out and spread them on the desk. He sat – somewhat meekly – in the Abbot's worn chair, unfolded the first scroll and scanned its contents. He was unable to read it. It was written in Scots, Abbot Ninian's native language. A single page document, it had been endorsed by several signatories, and sealed in red wax. His curiosity aroused, he unfurled another scroll, this one consisting of many sheets bundled together. To his delight, it was written in Latin, a language that Gunther was proficient at. Each document bore the same date in the top-right corner. It was recent: the fifteenth day of September 1592. Just two Sundays ago.

Gunther peered about him anxiously as if to check whether the dead Abbot's spirit wasn't in attendance, resentful of the intrusion. But the room was stilled in its airless silence. Gunther began to read:

My feet are cold and numb. When I try to walk they feel like millstones chained to my ankles. I often stumble over them as if they are somebody else's, not mine. Yesterday morning I woke with the horror of my breath being sucked out of my chest. My scream was no more than a wheeze of a dying man. For that's what is happening to me: I am dying. I can sense Death's presence at the foot of my bed, her chilling breath, her probing touch and her stare – deep into my soul.

I am an old man – three-and-seventy years of age. My time has come. I haven't got long left on this earth but I trust the good Lord will grant me time enough to complete this, my last deposition.

All my life I have been the Lord's humble servant, a protector of the true Religion, a deliverer of God's divine will. Although my hands are stained with blood, I acted in good faith, for the glory of Christ. If I was misguided, if I have overstepped my authority, the Lord will be my judge when the seven trumpets of the Apocalypse are sounded.

With Death at my bedside, I must now unburden my conscience before Christ.

The tolling of bells pounded Gunther about the head. He jumped with a start and took a while to steady his heart. His startled mind had to be calmed and tethered back to earth. What he was hearing weren't the trumpets of Judgment Day but the Angelus Bell calling him to midday prayer. Hastily he rolled the scrolls back up and returned them to the secret compartment in the wall. Then he hurried to *Jakobskirche* to join his brothers in prayer.

He had spent the rest of the day on his regular chores in the monastery garden, more prayer, the daily Chapter room meeting, Vespers, supper and the Compline service of night prayer. His mind had been wandering restlessly throughout the day, drawn back to the hidden vault in the dead Abbot's study.

At long last, the final note of the organ seeped away and Father Archibald blessed the monks and let them go in Christ's peace. Gunther pulled on his hood and hitched up his habit. He emerged into the night and crossed the cloisters towards the Abott's lodgings in the East Tower. He took care to sneak through the shadows so as not to be discovered. The night conspired with him in his endeavours. In the past hour the wind had picked up from the north, carrying on its back heavy rain. Nobody would venture out in this weather. Gunther's mysterious manoeuvres would hopefully go unnoticed.

He burst into the Abbot's scriptorium and threw his soaked cowl onto the floor. He lit the oil lamp. The room filled with a flickering golden glow. The flame was being tugged at by an invisible draught.

Gunther retrieved the scrolls, made himself comfortable in the Abbot's chair and started to read from where he had left off in the morning.

THE QUEEN'S AVENGER

I

Written on this the Fifteenth Day of September in the Year of our Lord 1592

I was a young priest at the time of Mary Stewart's birth, having entered Holy Orders only a few years earlier. Her birth should have been a joyous occasion, alas it was marred by the grave illness of her father, King James, who had succumbed to melancholy after his defeat at Solway Moss.

The memory of Mary's nativity is vivid in my mind despite the elapse of time. It was a bitterly cold December day — the Feast of the Immaculate Conception of the Virgin Mary. The loch lay frozen solid and the snow, knee-deep, capped the hills and valleys as far as the eye could see. On that day our lives became intertwined: she, a beautiful rose – I, a stake driven into the ground by her side to lean upon.

I was the provost of the collegiate church of St Michael. It stood near the main gate leading to Linlithgow Palace where Marie de Guise had been delivered of her daughter merely days before her husband King James's death. He was never to lay his eyes on his child and sole heir. I felt the babe's loss deeply in my heart. She was an orphan and thus easy prey to those who craved to subjugate her.

I could hear God's calling to guard and protect her. I made that vow as Mary's tiny form was handed to me by Archbishop Hamilton to hold at the font as he baptised her. She peered at me with her large, trusting eyes and in that moment she stole my heart, never to release it.

She would grow up to become a strong and courageous woman, but that day when I carried her from the high altar, she was as pale as the white taffeta of her christening robe and as light and frail as a petal kissed by frost. We were uncertain how long she would stay with us. Her survival was in God's hands. All we could do was pray.

After the ceremony, we proceeded to the palace to celebrate. We crossed the courtyard, past the fountain of mermaids, minstrels and beasts draped with icicles, and headed for the great hall. Tapestries warmed the cold stone of the walls and a brisk fire raged in the grate under the sprawling chimney breast. Food and wine were served. We soon warmed up and our moods lifted. Even little Mary's cheeks coloured pink before she was removed to her nursery to rest. Queen Marie watched her daughter with anxious eyes as the babe was carried away in her nurse's arms.

As her gaze turned to me, she gripped my arm and whispered, 'I fear for her safety, Ninian. Wolves are circling around her, hungry for power, keen to sink their claws into her. With her father gone – God rest his soul – she is the ward of the Holy Church. Swear to me that you will watch over her.'

'I will,' said I. 'As God is my witness. I would've done so even if you hadn't asked, Your Grace.'

THE QUEEN'S AVENGER

II

Written on this the Fifteenth Day of September in the Year of our Lord 1592

At the age of five, Mary was taken to the safety of France and placed under the protection of King Henry. She would be closely guarded by her powerful uncles, the Duke of Guise and Cardinal of Lorraine, both ardent defenders of the true Religion. I remained in office as Provost at St Michael's and became Master of Linlithgow Grammar School. My hands were full and my heart was filled with hope for the future of Scotland allied with France and the Holy Roman Empire. But hope is the mother of fools and ten years later I could scarcely recognise my homeland.

Heresy had seeped into Scotland and spilled like floodwater. Its propagators embarked on a mission to poison minds and corrupt souls. Soon they reached Linlithgow. Madness descended on the erstwhile decent and God-fearing folk of our town. Hysteria. Fear. Witch hunts. False prophecies and accusations. Bigotry. When the Devil knocked on the door of St Michael's, it was too late for me to fend him off. I had not seen him coming.

It was late spring, 1560. Seven years earlier, Dean Kinlochy had arrived in Linlithgow to seek a teaching post at the school of which I was Master. His blasphemous views had become all too transparent to me the moment he opened his mouth. I refused his application and sent him away, telling him that he should count himself lucky that I didn't have him interned and put on trial. Alas he stayed in town. I knew he would set out to destroy me, but I did not realise that he would also challenge the true Faith amongst my flock and turn them against it.

He began to parade himself as a man of God. He was no such thing. He was an imposter and a liar. A false prophet, he preached heresy and heralded the fall of the Holy Church. His venomous words filled the hearts of the good people of Linlithgow with hatred. He sowed division and mistrust, and soon built his private army of converts. I watched through my fingers and did nothing to stop him. I underestimated him. I was arrogant and a fool, may the merciful Lord forgive me.

On that momentous spring night, one that changed the course of my life, I was in my church, immersed in prayer. I was startled when suddenly the door flew open and Widow Ainsley burst in, her hair loose about her shoulders, a wild look in her eyes. She was wearing nothing but her chemise, her feet bare. They clapped against the flagstones as she tore towards me.

'Protect me, Father! I've done no evil!' She threw herself at my feet and wrapped her arms around my knees. I stared bewildered at her blood-stained hands and shift.

Before I could utter a word, a band of Kinlochy's partisans charged after her, carrying swords, clubs and pitchforks into the church. Kinlochy was at the head of the party, bellowing for me to surrender *the witch*.

'You're in the house of God. Lower your arms!' I demanded, but they only rattled them with greater menace and called for me to step aside. That sent Catherine Ainsley into fervent protestations of her innocence. She crawled on her hands and knees and cowered, whimpering, behind the altar. I knew Widow Ainsley to be a decent, law-abiding woman, a skilled midwife and a member of my dwindling congregation. She was no witch.

'Step aside and let us apprehend her. Do as you're asked, priest, lest you wish to be charged with harbouring a fugitive from justice,' Kinlochy was posturing before me, his naked dagger aimed at my throat. To this day I remember the whites of his eyes matted with bloody veins and the tips of his teeth flashing underneath his beard as he bellowed his wild accusations: 'She is a sorceress and the Devil's consort – a murderess of the innocent, a practitioner of black magic. A witch! Behold her bloodied hands, priest, and get out of my way!'

I snatched the liturgical Cross from beside the high altar and, heavy as it was, I raised it above my head. 'Do not dare break the peace of this temple! This woman seeks sanctuary on sacred ground,' I thundered. 'And she shall receive it. As long as she remains here you will not touch a hair on her head.'

'Seize her!' Kinlochy ordered his men as if I had not spoken.

THE QUEEN'S AVENGER

I stepped forward and brandished the Cross. 'You will have to go through me and through Christ Himself. You will have to shed blood in the House of God.'

'This hovel is no House of God!' Kinlochy's face coloured crimson. 'Seize her!' But the ruffians stopped in their tracks and began to withdraw. With the crucifix in my hand, I had drawn a line even they wouldn't cross. They sheathed their knives and lowered their pitchforks. A murmur of embarrassment rippled through them. Kinlochy saw it too and knew he was defeated.

'Mark my words, papist,' he spat at my feet, 'your end is nigh.'

When I finally soothed Catherine Ainsley with a cup of wine and a good word, she explained what I had suspected may have led to this. She had been called to assist Mistress Bryden in childbirth. Too late, for by the time she arrived, having been dragged out of her bed in her nightclothes, the babe's heartbeat was faint and slowing, and the mother was bleeding profusely. The poor woman fought valiantly but soon began to fall in and out of consciousness. Her soul was ready to depart her failing body.

Save my son! Master Bryden was yelling at the midwife, *Cut him out of her womb!* But Catherine knew that would achieve nothing. The babe's heartbeat had stopped and the mother lay lifeless in her own blood. *Call a priest,* Catherine advised, *We must pray for their souls.* But Master Bryden would have none of it. He grabbed her by the shoulders and screamed for her to bring them back. When she shook her head, he branded her a witch and a murderess. He screamed vile curses at her. Suddenly men were running towards the house with flaming torches and weapons, and with claims of witchery on their lips. Widow Ainsley fled through the window and headed for the sanctuary of St Michael's.

'You'll have to leave the town,' I told her. 'They'll be waiting for you in the morning, crying for blood. You can't stay here.'

She agreed, but tears welled up in her eyes. Linlithgow was her home. She had done nothing to deserve banishment.

We left before dawn. We slipped past two of Kinlochy's henchmen who had fallen asleep on the steps of the church while guarding the exit. I saddled a horse for me and a docile mule for her, and we headed west, to the town of Renfrew, my birthplace. I intended to plead for shelter for the homeless widow with my elder brother Douglas.

It was a journey of five days on horseback. Fearing pursuit, we travelled along lightly trodden paths and camped under the starry sky. Widow Ainsley was unaccustomed to the saddle and to wearing breeches (I thought it prudent to disguise her as a servant boy), but she did not complain and was able to conjure food out of what she could forage in the forest.

On the third night, as we sat over a campfire, I confessed to her my regrets. I had allowed a godless preacher – a charlatan and corrupter of souls – to take over my parish. Like a weed he had spread his tendrils unchecked, and they took root in people's minds. I blamed myself for his rise. I had let my flock down. If only I could turn back time! If only I could hold a mirror to Kinlochy's eyes and exorcise his demons!

'You can't reverse time, Father, but it is possible to give a man a glimpse of his soul. This I can help you with.'

I was intrigued albeit cautious. 'Only God can look into a man's soul. Only God... and the Devil,' I uttered my doubt and swiftly averted my eyes from her. For a moment, I almost believed that Catherine Ainsley was indeed a practitioner of the dark arts and that she could peer into my heart. That moment passed as soon as I heard her explanation.

'Man too can reach into his own soul. Isn't that what the sacrament of confession is about? Have faith in me, Father. I do not consort with Satan. I don't need to. I have my plants. There are plants that can take you to places buried deep inside you and make you see the naked truth about yourself. A man with his conscience clear will experience peace and joy. A sinful man will be haunted by his demons all the way to his grave. Isn't that what you want for Dean Kinlochy – for him to be confronted with his own wickedness?'

I had to concede the point, unchristian as that sentiment may have been.

At dawn, before we journeyed on, she took me into the woods to collect mushrooms. I was doubtful we would find any as it wasn't the season for mushroom picking, but I soon realised we were looking for a different type of fungi. Their caps were slimy, their stalks thin but sinewy. They were the colour of an old bruise, of decay. I had seen them before but considered them poisonous, or at least, worthless. Clearly, they had higher purpose. We picked a few handfuls – they were plentiful once we found them. Catherine fed them onto a piece of string and hung them from the pommel of my saddle. They were dry and wrinkled by the time we arrived at my brother's house. He and his good wife received Widow Ainsley hospitably once I explained to them the persecution that had befallen her at Linlithgow. They agreed to offer her a roof over her head in return for some light duties around the house. I stayed with them for a week to draft my testimony of Kinlochy's desecration of St Michael's and the charges I was planning to lay against him in the Ecclesiastical Court.

Before I departed, Catherine Ainsley asked for my blessing and kissed my hand in gratitude for saving her life. She pressed a small leather pouch into my hand. 'Powdered mushrooms,' she whispered. 'Sprinkle a pinch into Kinlochy's wine and watch him battle his demons. He may live if he wins, or else, the Devil takes him.'

III

Written on this the Fifteenth Day of September in the Year of our Lord 1592

Upon my return to Linlithgow, barely three weeks after my hasty departure, I was met with a vision straight out of the Book of Revelation. It appeared to me as if the world had come to an end and the town had been possessed by the forces of Satan hellbent on erasing me and my church from the face of the earth.

I rode into the town from the side of the west quarter, pulling the reluctant mule behind me, its reins tied to my saddle and as taut as lute strings. It was an old beast, on its last legs and, to add to its misfortunes, it had acquired a limp along the way. It would dig its heels in from time to time, and refuse to move. I should have put it out of its misery two days ago when the limping began, but I had no stomach for it. I resolved to stop at Angus Murray's, the blacksmith, to let him take a look at the mule's leg, and see if it could be salvaged.

Angus Murray lived on the western periphery of Linlithgow and in that quarter everything seemed as it should be. In truth, the day was pleasant, the sun high in the sky, doing its rounds over the green hills. Despite the obstinate mule that had delayed me in my travels, I was feeling sanguine. And I was energised in my plans to take on the scourge of Dean Kinlochy and liberate the good folk of Linlithgow from his clutches once and for all.

'Father Ninian!' Angus Murray's face was a picture of sheer terror. 'What are you doing back in Linlithgow? Is your life worth nothing to you?'

'What are you speaking of?' I asked, perplexed by his bizarre outcry.

'You've been put to the horn – expelled from this town! You're not safe here!'

You're not safe here... those were the very words I had uttered to Catherine Ainsley a month earlier. Had I made a mistake by leaving with her and letting Kinlochy reign free at Linlithgow in my absence? Should I have stayed, stood my ground and discredit his false allegations? I was in no doubt that my expulsion was the work of that false preacher. I would not give him the satisfaction of defeating me without a fight.

'That rabid dog, Kinlochy!' I spat out my anger.

'Indeed,' Angus Murray nodded. 'He had you shut out of the school, too. He is the Master now.'

That was the spur I needed dug into my side to fly into action. I rose to my feet, my fury boiling over. 'Look after my mule, Angus.'

'You're leaving, Father? Wisely so—'

'Oh no, my good man. I'm on my way to confront the imposter and have him incarcerated,' I declared, surprised that the blacksmith would have thought so little of me as to believe that I'd meekly submit to a small-time crook such as Kinlochy and be run out of my town.

'No, Father! You cannot!' the man stood in my way. He towered over me like a black mountain over a hill, he being a man of considerable height and muscular build, me – a willowy scholar accustomed to holding a quill, not a sledgehammer.

'Who are you to bar me?' I challenged him, unflinching. 'Have you sold your soul to that lout, too? I thought better of you, Master Murray. Was I wrong?'

'Father Ninian, trust my judgment. I'm loyal to the Holy Church and a good Christian. I beg you, flee while you can.'

'You think I can't take on a wee ruffian? You're telling me to bow to a heretic?'

'It's not just him, Father. It's the Lords!'

'Lords?' I repeated after him, perplexed.

'The Lords of the Congregation, Father. They came at dawn with their army. Kinlochy welcomed them into the town like he owned it. It began at sunrise… the desecration, the madness—' the blacksmith shook his mass of matted curls, desolately. 'You don't want to see it, Father. Every good man faithful to Rome will be wise to stay indoors and bolt their doors, and you, Father, you must flee!'

Every muscle in my body turned to stone and the weight of my heart chained me to the floor. I stood there, in the blacksmith's workshop, disbelieving, despairing and numb. I'd heard of the covenant of the heretic lords and their blasphemous war to overturn the true Religion and make Scotland into a Calvinist pit. I'd heard of their unholy rebellion and our Queen Regent's relentless efforts to quash it. I knew she had called for help from France where her brother Duc de Guise exerted strong influence over the young King Francis and his queen consort, our very own Mary Stewart. I was convinced that help was on its way and never imagined that the Confederates would dare strike at the Queen Regent's heartland – at Linlithgow. I was not aware that they had already overthrown her and that she was on her deathbed, dying from dropsy.

I told Angus that I had to go into the town to see the sacrilege with my own eyes to believe it. I had to bear witness.

I did see it and the sight burned into my mind, and it still brings bitter tears to my eyes.

Having to avoid the high street crowded with the Congregation mercenaries, we took back alleys, with the loch to our left. I wished to reach St Michael's to rescue our most precious relics, texts and some of my own scholarly writings. The town was indeed deserted, doors bolted, windows blinded with shutters. Linlithgow Palace, stabbed with the reds of the setting sun, cut an ominous picture. Soon I was to realise that it wasn't just the sun that lent the palace walls its crimson glow. It was also the bonfire that burned at the entrance to St Michael's.

We could smell the smoke before we saw the first glint of light reflecting off the church lead roof. Someone was tolling the bell. It was bound to be one of my novices. He had barricaded himself in the tower and begun sounding the alarm the moment the rebel troops descended on the town. Angus told me the clamour of bells had started soon after they arrived. The brave lad was as good as dead. A martyr. I said a brief prayer for his soul.

We reached the graveyard. I slumped behind a tombstone, down to my knees, partly for the weakness in my limbs, partly to beseech

THE QUEEN'S AVENGER

Christ for his much-needed intervention. I prayed to God Almighty to strike the desecrators dead. There were scores of them, armed, evil-looking, all with greed and frenzy burning in their eyes. By the time I arrived, the ancient stone statues adorning the exterior of the church building had already been destroyed: crushed to pieces like broken clay pots. The most precious one, that of St Michael, our patron, that crowned the south-west buttress, had been defaced. It was a sacrilege beyond redemption. The hellish fire in the churchyard was being fed with liturgical objects as if they were dirt. Priest robes and carvings of the Saints were being tossed into the flames. Even the statue of Holy Mary Mother of God was not spared. My heart bled.

'All of it! Burn popish trinkets to the last one!' Kinlochy was thrusting his heavy frame like a bull on heat. He dashed back and forth, shouting orders and dispensing vile blasphemy to which his henchmen responded with vulgar jests and barks of laughter. His cheeks were rippling with demonic hilarity, flushed red as if he was nearing an attack of apoplexy. Oh, I wished that upon him with all my heart! *Strike him dead, oh Lord,* I murmured under my breath.

But I had not seen the worst of it yet. Only when a soldier carried a dark-wood casket towards the flames, did I clasp my mouth to push back a cry of horror. That casket held a strip of St Michael's cloak, our most valued relic. The soldier hurled it into the fire which flared in a blinding eruption.

The clapper hammered the sides of the bell with force so great that it deafened me. The sun, unwilling to witness the sacrilege, dropped behind the hills, dragging with it its dying glow. I wept. I wept tears of hopeless impotency.

Angus touched my shoulder, 'I'm sorry, Father.'

I summoned all my strength to raise my eyes to him and give him hope. 'They'll pay. God is watching. He'll make them pay.'

I swept my gaze over the courtyard swarming with ungodly villains. My eyes halted on three nobles on horseback. They too were watching the destruction of St Michael's, but unlike me, their comportment signified approval. They were chatting amongst themselves casually, grins flashing under their red beards. Three of the Lords of the Congregation – Satan's consorts, leader-heretics and spiritual degenerates: Patrick, Lord of Ruthven, a fanatical Calvinist given to the practice of the black arts; James Douglas, the Earl of Morton, a perfidious scoundrel serving himself and himself alone; and Lord James Stewart, Queen Mary's bastard half-brother, a recent and most ardent convert to the side of Darkness, the most treacherous of the lot. That day he was leading an assault on the true Faith of Scotland. Next, he would set his sights on the Scottish Crown.

THE QUEEN'S AVENGER

IV

Written on this the Fifteenth Day of September in the Year of our Lord 1592

I fled to Edinburgh where I found safe haven as a protégé of John Leslie, a prominent canon lawyer and a Lord of Session, one of the last few Scotsmen who stood steadfast and unfailing on the side of righteousness. He had served our Queen Regent, Marie de Guise, to the bitter end, and he opposed the bastard usurper, James Stewart. Our longstanding collaboration in the service of the Holy Roman Church in Scotland and of Queen Mary had begun that year – the year of Our Lord 1560. There was much to be done.

Soon after my arrival in Edinburgh, in July of that year, James Stewart, the self-appointed Regent, had sold his loyalties to the bastard queen of England, Elizabeth. He had signed a treaty recognising her legitimacy in England and renouncing Mary's claim to the English throne. A month later he coerced the Scottish Parliament to establish the Protestant Church of Scotland and to outlaw the Catholic Faith and the celebration of Holy Mass. His treasonous actions would go unpunished while Mary remained in France, powerless against the rising tide of heresy drowning her kingdom.

With every fibre in my body and every spark of God's divine inspiration in my heart, I joined Leslie in combating the blasphemers. They were led by an infamous necromancer and heretic, John Knox. He was an abominable creature. A fallen priest ejected from the lap of the Holy Church like a rabid dog, he was now spewing his profanities from the lectern of St Giles' Cathedral which he had invaded and held under his occupation. His authority was propped on the tips of the Confederate Lords' swords. His countenance was as ugly as his demeanour. Sallow-faced, with eyes as black as the pits of Hell and small sharp teeth of a feral cat, he was thin and stooped, his mangy beard falling on his chest in tentacle-like wisps. He was a hater of the fairer sex. His venomous pamphlet *The First Trumpet Against the Monstrous Regiment of*

Women, which he had written a couple of years earlier against Mary Tudor, was by 1561 circulating the streets of Edinburgh. In it, he argued against the return of our gracious Queen Mary Stewart to assume her personal rule of Scotland and to restore her kingdom to Catholicism. I crossed swords with the wretched creature many a time by way of scholarly writings on my part and vitriolic bombast from the pulpit, on his. But I could not, I confess, contain the slippery, double-tongued snake with reason and verity, for he would distort it, twist and corrupt it, and spit it into people's eyes like poison, thus blinding them to the truth.

The war of words had to be abandoned in favour of actions. Mary, now Dowager of France consigned by her mother-in-law Catherine de Medici to idle irrelevance, had to be seduced back home to Scotland before the weed of Reformation took root.

In April 1561, Leslie and I, backed by the noble lords of Scotland faithful to Rome, headed for Champagne in northern France where Mary was rumoured to be paying a round of visits to her family to seek their counsel on her future. This was the most opportune time to put forward our proposals for her return.

We intercepted her enroute from Rheims to Nancy. She agreed to receive our embassy at Vitry. We were led into a marble-paved reception room with high windows letting in the dazzling noon sun. Mary's quartered cloth of state was hung from the ceiling, declaring her *Maria dei Gratia, Regina Franciae, Scotiae, Angliae et Hiberniae*. That was Queen Mary's fighting spirit on full display: she was the true sovereign of Scotland and England, and she wanted the world to know it.

'There is hope yet,' Leslie whispered to me, relief warming his features.

I only had time to nod as at that moment Mary entered the chamber and we dipped our heads and bent our knees in deep bows. She greeted us in a voice sweeter than nectar and fragrant with kindness. When I raised my gaze to her, I was stunned by her comeliness. I had half-expected to see a grown-up version of the weakly, blue-lipped babe I had held in my arms eighteen years earlier. Instead, my breath was taken away by a vision of unsurpassed beauty. Her posture was commanding, her bosom milky-white, her neck long and unblemished, her hair – coils of pure gold, and her lips moist and sculpted in the shape of butterfly wings. She moved with the fluidity of said butterfly and emitted a scent most enchanting, a blend of lavender and rose picked at the height of summer. I felt a stirring in my groin that I had never experienced before and would never experience again, a stirring I had to suppress with an immediate, humbling urgency and for which I would rake my skin in the night most severely.

Her white veil bristled in the sunlight, giving her an ethereal glow – a hint of the martyrdom to be visited upon her twenty-five years later.

I stood in her presence rigid like a pillar of salt, tongue-tied and bewitched, while Leslie pleaded with her to hurry back to Scotland. 'The Catholic lords will stand by you, Your Majesty,' he declared, 'the earls of Huntly, Atholl and Crawford have levied an army of twenty thousand men. They are at your disposal. The bishops of Aberdeen, Moray and Ross have pledged their full support. Arrangements are being made for your safe landing at Aberdeen wherefrom you will lead your army to Edinburgh. There you will overthrow the Protestant Parliament controlled by James Stewart, a Calvinist and a traitor.'

'A traitor?'

'I have it on good authority that he is a pensioner of the English Queen.'

'His devotion to our dear cousin Elizabeth does trouble us,' Mary said, her expression apprehensive.

'He sold his soul to the Devil, Your Majesty,' Leslie exclaimed. 'And he sold you and your kingdom to the English. The whole of Scotland is longing for your return, for you are a new dawn after a long, black night. Come with us, restore the true Religion and save Scotland from the clutches of that deceitful scoundrel—'

'This is our brother you're disparaging!' A dark cloud crossed her face. I could sense her discomfort. She could hardly contain it. 'It pains us to hear of his straying from the true Faith and of his pact with Elizabeth behind our back and without our assent, but we must not act with haste. Firstly, we must strengthen our alliances – with France and with Spain. We have to secure papal blessing and His Holiness's financial backing. My coffers aren't bottomless. I trust you can appreciate that.'

'Your Majesty,' both Leslie and I bowed in submission. I was astounded at the astuteness of her mind and her political acumen.

'We wish to dispatch you as our emissaries to Rome.'

'I am at Your Majesty's service,' Leslie replied.

'And you, Father Ninian?' She fixed me with her amber eyes.

'I am here to do Your Majesty's bidding,' I declared, remembering the day of her baptism when I swore to guard and protect her with my life.

'*Bien*,' she bestowed upon me a smile of an angel. 'Let us get down to work.'

THE QUEEN'S AVENGER

V

Written on this the Fifteenth Day of September in the Year of our Lord 1592

By the time we landed on the shore of Scotland four months later, we learned that Mary was indeed on her way back home. Knox was hurling insults from the pulpit of St Giles's, calling her and her ladies-in-waiting *jezebel whores* while the treacherous lords applauded and nodded their heads. I had to grind my teeth and hold my tongue. And wait.

At long last she arrived. I was among those few who were there patrolling the beach in the Firth of Forth and keeping the fires going in the night. Her two galleys emerged from thick fog, on the back of the foaming spray as if they had sprung from the bottom of the sea.

First, the lights of lanterns flickered in the night, then French voices urged the rowers to press on, and finally the outlines of the queen and her entourage appeared. Heavy rain had drenched them to the skin, but Mary appeared buoyant and full of vigour. She hitched her skirts and trod the waves. Her eyes were ablaze with excitement.

Cannons were fired and a messenger was dispatched to Edinburgh to announce her early arrival.

She recognised me the moment her gaze rested on my doubled down form. 'Father Ninian! I'm pleased to find you here. I take great comfort from your presence. Do not leave my side.'

My eyes misted somewhat in reply and again, just like previously in Vitry, I found myself lost for words and fell to my knees to kiss her hand which she graciously extended to me.

There was much to be done recovering her possessions and packing them onto wagons destined for Holyrood. There was mayhem and confusion due to the heavy mist and pounding rain.

We took shelter at a humble merchant's house in Leith where I shared a simple luncheon with the Queen. I was able to steal a few precious minutes of her time and brief her on the sad state of affairs in Edinburgh where Knox led the campaign of hostilities against her and against the Holy Church.

'Do not fear,' Mary squeezed my arm in a firm grip, 'all will be well. Have faith, Father.'

She was right. Soon the sun broke through the cloud and the downpours of the last few days ceased as if by magic. The lords, led by Chatelherault, skulked in with their tails between their legs and profound apologies. A larger and more organised welcome party arrived with fresh horses within the next hour: the Earl of Argyll and Erskine of Dun, and at last the man I had come to despise and fear: James Stewart, the Queen's bastard half-brother, the man who had overseen the sacking of my church.

I was aware that he had seen Mary in Vitry only a day after Leslie and I, and that he had given her assurances of tolerance of her personal practice of Holy Mass in return for her endorsement of the Reformist Church of Scotland of which he was the chief protector. For now, my hopes for the restoration of Catholicism in Scotland lay in ruin. I dreaded the influence James Stewart was bound to exert on our young, inexperienced monarch.

He put on the performance of going down on one knee before her and professing his undying loyalty and his purported delight with her return. She bid him to rise forthwith and embraced him not like his queen but rather his little sister. Her childlike trust in him sent alarm bells tolling in my mind. The snake had ingratiated himself into her favours. It would be hard to open her eyes to his treacherous designs.

As we set off for Edinburgh, a motley rabble of some twenty louts accosted Mary from the side of the track and a shabby man with an unkempt beard and bloodshot eyes threw himself under her horse's hooves. 'Mercy, my most gracious Queen! Have mercy on a poor convict!'

Amidst much shouting, pleading and copious tears, it transpired that the convict's name was John Gillon, a tailor by trade, and that he had been sentenced to death following some mischief and petty pilfering during the Feast of Misrule a month earlier. The pardon usually granted to the revellers on such occasions had been forbidden by Knox, and poor Gillon was to be executed the next day. His companions had managed to break him out of prison, but a pursuit by armed gaolers was afoot. Mary, with her authority overriding that of Knox, was the wretched man's only hope.

I saw a twinkle of girlish amusement in her eye as she commanded the condemned tailor to rise whereupon she declared with a giggle twitching on her lips that he was pardoned by the Queen's order and was free to go under the shield of her protection.

The party of ruffians broke into deafening cheers and accompanied our procession all the way to Edinburgh, shouting praises of adoration and gratitude to our handsome and merciful queen. Soon, they were joined by crowds that had lined the High Street to catch a glimpse of her. The word of Queen Mary's beauty, inside and out, had spread across the city like wildfire. I relished the image of John Knox cowering in his cellar like a big, black bat from Hell, biting his knuckles in powerless fury. Mary's entrance into her kingdom was an utter triumph and the common Scots worshipped the ground she walked on.

My hopes for the future however would prove short-lived. The following Sunday, 24th August, I said Holy Mass in the Queen's private chapel at Holyrood. It was attended by Mary and the Earl of Montrose while most of the lords sat at St Giles listening to Knox's incendiary diatribe. A number of his disciples, driven by the preacher's blunt calls to violence, clambered outside the walls, shouting profanities and threatening riots. Armed guards had to be posted at the chapel door to protect the Queen, and me, her humble priest. Alas, the protection did not extend beyond Holyrood Palace.

After the service and my short but most pleasant walk with Mary in the palace gardens, I headed back to my lodgings in Canongate. I spent the evening reviewing the obnoxious allegations published by Knox and drafting my measured albeit incisive riposte. On Monday, I proceeded to the printers in the High Street with a commission to print six scores of polemic pamphlets aimed at discrediting Knox's falsities. From there, I went to visit Leslie. We discussed our strategies over lunch and wrote letters to the northern lords loyal to our cause.

Warm and breezy dusk fell on the city as I finally walked back home, a bundle of leaflets bulging under my arm, my thoughts and plans swarming in my head. I was so deep in contemplation that I failed to see the tongues of flames rolling behind the cracked windows of my lodgings. Neither did I smell the smoke. Only when I opened the door was I hit by a wave of heat. My home was on fire!

A sulphurous breath straight from the pit of Hell engulfed me. I was hurled onto my back, whether by the shock of my discovery or the impact of the raging heat, I cannot say. The string holding my leaflets broke, and they became airborne and slowly, unhurriedly drifted into the cloud of black smoke that broke out of the house. I stared into the inferno, mesmerised by the flames. My mind raced to all my texts and precious volumes devoured by the fire. They were beyond salvaging.

I could hear rapid footstep and shouting in the street behind me. People ran to the rescue, buckets of water in hand, screams for help echoing in steep alleys below. Someone grasped my shoulder. I looked up but did not recognise the face. It was bleary, shivering in the heated air. 'It's arson! They tried to fry you alive, Father! You are not safe here!'

I'd heard that before – *you are no safe here.* Angus's words rang in my ears, clapping against my temples. I had fled then, and now I would again have to go on the run. This time I had to go further; I had to vanish. As a Catholic priest, I was not safe anywhere in Scotland. The country was ablaze with heresy and persecution. Heathens, chancers and fraudsters were riding the wave of religious unrest. Scotland was doomed.

THE QUEEN'S AVENGER

PART 2

30th September 1592, Ratisbon, Bavaria

A stab of pain stung Brother Gunther into alertness. He jumped to his feet, his eyes ablaze with the livid flames that were devouring his sleeve. He waved his arm manically, his panic fanning the flames and causing them to flare up. They crackled in his ears as they singed his hair and burnt his cheek. The acrid smell of burning hit his nostrils. Gunther threw himself on the floor and rolled across it, pitting the weight of his body against the flames. As suddenly as the fire broke out, it was smothered.

Gunther sat up, his legs wide apart, and blinked away remnants of smoke. His sleeve was in tatters, burnt up to his elbow, and blackened beyond it. He would have to explain it somehow to Father Archibald. Gunther heaved himself to his feet and searched the room for the source of the fire. All he found was the weak flame of the oil lamp flickering harmlessly. The candle was long expired and reduced to a puddle of beeswax clotting under the sconce. The sheets of the first scroll lay untouched by the fire, their edges furling over the inkwell that was weighing them down. Gunther must have fallen asleep. The hem of his sleeve must have brushed over the flame of the lamp and caught fire. Fortunately for Gunther, he had been stirred awake by the fire before the poisonous fumes could lull him into a deadly slumber.

The tower bell was calling the brothers to Vigils. Gunther hesitated. Should he be taking his discovery to Father Archibald or should he keep it to himself for a while longer, at least until he had a chance to examine all the scrolls? He was sure that once he let them out of his hands, he would never find out what they contained and he would never hear the rest of the late Abbot's deathbed testimony. He silenced the vexing voice hissing into his ear that it wasn't his place to receive his superior's confession. Gunther's curiosity was stronger than his principles. He rolled the sheets of the first scroll into a bundle and bound them with a singed ribbon of flax. He then swept all of the scrolls from the desk and shoved them back into the secret compartment in the wall. He would be back tonight.

The morning was grey and dreary with the sun gagged by the thick fog and leaden cloud. The cold wet air touched Gunther's raw cheek and eased the searing pain. Gunther pulled up his hood to hide the burn. He slipped his left arm inside the other sleeve and hooked his finger around his elbow. Bracing himself, he hobbled into the chapel.

He was late. Father Archibald shot him a scornful glance from the height of the pulpit. The other monks, lined along the nave, singing morning praise, watched Brother Gunther run the gauntlet as he headed to his usual place between brothers Loui and Cornelius.

After the service, Cornelius accosted Gunther in the quadrangle. 'What mischief have you been up to in the night?' He gripped Gunther by the sleeve, dislodging his bare arm from its hiding place. Cornelius stared aghast at the stump of Gunther's sleeve. 'And what in Lord's name is that?'

'An accident,' Gunther lied smoothly. 'I had overfilled my oil lamp. It leaked and the flame caught onto my cassock.'

'That's so reckless of you, Brother Gunther. You could've sent the whole monastery up in smoke. You know how little it takes—'

'It was an accident, I told you!' Gunther snapped. He was feeling rather ill-tempered and tired. The last thing he was prepared to endure was a sermon from the excitable little do-gooder.

'And what will you do about your ruined robe?'

'I haven't thought of it yet,' Gunther admitted, his eyes searching Cornelius's for advice.

'Come, we'll have to mend it before Father Archibald discovers the damage. He wouldn't be too pleased to learn how irresponsible you've been.'

'I'd hear no end of it,' Gunther concurred.

'No, you wouldn't. And quite rightly so,' Cornelius's eyes narrowed in a supercilious squint but his puckered lips seemed to smile, 'but I do have a soft spot for you, God knows why! I think we can mend your cowl. I was about to take some old robes to the town, for the poor. Let's see if we can find a spare sleeve.'

They rummaged through the rejected old garments stored on the cart, ready for delivery to the doorstep of the cathedral where a growing population of beggars huddled together, bracing themselves for the chills of winter. Cornelius pulled out a threadbare black cape. 'We can do something with this.'

Gunther nodded keenly. He had no sewing skills and was more than happy to follow Cornelius's lead as long as it culminated in the reconstruction of his ruined sleeve to its former glory.

They retreated to Cornelius's cell where Gunther was instructed to disrobe down to his shirt. Cornelius ripped the shreds of the burnt sleeve from the cowl and matched the better side of the rescued cape with the other sleeve. He reclined on his bed, threaded a needle and began attaching the new sleeve, his fingers as dexterous as those of a seasoned seamstress.

'Don't stand there like a halfwit,' Cornelius peered at Gunther, mockery twinkling in his small, quick eyes. He patted the foot of his bed. 'Sit down.'

Gunther did as he was told. He slid gingerly to the edge of the bed. The room was cold and smelled like mouldy cheese. Gunther had goosebumps on his bare arms. He folded them across his chest and hunched his shoulders.

The needle in Cornelius's hand worked its way between the layers of fabric with brisk efficiency, pulling the thread in and out. Gunther would be indebted to this little, odious monk whether he liked it or not. Cornelius was a bag of hot air and many good intentions – too good to be true. There was something sticky and black under the surface of his magnanimity, like a layer of tar.

'There,' Cornelius bit through the thread and tied a knot to secure it in place. He shook the cowl, holding it by the shoulders. His eyes smiled, 'As good as new.'

'Thank you, brother,' Gunther was grateful. He reached for the robe.

'Let me,' Cornelius pulled back. 'I'm best placed to see if any alterations are needed. Put your hands up.'

Gunther obliged. Cornelius lifted the cowl over Gunther's head and for a moment Gunther found himself blinded and trapped inside the folds of the fabric. He felt Cornelius's chubby fingers slide down towards his armpits and further down along his ribs. They were quick like spider's legs. Gunther shuddered and pulled away forcefully, his back colliding with the door frame. He battled with the garment until, at last, it fell into place.

Cornelius gazed at him with a guilty expression, his cheeks burning red, 'Clumsy old me...'

'Sorry,' Gunther mumbled and flapped his arms like a lame crow. 'As good as new, see? You're a miracle maker. Thank you,' he was blathering nervously. 'You saved me the embarrassment of having to—'

'Don't mention it. I'm glad I could be of service,' Cornelius smiled again, somewhat coquettishly. The pout on his wet, pink lips repulsed Gunther.

'I'd better be going. So much to do.'

'Yes. Me too. I'll see you at Mass, Brother Gunther. Don't be late.'

Gunther spent the rest of the day shaking off the memory of Cornelius's fingers on his skin and convincing himself that there was nothing to it. At Mass, Cornelius didn't as much as glance at him. That re-assured Gunther that he had overreacted earlier. Cornelius was just a harmless old fool and, after all, he had saved Gunther from considerable trouble.

After Compline, Gunther retired to his cell and waited for the night to fall. As soon as every last footstep faded in the cloisters, he stole to the common Chapter room to resource a few candles and from there proceeded to the Abbot's quarter in the tower. He did not see that he was being followed.

A rotund male figure ensconced in woolly robes crept behind him across the quadrangle and up the spiral staircase. The spy stood, a little breathless, with his ear to the door, listening attentively to the squeak of an unoiled hinge followed by a rustling of parchment. Then there was a long silence. The flickering of light within the chamber told the spy that Gunther was awake, busy with some night-time task, but mysteriously motionless and silent. As curious as that was, the spy didn't enter to find out what Gunther was up to. He left quietly and vanished down the stairwell.

Meantime, Gunther had made himself comfortable in the Abbot's chair and unfurled the second bundle of parchment. He noted that it was written the day after the first one. Standing on the threshold of death, Abbot Ninian hadn't been wasting any time.

VI

Written on this the Sixteenth Day of September in the Year of our Lord 1592

Driven out of Scotland, I fled to the Continent and settled in Leuven where, for the next four years, I devoted myself to the study of theology, philosophy and canon law. I deployed my wits and quill to extinguishing the wild fires of Calvinism that had engulfed the Low Countries and threatened to devour the whole of Europe: from the Lutherans in Saxony to the Huguenots in France.

Although my hands were full, my hunger for news of my Scottish Queen never diminished. Powerless to intervene, I looked in horror on the exploits of her half-brother, James Stewart. She had made him Earl of Moray, bestowed upon him Darnaway Castle and entrusted the rule of Scotland into his hand. He had wasted no time assuming full control of her mind and led her into making grave errors of judgment which pleased neither her uncles in France, nor the Holy Father in Rome. Catholic Europe watched speechless as the young Queen, beguiled by the servants of Satan, had recognised the Reformist Church of Scotland and allowed for Holy Mass to be outlawed.

I could not blame her. She was but a child surrounded by masters of deception. She was becoming increasingly isolated on the northernmost, windswept confines of Europe. I craved a chance to return to Scotland to stand by her side, be her champion and deliver her from evil.

My chance came in April of 1565. I was summoned by the Cardinal of Lorraine to Joinville, the seat of the House of Guise. His letter was intriguing, if laconic: I had come highly recommended by his late sister Marie de Guise, Mary's mother. I was to present myself forthwith; my services were urgently required. The following morning, I set off for France, travelling on horseback for expediency.

I arrived after nightfall the following day. The Cardinal had already retired to bed. He would receive me in the morning. I was offered lavish hospitality: was fed like a king and accommodated in a bedchamber the size of an auditorium. A fire was lit in the grate for which I was more than grateful. That year, winter held well into April, ground frost shackled the earth, unyielding, and the cold wind could throttle a grown man. I was chilled to the bone and weary. My chest seemed filled with lead which I could not shift.

The next morning, I was awoken by a servant who came to rekindle the fire and brought me a jug of water to refresh myself. I splashed my face and washed off sweat and the dirt of the road with a wet cloth. I said my morning prayers hurriedly, conscious not to keep His Eminence waiting. As I stepped out of my room, I was informed that the Cardinal would receive me in the grand chambre d'apparat of Chateau du Grand Jardin. I was directed across the frost-bitten garden to a magnificent pavilion. The early-morning sun drove through the glass panels of tall windows, giving the interior an eerie, otherworldly quality. I was led, blinking and bewildered, through a grandiose festive hall paved with marble floors, to an ornate staircase that spiralled its way up to the reception room. There I met Charles de Guise, the Cardinal of Lorraine.

He looked magnificently commanding, seated in a gold-rimmed chair, wearing a crimson robe symbolic of his status. There was something in his features reminiscent of Mary. Whether it was the length of his prominent nose or the shape of his large eyes, I could not tell, but the resemblance, however remote, was there. His beard was trimmed closely, bearing only a hint of silver.

'Your Eminence,' I approached to kiss his ring, which he offered to me, his hand extended over his lap. I couldn't help noticing the length of his translucent nails.

'My dear-departed sister had only good things to say about you, Winzet.' He gestured for me to take a seat. 'She trusted you and that's enough for me to do likewise.'

I bowed in reply.

'I have a highly sensitive assignment for you. You're a Scot, fluent in their language and their ways. I need a pair of eyes in Scotland, someone I can rely on to tell me the truth about what goes on there. Mary— she is young and inexperienced, ruled by her heart. She's easily impressed upon, easily manipulated... Vultures are circling over her head, relentless in their quest to subjugate her.'

'Moray holds her in a tight grip,' I commented.

'Ah, the bastard half-brother! Indeed,' the Cardinal inclined his head and teased his beard on his chin. 'She gives him dominions and titles. He takes them and leads her further astray, into the arms of the Reformists and under the thumb of that scrawny whore perched on the English throne.'

'He is on Elizabeth's payroll,' I added.

'He, and many more Scottish nobles. They're happy to sell your country to the English for thirty pieces of silver and a promise of personal gain. Our Scot-French alliance is under threat, as is the Catholic faith in Scotland. Mary is doing her best to prevent it all from unravelling, but, like I said, she's only a young woman, alone in a nest of snakes. I can advise her, but I'm not in possession of all the facts. Besides, she often acts before seeking my counsel.'

'The prerogative of youth,' I said.

'Alas not something I can afford, or am prepared to, indulge. And that's why I need you there, by her side – a voice of caution.'

'I am at Your Eminence's service,' I pledged myself without hesitation. 'The fate of our Queen has always been at the fore of my mind. Besides, I promised the late Queen Regent that I'd watch out for her daughter.'

'I'm aware of that and I have trust in you to keep that promise.'

'When would you wish me to leave for Scotland?' I inquired. 'I've a few matters to conclude in Leuven before departure, but that shouldn't take longer than a fortnight.'

'Ah, first thing's first,' the Cardinal raised his long-nailed forefinger; the blood-ruby of his ring caught the light, bringing the gem to life. 'And firstly, I have a mission for you in Rome.' He rose from his chair. 'Join me for a stroll in the garden. In an hour. We'll discuss the details.'

When I accompanied the Cardinal on his morning walk an hour later, the previous night's frost was but a distant memory. The sun had by then climbed into the cloudless sky and beat down on earth with all its might. I could feel its life-giving warmth on my back, my tight chest loosening a fraction.

We took a footpath that weaved among the neatly cropped hedges of sturdy hornbeam whose green foliage had withstood the chills of winter. The Cardinal had discarded his formal attire in favour of a simple black cassock. I walked a couple of steps behind him out of respect for his station.

'I want us to talk in private, Ninian. I've sensitive matters to divulge to you.'

I noted, with a tickle of pleasure under my chin, that the Cardinal had moved to addressing me by my first name. I was flattered by his cordiality and listened attentively to what he had to say.

'Mary cannot rule on her own. She's but a woman. She needs a man to guide her. A strong man with a clean royal lineage. And above all, a Catholic.'

'A husband for the Queen?'

'It's time. Her mourning for Francis has long run its course. She's a woman in her prime. She needs to ensure the continuity of her line. We can't let her end up like that shrivelled old prune of England, can we?'

True, Elizabeth of England was now past her child-bearing time, deluded as some of her nobles may have been about her prospects of ever producing an heir. Mary, however, was the best catch in Europe. And the most beautiful one. I nodded my agreement.

'My preference for her was Archduke Charles of Austria,' the Cardinal said.

'The Emperor's brother?'

'Yes. I entered into some tentative – very delicate, you'll appreciate – negotiations with the Archduke but Mary put a swift end to it. *A pauper*, she said, *commanding no army to support me in Scotland*. I conceded defeat. There were – still are – many other eligible candidates across Europe. The kings of Denmark and Sweden have expressed their interest in exchanging nuptials, but again, my dear niece wouldn't entertain the idea of either of them. Having been married to the King of France, she has set her sights high. Understandably so, alas to my chagrin,' the Cardinal flicked his wrist with elegantly expressed disappointment.

'Our Scottish Queen has a mind of her own,' I commented.

'Oh, that she does! But with some patience... Suffice to say, the tide changed in my favour when she expressed interest in Don Carlos.'

'The son of King Philip?'

'And the heir to the Spanish throne.'

'And a Catholic. Excellent news!'

'Oh, he has his disadvantages. It's all a big secret but my spies tell me something is terribly wrong with the prince. Apart from his disfigurement, he may be teetering on the edge of madness. Still, he would have been quite agreeable—'

'Would have been?'

'— had Mary not changed her mind. She fell—

VII

Written on this the Seventeenth Day of September in the Year of our Lord 1592

I fell asleep last night, mid-sentence, quill in hand. I didn't hear the bells toll for Vespers. I woke with a start when I slid from my chair and hit the floor. Luckily, in my ripe old age, I have learned how to fall without hurting myself. My side is bruised but then I do bruise easily these days. And I tire quickly and fall into a daze. I can't remember much when I come out of it. It is as if I have died and several hours later, I am brought back from the brink of oblivion. My memory of the distant past however is as clear as crystal. More and more often, as I sit here crouched over my desk, my quill scratching the parchment ferociously, I feel the past take over my mind, every recollection sharp and vivid before my eyes. It is the present that has fallen into a bottomless well. I have no desire to recover it. Nor do I care for the future. My only desire is to make peace with the past. I have a long way to go yet, God willing.

'She fell in love,' the Cardinal spoke with a sneer. 'Queens do not fall in love. They cannot afford the luxury of lowering their guard.'

'Who is the lucky prince?' I asked, politely, disregarding his remark about queens having no hearts.

'He's no prince, certainly not one with a kingdom or any wealth to speak of.' The heavy sigh unfurling from the Cardinal's lips conveyed his deep disappointment. 'Lord Henry Darnley.'

'Matthew Lennox's eldest?'

The Cardinal nodded. 'I wrote to Mary to dissuade her from the foolish idea of marrying her lesser, but – true to her nature – she won't listen to reason. Ever since Darnley succumbed to some form of measles and became bedridden, she took it upon herself to nurse him back to health, and that did it! She's taken it into her head that marriage is about healing the sick and keeping vigil by their side. I blame her late husband.'

'Francis? The French king?' I admit I was taken aback by his remark.

'Yes, Francis. The wretched boy was a weakling. Mary spent her days caring for him, and she did it with love and devotion, alas—' the Cardinal cleared his clouded throat, 'Alas, that gave her the wrong idea about marriage. You know that their nuptials were never consummated?'

'Ah!'

'Never mind. We can't turn back time. She's now hell-bent on throwing herself and her kingdom at the feet of a spoilt reprobate.'

I didn't comment on the Cardinal's choice of words, but they gave me cause for concern.

'I wrote to her,' he continued, 'but my warnings fell on deaf ears. She will marry him. I can only try to mitigate the damage. She assures me that the boy – he's only but eighteen – comes with some advantages, other than the pretty face.'

'Royal blood runs through his veins,' I agreed. 'He's the grandson of the king of England, Henry VII.'

'And that strengthens Mary's claim to the English throne. That is something we can exploit to our advantage. Mary informs me that Elizabeth approves of the union though I find it hard to believe. Two legitimate successors to the Tudor throne, united in marriage, will pose a threat to the Protestant bastard-queen. But she's without a child, and without a chance to produce one, so perhaps she's finally accepted that her cousin succeeding her to the English throne is better than another civil war.'

'That'd be a wise course of action although I'm convinced that the English would much rather subjugate Scotland than join it in a union of two equals under a Scottish Queen,' I expressed my reservations. Considering that I was speaking to a French nobleman, I didn't go on to add that so would the French, given the same opportunity. Both the French and the English behaved as if Scotland was a trophy to be won and owned.

'That is an astute observation, Ninian,' the Cardinal's eyes hovered over me as if trying to penetrate my thoughts. 'Be it as it may, Mary's move to marry a Tudor heir will do no harm to her own claim. Secondly, she assures me that supported by Darnley she will be in a stronger position to champion the Holy Mother Church in her kingdom.'

'The true Faith in Scotland has been under assault for years. The Queen is powerless against the growing ranks of heretic militants. I heard she couldn't even grant safe conduct out of Scotland to papal nuncio Gouda. He had to flee under the cover of night. In truth, so did I. My life was in danger from the fanatics, my house set on fire... Catholicism is on its knees in Scotland.'

'Indeed, we are aware of the crippling damage inflicted upon it, but this may change when two Catholics sit on the Scottish throne and shake off the influence of the Protestant Lords. Of course,' the Cardinal pursed his lips pensively, 'I'm well aware of Darnley's shortcomings. He's a Catholic in name only, a child of limited intelligence and high ambitions.'

'A lethal mixture.'

'Indeed, it can be. That is why I intend to ensure that my dearest niece and her boy-husband are surrounded by advisers sympathetic to our cause. That is why I need you there, Ninian.'

I inclined my head modestly, but I won't deny I was rather flattered by the Cardinal's confidence in me.

'You will watch and you will report to me. Beware of Darnley. He may be an agreeable buffoon but he was brought up in Protestant England and he is an English subject. For all we know he could be Elizabeth's Trojan horse. His loyalties could turn inside out, depending on which way the wind blows. Mary intends to grant him extensive titles and proclaim him King of Scotland. I can't dissuade her, but I have warned her against giving him the Crown Matrimonial or else she could become superfluous in her own kingdom. I hope she heeds my advice, but I won't leave it to chance. You'll be there to keep an eye on her and give her the benefit of your counsel. You'll go there as her priest and confessor. I'll furnish you with official letters of introduction.'

'Her Majesty knows me well. I was at Linlithgow when she was baptised, and five springs ago I beseeched her to return home on behalf of Scottish Catholics—'

'I said *official*. Many eyes will be on you when you arrive in Edinburgh, trying to work out your purpose. We must avert suspicions or else you'll be paralysed in your mission.'

'Of course.'

'But firstly, I need you to travel to Rome to petition the Holy Father for dispensation for Mary and Henry's marriage. They are cousins as, I'm sure, you are well aware, but it will be just a formality. His Holiness will be expecting you and will treat our request favourably. My brother Francois is making a significant donation to fund Pius's latest building project. I hear the Basilica di Santa Maria degli Angeli requires patching up. With money on the table, Pius won't be able to say no.'

THE QUEEN'S AVENGER

VIII

Written on this the Seventeenth Day of September in the Year of our Lord 1592

Upon my return to Leuven, I was struck with ague so severe that I found myself drifting in and out of consciousness. I was unable to rise from my bed, take food or drink. It didn't help that initially I was treated by the university physicians who prescribed leeches. I was bled nearly to death. A month into my illness, fearing I was dying, Neesken, my housekeeper, sent away the physicians and brought in a wisewoman. Wrinkled, her hair bleached of colour and her eyes hooded with the weight of years, the wisewoman had to be as old as the earth itself and that gave me hope that she knew what she was doing. Indeed, she did. Slowly, my health improved. I could again breathe without my chest imploding. My appetite returned and one sunny July day I sat up in my bed. I re-learned to walk and built strength in my muscles over the next fortnight, and finally, delayed by three months, I was on my way to Rome.

The heat of the summer filled the piazzas with lingering odours of sweat and staleness while the exotic aromas of Italian cooking wafted through the stench. I noted the extent of building works being carried out on the Basilica di Santa Maria under the supervision of an architect called Michelangelo. Scaffolds were swarming with workers, marble, wood and other building materials transported into the Holy City by the wagonful. Francois Guise's donation was already being spent.

Pope Pius IV received me soon after my arrival. He was an ailing old man, seated in his gestatorial chair like a crumpled string puppet. His head was tilted towards his left shoulder as if it needed somewhere to rest. He let me kiss his signet ring and listened to my submission with a clouded, passive expression in his eyes. A sneaky suspicion crossed my mind that he had fallen asleep. When I finished, I handed Cardinal de Lorraine's letter and supporting documents to the Pope's Personal Secretary, who informed me that His Holiness would carefully consider the request and I would have his answer as soon as possible.

I was made to wait for two weeks, which I took in my stride. Clearly, although the dispensation was a mere formality, I and, most of all, the French cardinal had to be reminded of who was in charge. I spent my spare time loitering around the Holy City, admiring its wonders. At long last, the Personal Secretary summoned me to his gold-gilded office and presented me with a dispensation document signed and sealed by the Holy Father. It was also backdated to the time when I was lying on my sickbed in Leuven. I stared at the man in puzzlement.

'It had to be done. It is our understanding that the petitioners have already exchanged their vows. They obviously couldn't wait,' the Personal Secretary explained, his face contorted in a grimace of disapproval.

I was befuddled by the news. It meant that Mary and Henry had married without papal dispensation and thus their marriage was technically invalid. The backdating would address the problem but if it became public it could be successfully challenged in court. Their offspring would be considered illegitimate. I expressed my heartfelt gratitude to the Personal Secretary, and through his proxy, to His Holiness himself, for this indulgence. I would of course take the knowledge of this irregularity to my grave.

THE QUEEN'S AVENGER

IX

Written on this the Seventeenth Day of September in the Year of our Lord 1592

Edinburgh presented itself in its full autumnal glory when I finally arrived there at the end of September, the year of 1565. The false prophet Knox was still slithering about the city and spitting his venom, but there was hope in the air. Queen Mary was married to a Catholic. At long last she was in charge of her mind and fortune. Her brother, Lord James, who had revolted against her, had been crushed and put to the horn. He had fled to England to hide in the skirts of his Protestant paymaster, Elizabeth. The whole of Scotland was breathing a sigh of relief. The Queen was riding high in the opinions of her subjects. My first report to the Cardinal stated that his niece was happy and that she was well loved by her people.

She welcomed me with tears of joy. I handed her letters from her uncle and the dispensation grant from the Pope. She was hungry for news from the Continent. We talked well into the night about her marriage and how she had defended it. She described to me how she had tracked down the rebels – *like a husk of fleeing hares*, she joked – and defeated them in open battle. She looked tired and pale but radiant with the glow of her victory.

She also spoke passionately about her undying devotion to the true Faith and about her hopes for it to be resurrected in Scotland. She told me about her loyal supporters, mentioning to my surprise James Douglas, the Earl of Morton, and James Hepburn, the Earl of Bothwell, both rotten Calvinists. She explained that Morton stood firmly behind her marriage to Henry as he was his mother's kin, and Bothwell was apparently the most skilled general in her army and a sworn enemy of the English. She needed both men to neutralise her ungrateful half-brother. Tears glistened in her eyes as she spoke of the honours and domains he had received from her only to betray her and challenge her God-given sovereignty. I remembered him bitterly from the sacking of my church at

Linlithgow all those years ago. There wasn't a spark of Christian forgiveness left in my heart for the wretched man. Already then I knew that he posed the greatest threat to my queen.

The following day I met with my old friend, John Leslie. While I was rattling about on the Continent, he had stayed behind in Scotland to fight for the cause and had since been elevated to the position of the Bishop of Ross. He was a man I could trust with my mission. We were like brothers. He, too, would stand by Mary's side to the bitter end and he too was an ardent defender of the true Religion.

Leslie introduced me to the Queen's secretary, David Rizzio. He was a small man with a swarthy complexion, dolefully bovine eyes, an effeminate manner and very expensive taste in clothes. In puritan Edinburgh he stood out like a peacock amongst grouse. He was yet another loyal servant of the Queen and a keen supporter of her marriage to King Henry.

Speaking of King Henry, he was nowhere to be found. I didn't clap my eyes on him until late November for at the time of my arrival he had been busy hunting in Fife, then hawking and indulging in a variety of pleasurable pursuits on his father's estate near Glasgow. Curiously, no one, not even the newlywed Queen seemed to be missing him. An iron seal with his signature etched into it had been made to be used in his absentia. It was given into the custody of Rizzio so that urgent matters of State could be dealt with expeditiously.

The King returned to Holyrood with the first snow. I was introduced to him by Leslie. I bowed and bent my knee to his authority. Discourteously, the King's eyes barely skimmed over the top of my head, and he was off, muttering something about a lame horse.

He was a beardless youth, exceedingly tall and long-limbed, with the deportment of a feral dog. I heard many accounts of his ill-tempered outbursts and I witnessed one when he drew a dagger at a humble justice clerk who brought him some unwelcome tidings. The poor man fainted on the spot and had to be revived with salts.

THE QUEEN'S AVENGER

The King was most unpopular with just about everyone at court. His only friend seemed to be Rizzio, but I detected it to be more of an unnatural infatuation on Rizzio's part than a friendship based on the merit of Darnley's character.

The King returned to Edinburgh soon after the Queen had departed. She'd gone to Linlithgow to convalesce after suffering ill health that had gripped her with agonising pain for several gut-wrenching days. Carelessly, though I could think of a stronger word to convey my condemnation, her husband didn't deem it fit to follow her. Instead, he held an impromptu banquet. I was not invited, but even if I had been I wouldn't have attended. The masque that was held at the end was nothing short of an orgy, a trusted courtier told me the next day. I didn't inquire about details.

I wished I could have travelled with Mary to my old parish of Linlithgow. Alas I had important commitments in Edinburgh to take care of. I had established contact with Edinburgh's Catholic community. It was a clandestine network of the faithful: burghers, courtiers and nobles alike. They met every Sunday at a different location to hear Holy Mass. If caught, they faced incarceration, possibly death. Mass had been banned in Scotland by an Act of Parliament; only the Queen was exempt.

I had been approached by Lord Seton to join the network. I agreed without hesitation. It would be dangerous, he'd warned me, but I didn't need to be told that. I'd had personal experience of Calvinist militancy. Protestant converts were the worst – the most violent – breed of fanatics. If apprehended, I'd be lynched on the spot, no questions asked.

A piece of paper with the address of each new venue would be slipped under my door the night before, with instructions to memorise and burn it. The following day after sunset, I would dress in tattered old garments befitting a travelling merchant, conceal my face in a deep hood, hide the Holy Book and my peripatetic liturgical objects in purpose-sewn internal pockets of my cape, and steal out of my palace lodgings. I would say Mass in cellars, chambers concealed behind secret doors, shop storerooms and twice in a church underground vault, with coffins looming over my congregation.

One night in early December, I was sneaking in the shadows of the High Street, heading back to my lodgings after delivering Mass in town when I spotted a tall figure dive into a deep alley. Even though the night was black and the figure was but a silhouette, there was no mistaking it. It was the King. He was unsteady on his feet, staggering and sliding on icy cobbles, with the most foul language flying off his tongue.

I asked myself what his business was traipsing the city, drunk and alone, under the cover of night. I had to know the answer. I followed him.

We were descending into the criminal underbelly of the city: backstreets and dead-end alleys, filthy, stenchy, resonating with cries and curses, and populated by all manner of cut-throats, prostitutes and pickpockets.

His Majesty seemed to know his way around these parts. He headed resolutely towards a ramshackle tavern with small windows and dimmed lights still flickering inside despite the hour being well past curfew. He kicked the door open and tumbled inside.

In the moment that the door shuddered ajar on its hinges, I was able to discern a large mob of drunken patrons and a few half-naked whores weaving between them, selling their wares. I entered.

I had no fear of being discovered. I was dressed shabbily and my face was concealed under the hood. I mingled with the crowd, one eye searching for the King. A serving maid, her full bosom heaving under her corset and her lips scarlet as if she'd just sucked blood out of a lamb, accosted me, offering me a tankard of ale, and anything else I might be after. I took the ale and threw the wench a coin.

The King, a chuckling harlot hanging on his arm, swayed into a narrow corridor behind the bar and disappeared from view. I left my ale untouched and crept after him. I took care and some time before I entered the passageway in case it was guarded or I, in my turn, was being followed. Assured that wasn't the case, I stepped into the darkness.

THE QUEEN'S AVENGER

Grunts and heavy panting greeted me there. A room with a rag draped from the ceiling in place of a door was the place where the noises were coming from. A sound of a slap resonated, and another one, and then fruity curses and blasphemies uttered with a distinctly English tilt. I recognised King Henry's adolescent twang.

My fingers trembling, I pushed the curtain just enough to steal a one-eyed peek. And there I saw him fornicating, his white arse rising and falling, and jamming, each thrust supplemented with another grunt, another curse.

I would have made little of this indiscretion. The King was young and the Queen had been indisposed for weeks, unavailable to discharge her marital duties. One could forgive him the urge to unburden himself with a random harlot. But when he was done, I realised the extent of his depravity. He pulled out and fell into the arms of the whore he'd walked with. She had sat through the spectacle, watching but not partaking. The other whore, sprawled on a pallet, was revealed to me, and it wasn't a maiden. Young and supple he was, his skin white and hairless, his tresses long and bright with lustre, but it was a man.

I recoiled in horror, my back catching against the wall before my legs buckled under me. The King was a sodomite.

X

Written on this the Seventeenth Day of September in the Year of our Lord 1592

As soon as I dispatched my letter to the Cardinal, informing him of my discovery, I set off for Linlithgow. The Queen had to be advised forthwith. My journey was arduous. Fresh snow had fallen and was still falling, thick and unrelenting. I was making haste to ensure that I made it to Linlithgow before nightfall. I wasn't adequately clad for the sharp bite of Scottish winter. The freezing air seemed to be punching a hole in my chest. I could tell my lungs hadn't quite recovered from my earlier illness. Nevertheless, I didn't measure my pace. Slowing down could mean a night in the wild and certain death.

I arrived at dusk, just as the last ray of daylight faded away and before the moon rose in the sky to illuminate my path. Had I not known the area like the back of my hand, I would have become desperately lost. Fortunately, it had all come back to me. I recognised the shape of the snow-capped hills and could delineate the form of the loch buried in two feet of all-levelling white blanket. The spire of St Michael's pierced the sky like an upturned icicle and it glowered with its own eerie light. Seeing it brought a tear to my eye. I was home.

The Queen saw me without delay. She invited me to join her for supper. I shed my wet and soiled attire and was given dry clothes. I sat with my back to the fire, feeling my blood thaw slowly and carry warmth to my limbs.

I asked the Queen to send away the servants whereupon I conveyed to her, without embellishment or suppression, what I had seen the King get up to in the whorehouse. Her face dropped and the colour drained from it as she listened. She didn't interrupt me, bar a gasp when she heard me repeat one of the blasphemies he had uttered at the height of his exultation.

'Sodomy is a ground for annulment, Your Majesty,' I advised her.

THE QUEEN'S AVENGER

'It cannot be done. It cannot be done,' she spoke in a haze.

'But it can,' I assured her. 'And that's not the only ground. The Holy Father's dispensation for you to marry your cousin was granted after you exchanged your vows. My fault entirely. I had been struck with ague. My embassy was delayed by weeks. By the time—'

She reached to me, gripped my shoulder and gazed at me with burning intensity, 'I tell you, it cannot be done. Not now. Our nuptials stand. It's too late.'

'But why?'

'I'm with child,' her hands travelled to her belly. She lifted her eyes to me. Her gaze was steely. 'I carry in my womb the future king of Scotland, England and the Hebrides. His legitimacy cannot be put into doubt. Under no circumstances. I will hear no more of it.'

I hung my head in concession.

We ate in silence. I had no appetite and neither did Mary. After a while of disquiet, she squared her shoulders and lifted her chin. 'I knew,' she said. 'I knew before you told me, Father. My affections for him died on our wedding night. He was drunk. Angry. Vile. Raving. He couldn't bring himself to touch me. He ran away that night in a huff. Took himself down to his bedchamber. To sulk, I thought. I lay in bed, dejected. I couldn't sleep, wondering what I did wrong, pondering how it was to be done correctly. I... I was confused and ashamed. My gut hurt as if he had punched me.'

'Ah!' I remember blood rush to my face and burn my barely thawed cheeks. The queen had been a virgin when she'd married Darnley. She'd had no experience in carnal pursuits.

She pursed her lips; her nostrils flared. 'Then I heard peculiar sounds rising from under the floor. His bedchamber is right below mine. I picked a lamp and crept down the staircase leading to his room. I saw it then. My husband with another man.'

'Forgive my impudence, Your Majesty, but is the babe you carry—'

'It is Henry's. Never question that. I found a way to make it happen, that's all you need to know.'

She rose from her chair. The supper – and our audience – was over.

I took a few days to recover my strength and my wits. The breakneck journey through snow had brought me down like a felled tree. I succumbed to fever, my body on fire, my joints twisted with inflammation. My mind was equally disturbed. I endured nightmares and visions: unnatural and wicked. It was as if I had been cursed.

My Queen visited me every day and sat by my bedside, wiping my brow with a wet cloth and whispering encouragement into my ear. Her sweet voice, her angelic face and the touch of her soft hand gave me the strength I needed to fight on.

I overcame the malady on the fifth day and that night I slept without waking. Nightmares fled from my mind. In the morning, I ventured back into the world.

I crossed the town to the West Quarter. I could hear the metallic clanging of the blacksmith's hammer as I approached Angus Murray's workshop. Drowned in the noise, he was oblivious to my arrival.

'Master Angus!' I called out.

He looked up. A wide grin cut his face in two. He dropped his iron tongs into a pail of hissing water and put aside his hammer. He wiped steam, smoke and sweat from his brow and greeted me.

'Father Ninian!'

We embraced.

'What brings you to Linlithgow, Father?'

'Visiting Queen Mary. I had matters to take up with Her Majesty, matters that couldn't wait until her return to Holyrood.'

'You know our Queen? In person, like?' Awe flashed in his eyes.

'I'm her priest and confessor.'

'Isn't she a vision of loveliness?'

'Aye, that she is.' I stretched my hands to warm them against the fire in his hearth.

'Dean Kinlochy is dead,' Angus said. 'Two Sundays ago he passed. He was struck dead with apoplexy.'

THE QUEEN'S AVENGER

'May his soul rest in peace,' I uttered and drew the sign of the Cross on my chest.

'Good riddance, if you ask me,' Angus shrugged. 'The Devil got him at long last.'

He said what I was thinking only it didn't become a priest to say it out loud. I bid the blacksmith farewell and walked back to the palace with a spring in my step. God's justice is slow but certain, I pondered. I still had the pouch with the powdered mushrooms Widow Ainsley had given me to conjure Kinlochy's demons, but I wouldn't need it after all. The good Lord had taken care of that for me. Still, the powder might come in handy one day. I decided to keep it.

PART 3

1st October 1592, Ratisbon, Bavaria

Gunther paused. He recalled seeing a small leather pouch in the secret compartment in the wall. He had not made much of it when he first discovered it, his attention captured by the seven bundles of the Abbot's writings, but now, upon reading the Abbot's remarks, he decided to take a better look at the pouch.

He left the parchments spread on the desk, held down by the weight of the inkhorn. The panel in the wall opened with a rusty clank. Gunther held a candle over it, reached his hand into the cavity and rummaged through the scrolls. His hand came across a small parcel of soft leather. He carried the pouch to the table and untied its drawstrings at the neck. Inside, he found remnants of dry powder, like coarsely ground pepper. He pinched a small quantity which he proceeded to examine. It smelt musky. He considered tasting it, but then remembered its properties. What if it caused him to meet his demons? It was after all a witch's draft. On the other hand, he'd be curious to—

A strange noise outside the door startled Gunther. He froze and listened. It sounded like the shuffle of a misplaced foot or a scratch of wings. Was it a man spying on him, or an owl trapped in the tower?

'Anyone there?' Brother Gunther called out.

A soft patter receded hurriedly. It was a man!

Gunther grabbed the pouch and threw it back into the secret compartment, making sure it closed. Then he set off after the intruder.

He hurried down the spiral staircase, a couple of times losing his footing on the narrow steps in the disorienting, jet-black shaft of the tower. He burst out into the quadrangle just in time to see a hem of black robes swishing into the cloister. The spy was one of the brothers. Gunther ran after him. His head was buzzing with angry accusations against the spy and panicky excuses to explain his own night-prowling in the dead Abbot's lodgings. He crossed the courtyard, shot through the cloister and entered the dormitories. The lobby was empty, the footsteps long silenced.

Gunther crept from door to door, pressing his ear to each one, listening for any sounds. All was quiet. Dismayed, he abandoned the search. He noticed the new day had already dawned, the first rays of light timidly filtering through the night. He decided to use the few precious minutes to catch up on lost sleep before the bells tolled for Vigils.

He jolted awake three hours later, roused by the ringing of the Angelus bell. He had not heard the first call of the day and had failed to attend Vigils. If he hurried, he would just make it to the morning service of Lauds. He splashed his face with ice-cold water to shake off the remainder of sleep still lingering heavy on his eyelids.

He entered the chapel together with the others. As was the rule, they all proceeded silently, held their heads low, their eyes downcast and minds filled with pious musings. Perhaps nobody had noticed Gunther's absence at Vigils. He wedged himself between Loui and Cornelius. He peered between his lashes first to the left at Loui, who didn't as much as glance at him, and then to the right at Cornelius whose quick eyes caught Gunther's gaze in an instant. Cornelius tilted his head to gaze at Gunther sideways and bestowed upon him an affable smile. Gunther's lips twitched nervously in reply.

The service proceeded without a hitch. Towards the end, Gunther relaxed enough to join in the psalm. His youthful voice hovered an octave above his neighbours, creating a pleasing harmony.

Alas, as soon as the service was over, Brother Cornelius accosted Gunther in the gallery. 'Brother Gunther, wait! I'm gravely concerned about you. You missed Vespers, and you look…' his eyes gripped Gunther like a pair of pincers, 'like you haven't slept all night. Are you unwell? Troubled about something?'

'No, I'm fine.' Gunther stepped back, trying to avoid Cornelius's stale mead-breath. 'I… I overslept. That's all.'

'That's what I mean!' Cornelius exclaimed and raised his forefinger ominously over Gunther's head. 'It never happened before. It's not like you. If you hadn't arrived for Lauds, I would've been obliged to bring the matter to Father Archibald's attention—'

'Don't!' Gunther said, a bit too loudly. He quickly moderated his tone. 'Please, don't. There is no need. I've had a bad night, and I overslept. It won't happen again.'

'I'm glad to hear that,' Cornelius moved closer and lowered his voice to a whisper, 'but if there's something that troubles you... Unburden your soul, Brother.'

'No. There's nothing at all.'

'Well, you know where to find me if you want to talk.'

Cornelius walked away, wobbling and flapping his arms like a big lame goose. Only now did Gunther notice that Cornelius had developed a slight limp. Was he the spy that had been following Gunther in the night? Had he twisted his ankle last night when fleeing from the tower? It was unwise to jump to conclusions but Gunther had his suspicions about Cornelius. The man was insufferably curious and in recent days had developed an odd fascination with Gunther's affairs. Gunther would have to keep an eye on him.

The rest of the day passed torturously slowly, dedicated to tedious tasks. It felt to Gunther like he was pouring thick, sticky honey through a keyhole. By suppertime he was exhausted beyond description and found himself nodding off during Compline. At one point, he must have leant against Loui; a sharp nudge into his ribs and a dour frown from the elderly monk brought him back to full alert. Gunther mouthed a silent apology, but Loui was no longer looking at him.

After sunset Gunther headed for his cell and collapsed in his bed as he stood. He'd decided against a visit to the Abbot's lodgings tonight. Firstly, because after three sleepless nights in a row he couldn't keep his eyes open, and secondly because he wanted to confuse his mystery follower into thinking that his business in the tower was at an end.

THE QUEEN'S AVENGER

His sleep was turbulent, haunted by visions of naked harlots with blood-red lips, dancing on tables and fornicating with demons, then morphing into young beardless men, all wearing Gunther's face. Gunther jolted upright, gasping for air. Cold sweat blistered on his brow. He ran his fingers through his wet hair. There was no way he would go back to sleep. His nightmare was still raw in his mind like a gaping bloody gash.

He peered out of the narrow slash of his window. The moon was still high in the sky but its light was beginning to dim in the east, giving way to the first hint of rising sun. Another hour or two and the bells would toll for morning prayer. Despite his earlier resolution to stay away from the tower, Gunther decided to use this gained time to delve into Abbot Ninian's deathbed confessions once more. He couldn't help himself, as if he had been bewitched by the dead priest to read on, and commanded by him to shield the scrolls from prying eyes.

If nothing else, he would at least go to check that all was in order. He headed for the tower, the key to the Abbot's lodgings heavy in his cowl pocket, crashing against his thigh as he strode.

As he thrust the key into the keyhole and attempted to turn it, he realised that the door wasn't locked. He froze, more cold sweat chilling his temples. Had someone else been snooping here? Had they found the secret vault? But then it occurred to Gunther that last night, in his haste to catch the spy, he had dashed out without locking the door behind him. Gunther steadied his breath and ventured inside. He lit the oil lamp and the two half-burned candles. The chamber filled with a soft and reassuring luminosity. Candle flames, fleeting though they were, gave Gunther a curious sense of calm and permanency.

Firstly, he checked that the pouch was still there. It was. That convinced Gunther that no other man had, as yet, discovered the secret compartment. Probably nobody knew it existed.

Gunther retrieved the next bundle of parchment from the wall and settled down to read.

XI

Written on this the Eighteenth Day of September in the Year of our Lord 1592

On her return to Holyrood, Mary made it clear that Darnley was out of favour. She withdrew her company from him and excluded him from the affairs of state. She was now firmly in charge of her own government. I was one of the few whose counsel she relied upon, as was John Leslie and David Rizzio, all true Catholics. Bothwell, although a Protestant, remained loyal to the Queen. He focussed his efforts on rebuilding her army and protecting her southern borders, and on that front he could not be faulted. Her Secretary of State, Maitland dithered in the shadows, pretending to do Her Majesty's bidding but, according to our spies, keeping lines of communication open with the banished James Stewart, who was still, but I hoped not for much longer, the Earl of Moray.

Darnley who, outside his earshot, we no longer referred to as King Henry, sulked, drank and whored. He too was conspiring with the Lords. At the beginning of March, Leslie's men intercepted a letter Darnley wrote to Moray, instructing him to go to Berwick and await further orders from himself, *the King*. I was baffled by that – Moray despised Darnley and had been objecting most vociferously to his marriage to the Queen. He had openly revolted against her over that very matter. His sudden familiarity with Darnley represented a drastic change of heart. I suspected Moray had contacted Darnley in the first instance, alas the exact nature and purpose of his approach could not be established. All I could tell was that something sinister was afoot. Mary had to act quickly to neutralise both men. Her best course of action was to call Parliament with the view to attaint Moray and his cronies in exile, and to have them divested of their titles and estates.

The second equally urgent objective was to enact legislation decriminalising Catholicism in Scotland.

The new session of Parliament opened in the Tolbooth on 7th March. The ceremony had been planned in minute detail to

THE QUEEN'S AVENGER

demonstrate to the people of Scotland that their Queen was in command and that the government of her realm was running smoothly. Wearing a jewel-studded head-dress, Queen Mary arrived with the lords Bothwell and Huntly by her side. Bothwell was carrying the sceptre, Huntly holding the crown. Although formally summoned to Edinburgh to face justice, none of the rebel-lords attended. Moray was on his way, but he wasn't coming to atone for his sins. He had been granted safe-conduct by Darnley to return to Scotland, and his intentions were to use the young fool to regain power. Like a puppet-master operating from the shadows, he would soon put his plans into action and would almost succeed at having his half-sister, our most gracious Queen, murdered.

The events of that Saturday night will forever remain carved into my memory.

Mary was holding a supper party attended by her few closest intimates. We gathered in a small room draped in crimson and green. It was adjacent to the Queen's bedchamber and accessible to the King through a narrow privy staircase. He however had not been invited.

The mood was buoyant. We were chatting merrily, Rizzio played lute for Mary's entertainment and fooled about, flapping his furred damask cape and making crowing noises. Mary's little dog sat in her lap, warming her belly that was now visibly swollen. She was stroking the dog's long silver hair and tickling its pricked ears. From time to time she gave it a morsel of meat from her plate. The creature peered at its mistress with adoring eyes. Mary was in good spirits. Her laughter rang out, sweet and resonant. It died on her lips when unexpectedly her estranged husband entered the room.

Darnley emerged from the door to her bedchamber hidden behind a tapestry. A few of us stood up to bow to the King, but most remained seated in defiance. He didn't react to the snub with his usual petulance. His face seemed set in stone. He sat next to Mary and placed his arm on her shoulder as if asserting his authority over her. He said something I cannot recall now, but it was at that moment that the white-faced spectre of Lord Ruthven swept into the chamber, his steel cap and armour glinting in the candlelight with unholy menace. Waving his pistol, he demanded that Rizzio step forward. Rizzio did no such thing. Nevertheless, Ruthven proceeded to charge him with all manner of crimes against the Scottish nobility, as well as treason, dishonouring the King and destroying the commonwealth.

Before he could be overpowered, his heavily armed accomplices burst into the room. One of them, I noticed with disgust, was a fallen Catholic priest, now a killer for hire – Henry Yair.

Rizzio crawled behind Mary, crying for help. Her little dog jumped from her lap and charged at the attackers, barking in her defence. One of them kicked the wretched creature out of the way and it flew against the wall with a dying yelp. Outraged, Mary demanded that they leave or be arrested for treason.

Ruthven shook with laughter: we were surrounded by Morton's armed guards; all exits were secured; the Queen was to do as she was told. When Mary demanded an explanation, he informed her that everything being done here was with the King's assent.

He then pushed Mary into Darnley's arms. 'Take your wife in hand, *Your Majesty*,' he pronounced with a sneer. 'Remove her to her chamber and for once keep an eye on her. We will take care of the bastard who made a cuckold of you.'

It was clear who was in charge. Mary was too confounded to protest. She coloured deep red with indignation but words failed her.

What transpired next is a blur of blinding violence. The table was overturned, plates and cups catapulted into the air, chairs crashing to the floor, candles spilled and extinguished. Ruthven lunged at Rizzio who was clawing at the Queen's skirts and screaming with horror. She attempted to shield the Italian but Lindsay rammed a chair at her stomach and trapped her in the corner. George Douglas seized Darnley's dagger and thrust it at Rizzio over Mary's shoulder, narrowly missing her throat. The dagger pierced Rizzio's side and there it remained embedded as the slaughter proceeded.

My breath was punched out of me when one of the assassins, whom I recognised as Andrew Ker of Fawdonside, pressed his loaded pistol to the Queen's womb and pulled the trigger. That moment still unfolds in my nightmares in slow motion. I can still hear the dry click of the hammer. I can still see Mary's eyes frozen with dread. I can hear her scream. I envisage her standing still and numb, in the grip of mortal fear.

Praise be that God protected her and her unborn babe for no man could. By the Lord's agency, the pistol did not fire.

They detached Rizzio from the Queen's skirts and dragged him across the chamber, and hauled him up the stairs like a child's rag doll. After that, left behind in a morbid silence, we could hear his cries of agony as the bloodthirsty butchery continued above our heads, in the presence chamber.

Holding her around the waist, Darnley led the Queen to her bedchamber as she swore bitterly, 'I shall cause you to have as sore a heart as I have right now.'

'I am your husband and you promised me obedience the day I married you,' he lectured her in return, 'and that I should be your equal in all things—'

Her eyes fell on me, a cry for help crumpling her features. I saw rather than heard her mouth to me, 'Find Bothwell. Warn him.'

XII

Written on this the Eighteenth Day of September in the Year of our Lord 1592

Under the cover of the unfolding chaos, I was able to run out of the closet unobserved. I crossed the Queen's presence chamber where David Rizzio's lacerated body lay abandoned by his assassins. I witnessed porters tearing David's fine furred cape from his shoulders and stripping his doublet from his body. His leg became momentarily animated as one of the porters tugged at the corpse's velvet hose. I shuddered at the sight of David's naked chest punctuated with bloody gashes. I could not stop to deliver the rites over the poor man's earthly remains for fear of being identified and thwarted in my mission. I ran past the armed guards posted at every exit by Morton. I was heading to the other side of the palace where the lords Bothwell and Huntly were lodging.

I burst upon them as they were having supper and described to them, between gasps for air and cries of horror, everything that had occurred in the Queen's apartments. Hot-headed Bothwell seized his sword and threatened to confront the attackers and single-handedly free Mary. Lord Huntly and I had to wrestle the weapon out of his hand as I impressed upon him Her Majesty's will: he was to rally her supporters and organise a rescue party, not throw himself onto the swords of her captors.

The palace was swarming with armed guards. Bothwell listened for a while to the din of many feet outside and at last realised that he and Huntly stood no chance of taking them all on.

'Tell Her Majesty that we will come back for her with an army,' he said before he and Huntly squeezed through a narrow back window overlooking the lion garden. I watched their doubled-down figures slink away until they were embraced by the night.

I headed back to the Queen's apartments. I was diverted on the stairs by the arrival of Ruthven with a score of guards. I decided to take an alternative route via the Queen's private chapel.

THE QUEEN'S AVENGER

It was quiet in that quarter but as I was sneaking through the lobby, my eye was caught by the figure of Henry Yair. He had emerged from the bedchamber of my good friend, Father Adam Black. Yair had a crazed look in his eyes and was holding a dagger dripping with blood. I pressed my back against the wall and let the unholy fanatic pass, unchallenged. As soon as he was gone, I ran to check on Father Black. I found him in his bed, his body perforated with multiple stab wounds. His breath bubbled with red foam.

'Adam...' I heard myself whisper in horror.

His hand reached for mine and with a strength I didn't expect, he pulled me close. His lips moved, spitting blood and the name of his assassin, 'Henry Yair—'

'I know, I know,' I told him. 'I'll bring him to justice, rest assured.'

A shadow of a smile crossed his face and he relaxed his grip on my arm.

'Pray for my soul,' were his last words.

Alas, I had not time for prayer. I had to tear myself away from my friend's dead body and find a way back to the Queen. I was intercepted in the lobby by Leslie. He gripped my arm painfully, 'Ninian, where are you heading? There's no return to the apartments.'

I told him I was going to see the Queen; I had a message for her.

'Haven't you heard? We've been permitted by the King to leave the palace. We must make haste before they make him change his mind. Come with me. I have a carriage waiting—'

I unbent his fingers that were still clawing at my arm and pushed him away. 'No, my friend. I'm not leaving. She needs me here.'

To my dismay, I was prevented from seeing the Queen that night. Armed guards remained posted at the door to her bedchamber. They were under strict orders from Morton not to allow her any contact with the outside word. I feared for her life and for the life of her unborn baby. I didn't retire to my lodgings but stayed put near the door, perched in a chair, awake, watching the manoeuvres of her captors. A dagger was concealed in my sleeve in case I too, like Father Black, was on Henry Yair's list.

In the early hours of the morning, a commotion ensued. I could hear Mary's cries and whimpers in her bedchamber. Darnley shot out and yelled for a midwife. The guards stood confounded, unsure what to do until he threw a tantrum and began waving his dagger – one thing he was good at. The midwife and the Queen's physician, a Frenchman, were sent for.

Tense minutes passed as she was being examined behind closed doors. I was beside myself with anxiety. Had the bloody events of the previous night sent Mary into premature labour? Was she about to lose her baby? If that was the case, her captors had the blood of yet another victim on their hands: the future king of Scotland.

At last, the Queen's cries subsided and the doctor came out of her apartment, an expression of grave concern on his face. Morton accosted him right next to where I was sitting and demanded to know if Mary had miscarried. He had his back to me so I could not see his eyes, but his voice alone betrayed something bordering on keen expectation.

'She has come close to losing her child, my Lord,' the physician replied in accented Scot. 'She is not out of danger yet, but she's strong and she's a fighter.'

'Is she now?' a note of disappointment, even nervousness, rang in the Lord's voice.

'She's in need of her ladies in waiting and she's been calling for her confessor. In case it comes to the worst, she wants to clear her conscience before God.'

'I must see her!' I sprang to my feet and fixed the nasty bull of a man with a firm, uncompromising eye. 'I'm her priest and confessor. It's my duty before God to hear her—'

'Ninian Winzet, fancy finding you here! Round and round you go, like a bad smell,' Morton frowned, displeased.

'Her Majesty requested my presence,' I insisted.

'Oh, just go in!' Morton waved his arm in dismissal, muttering something under his breath about *rotten papists* and *stubborn women*. 'Get on with your hocus-pocus.'

THE QUEEN'S AVENGER

Mary was reclined on the bed, looking comfortable if in a state of agitation. When she saw me enter, she sat up and outstretched her arms towards me, 'My dear Ninian! Come closer. We have much to discuss.'

I folded myself into a deep bow. 'Is Your Majesty feeling better?'

'I'm well. As well as I can be under the circumstances of my imprisonment and threats to my life.' A tear glistened in her eye, but she quickly recovered her composure. 'No more tears,' she said. 'It's time to think upon escape, and then – revenge.'

I couldn't agree more but I hastened to inform her of the gravity of the situation: Rizzio was dead, so was Father Black, most of her allies had fled and the palace was swarming with armed guards under Lord Morton's command.

'What of Bothwell and Huntly? Have you passed on my message?'

'Indeed, and they have both escaped. Lord Bothwell pledged to organise rescue.'

'Which he will. I have faith in him. But we can't wait idly. I have a plan and I will need your help.' And she proceeded to apprise me of the events of the previous night.

XIII

Written on this the Eighteenth Day of September in the Year of our Lord 1592

A knock on her door had stirred Mary from a fitful sleep in the dead of night. She sat in her bed, listening, her heart pounding in her chest. Having witnessed Rizzio's death, she was fearful for her own life. Her lords had rebelled against her. They had abandoned all pretence of loyalty to their sovereign. Had they now come to murder her and her unborn heir? Perhaps they wouldn't dare do it in public view, but under the cover of darkness they could dispose of her quietly and claim she had taken her own life, out of shame, or grief for her alleged lover.

Clutching her small but deadly Damascus steel dagger, she tiptoed to the back door, and whispered, 'Who's there?'

'It's me, my love,' another tremulous whisper answered her. She recognised Darnley's voice. Gone was his earlier bravado. He sounded frightened. 'Let me in, Mary. I slipped past the guards, gone by our private staircase, but they're watching and when they discover I'm gone—'

'I don't believe you,' she hissed through the keyhole. 'They sent you to kill me. And our son!'

'I would never, I swear!'

'Wouldn't you? You didn't think twice of taking Rizzio's life.'

'Mary, my love, I didn't... I loved him, too. But I couldn't turn a blind eye to the rumours or impropriety. Voices... so many voices crying that the babe you carry in your womb isn't mine—'

'You'd take the word of cowardly gossipmongers over mine? Go away!' She was barely able to control her indignation. Fury was building up in her chest.

'I can't. I'm scared, Mary, scared for my life. They put sentries by my door. God alone knows what they are planning to do to me in the morning. They played a cruel trick on me. They'd made pledges they didn't keep. They laughed in my face when— They

THE QUEEN'S AVENGER

told me to mind my place! Told me, their King! Oh, Mary, please let me in, let us stand together against the traitors.'

Listening to his whinnying, Mary made a quick calculation in her mind. He was seeking her protection. Granting it to him could help her expose the conspirators and bring down their leaders. She could play them against each other.

At dawn, Mary admitted Darnley into her bedchamber.

He threw himself to his knees, all atremble. 'Oh Mary, my dearest love, will you ever forgive me!'

She commanded him to rise and tell all he knew.

'I've been betrayed,' he lamented, selfishly focused on his own wretched person. 'They confined me to my bedchamber and banned me from seeing you, my Queen, other than under their supervision. Oh, the humiliation! The betrayal! I shall not forget!'

'And neither will I. But this isn't the time for recriminations,' she admonished the fool. 'We have to be prepared, Henry. What are their plans? Do you know?'

'I've heard Ruthven and Morton consort outside my apartments about sending you under guard to Stirling and their taking charge of the government of Scotland. They have discarded me, Mary! I'm king in name only, and soon I will be dead…' The last word he pronounced with such dread that it came out as a whimper of a hapless babe.

Watching his pathetic capitulation, Mary squeezed her fists. Her resolve grew stronger. She quickly realised the extent of the conspiracy against her person, the identity of the leader of the coup and the perfidy of his intentions. Like the strike of a blacksmith's hammer, every new revelation hardened her heart and forged it into a nugget of steel.

And then came the final assault. 'They promised me the Crown Matrimonial,' Darnley whined, 'Moray pledged it to me—'

'My brother? But he's in exile, in Newcastle.'

'He's here, in Edinburgh. I granted him safe passage and promised him a royal pardon in return for the Crown Matrimonial – which you had obstinately refused to grant me – but they,' Darnley sniffled, self-absorbed and oblivious to the effect his words were having on his wife. 'But they reneged on it, and now, my dear Mary, I fear their next step is to get you and me out of the way. My life is in peril. I'm certain of it!'

Mary calmed him and questioned him further, 'These are grave accusations you're making, Henry – accusations of treason against my brother. Without any proof—'

'You ask for proof? I have it! We signed a bond while Moray was still in Newcastle. It's all been agreed in writing, signed and sealed: the removal of Rizzio, a safe passage and royal pardons for the exiled lords and my... *my* Crown Matrimonial! What was I to do? How could I refuse?'

'You could have spoken to me – trusted me – your wife and queen!'

'The rumours, Mary, the cursed rumours! Rumours were rife about you and Rizzio. How much time he was spending by your side, locked alone with you in your apartments ... How he carried himself about the court – a painted, boastful peacock! I couldn't stomach that any longer! You'd been denying me familiarity and your company, and I began to think ... Oh, my dear Mary, how sorry I am!'

Mary soothed his bleeding ego with kind words and assured him of her constancy. She later told me of the physical repulsion she'd felt when she touched the quivering muck of her husband.

'But the rumours, Mary! There's no smoke without fire. Rizzio was a whore, and I should know—' Darnley paused and swallowed the rest of the insult for he would have incriminated himself. 'He had to be eliminated. He had offended my honour – your honour, my dear Mary. There're doubts about your child's paternity—'

'That's preposterous! I am carrying your child in my womb,' Mary protested, aggrieved beyond reason. 'Can't you see? My wicked brother has orchestrated this. He played you for a fool so that he could eliminate us both, undermine the legitimacy of our child and claim the crown of Scotland for himself! Open your eyes, Henry! There'll be no Crown Matrimonial for you! James will deny ever promising you anything—'

'He can't. I have proof!' That was when Darnley handed her his copy of the bond with the words: 'If it is ever known that I gave it to you, I will be a dead man.'

Mary read the document with horror. If she had been harbouring any hope before, she now knew her life was in mortal peril. Moray would not stop at having her servant murdered. Once she was trapped at Stirling, away from the public eye, she would be as good as dead. She had to do everything in her power to get away from the rebels and mobilise her army. She had to outsmart her captors, divide and conquer them. First of all, she had to escape, and that was where I came in.

She had feigned labour pains so that she could call for me on the pretext of making peace with God in the event of her death. A deathbed confession was the last thing on Mary's mind however. As soon as she relayed to me what had occurred in the night, we formulated a plan of action.

While Darnley, who was now back, snivelling at her heel, continued with the charade of proclaiming the royal pardon for Moray and reintroducing him into the lap of the Queen's favour, I worked in the background organising the grand escape. I took a message to Lady Huntly who in her turn organised Bothwell and Huntly to wait for us at Seton wherefrom they would escort the Queen to her stronghold at Dunbar Castle.

Repulsed as she was by her half-brother's duplicitous dealings, Mary received him the following day. She put on a grand performance when she embraced and kissed him, wept most convincing tears of joy and declared, 'Oh, my brother, if you had been here I should not have been so uncourteously handled!'

Moray swore his indignation at her captors, betraying not a word of his own involvement. He too wept and bent his knee before her, declaring his undying loyalty to his queen and offering his service and protection. Had I not known the truth, I myself would have been moved to tears by his magnanimity.

The next morning, Darnley again sneaked into the Queen's apartments unnoticed and in my presence apprised her of the lords' secret meeting in the night when they agreed to persist with their original plan to remove Mary to the castle of Stirling while they took control of Parliament. Should she refuse to formally relinquish power to Moray, they would put her to death or detain her in perpetual captivity.

I watched Mary's complexion pale upon hearing that. She was but a young lass, an orphan, with an idiot for a husband, vulnerable and frightened for herself and the babe she was carrying in her womb. I wished I could embrace her, shield her with my own body, but I knew not to offend her dignity.

She thought on it for a long while. Darnley and I sat in grim silence, waiting for her decision. At last, she spoke, and her composure astounded me, 'We will give them what they want. Tell them, Henry, to start drawing up their pardons, ready for us to sign.'

'You can't possibly trust them, my dear Mary!' Darnley spluttered, his voice high like that of a choir boy.

'We do not trust them. Far from it! And we don't intend to ever forgive them, but don't you think that by pleading for our forgiveness they will inadvertently admit their wrongdoing? It will be a confession of guilt on their part, in writing.'

Darnley took a moment to contemplate her words and at long last, smiled.

'Good,' the Queen smiled back. 'Meantime, Father Ninian will finalise our escape plans for tonight. Be ready.'

After supper, Darnley went to see the traitors to collect their petitions for pardon, excusing Her Majesty for not appearing in person on the account of her poor health. He had succeeded at convincing Morton to remove the armed guards from her apartments. All along, he had been trembling like a leaf and whinnying about his personal safety should the Lords discover how he had double-crossed them. It was too late for second thoughts, Mary warned him and he took the chastisement with a low growl, like a caged wolf.

Meantime, a messenger had arrived from our allies: Bothwell and Huntly had gathered four thousand armed Borderers and were on their way to Seton to await the Queen. There was just the minor matter of the Queen escaping from under the watchful eyes of her captors, and that was down to me.

THE QUEEN'S AVENGER

I had enlisted a few men whose loyalty to the Queen I was certain of to saddle horses. They were waiting for us outside Canongate cemetery. At the stroke of midnight, a small party of fugitives gathered on the back stairs outside the Queen's chamber. There was just five of us: the Queen and Darnley, Her Majesty's gentlewoman Margaret, and her page Anthony Standen. We proceeded stealthily through the servants' quarters, down to the wine cellar which led out into the cemetery.

We emerged into a chilly night. An owl hooted ominously as if counting us down to a fatal end. Headstones stood stone-silent and cold with the exception of a mound of fresh soil: wet and glistening in the ghostly light of the moon. It was David Rizzio's hurriedly dug grave. Darnley confirmed as much, looking contrite and bemoaning, hypocritically, the passing of his faithful friend and servant. I nearly spat my indignance in his face, but Mary only hushed the fool for fear that we should be overheard and discovered.

We made it to the outskirts of the cemetery where our horses were waiting. Mary mounted behind Arthur Erskine, her Master of Horse, since Darnley was too shaken to offer her his assistance. With the cold moon looking down on us, we rode east at a breakneck gallop.

The journey was gruelling but Mary uttered not a single word of complaint. Darnley, on the other hand, groused and grumbled to everyone's silent annoyance. The man was a quivering wreck. On a few occasions, I wished I could wring his neck and be done with him once and for all.

As we approached Seton, we were confronted by black, unmoving silhouettes of several horsemen on the road. It looked as if they had formed a blockade. Darnley squealed in terror, convinced those were his erstwhile co-conspirators, Morton and Ruthven, out to get him. He whipped Mary's horse, spurred his own and urged her to flee, crying: 'By God's blood, they will murder both you and me if they catch up!'

He was bereft of reason or any regard for the Queen's condition. I called upon him to restrain himself and mind the wellbeing of his unborn son. To that he responded with callousness so acerbic that it burnt a hole in my gut, and no doubt, in Mary's. 'If the child dies,' he declared, 'we can have another. Hurry! Let's go before we're all dead!'

The man was a monster.

I ground my teeth and rolled my fist in impotent anger. Perhaps he wanted the baby dead; perhaps he truly believed that the child wasn't his?

As the coward galloped away, the mysterious horsemen drew level with us. We greeted our saviours, Bothwell and Huntly. They led us to the safety of the castle of Dunbar. Within hours, Her Majesty's faithful supporters began to arrive in numbers to pledge their loyalty to their true monarch.

Two days later, Mary dispatched me with a letter to Queen Elizabeth with the news of the rebellion. In my saddlebags were also letters written in code addressed to her uncles in France and to Philip of Spain, and one final epistle to the Holy Father in Rome. At this point, she was still uncertain of her victory over the rebels. She needed every help she could get. As much as I wished I could stay by her side, I knew my mission could save her life should our worst nightmares come true.

'Be careful, Father. Avoid Edinburgh.' She always had the presence of mind to think of others, even in distress when her own life hung in the balance. 'God's speed.'

I offered her my blessing and departed.

XIV

Written on this the Eighteenth Day of September in the Year of our Lord 1592

Three months later I was travelling back to Scotland. I had delivered the Queen's letters and had been graciously received by the Cardinal of Lorraine and the new pope, Pius V. Both had expressed their commiserations at Mary's misfortune and their unequivocal condemnation of the rebellion, yet neither could offer her more than the empty words of their moral support. Both claimed to be thwarted by circumstances beyond their control.

The Cardinal had lost his influence at the French court after the pubescent King Charles succeeded Mary's late husband, Francois. The new king's mother, Catherine de Medici had taken the reins of government on the day of Francois's death and sent the de Guises away, one by one. She had asserted full control over Charles and the affairs of state. Her loathing of Mary was well known. She would not come to Mary's rescue and would, in fact, relish her fall.

The Holy Father, as much as he longed for the restoration of Catholicism in Scotland, complained of his empty coffers depleted by his predecessor. He promised to have a word with Philip of Spain about deploying his army and organising a landing from the shores of the Low Countries, but they would firstly have to break down the English. It would be a long wait yet.

I was traversing the rolling, verdant planes of northern England with a heavy heart. My saddlebags were weighed down with pages of meaningless reassurances from the rulers on the Continent and their even more meaningless – and insulting – wishes of enduring good health for my Queen. Words are cheap. Actions cost money and help doesn't come to those who can't pay. I have learned these tough lessons in my long life, but thirty years ago I was heart-broken for Mary. I dreaded the new reality I would be faced with upon my return. Would I find Mary defeated, humiliated, subjugated by her bastard half-brother? Would I find her supporters scattered, some hiding in exile abroad, others in the Highlands under the protectorate of the last few Lords who remained faithful to Rome and to our Queen? I was too fatigued to contemplate those unsavoury possibilities, or perhaps, too disheartened.

As the sun went down in a hue of crimson, I stopped at an inn on the southern periphery of Newcastle. I watched scarlet sunrays skid over the crenelations of the castle towers across the river. I would cross the Tyne Bridge at first light. For now, my backside was raw with discomfort after hours in the saddle. I threw the saddlebag over my shoulder and handed the reins to a young groom with hair as white as dove feathers and eyes equally pale, as if bleached by the sun. I instructed the urchin to take good care of my horse and threw him a coin for his trouble, promising another one the next day.

The inn was full to the brim, buzzing with drunken hubbub, laughter, bawdy quarrels, the clatter of plates and tankards, the chiming of naked blades and coins tossed across the counter. Busty English barmaids with their cheeks and lips pinched red flounced amongst the tables, serving steaming pottage and ale. Their skin glistened with sweat. The whole place was like a reheated brew of stale breath and farts.

I took a table by the window, for some air, and ordered my supper: bread, cheese and a cup of wine. When it arrived, the wine tasted like dog's piss and the bread was harder than nails. I didn't wish to complain. I was hungry enough to eat a dead rat.

I enquired after a room for the night and was told that they were full, what with the other Scottish travellers, noblemen nonetheless, who had arrived two months ago and showed no inclination to carry on their way. It was at that moment that I picked up the sounds of Scots cutting through the drool and drivel of the English twang.

My curiosity aroused, I peered discreetly in their direction, my face partly obscured by the hood of my cape.

My eyes glazed with fury when I recognised the vile faces of Morton and Ruthven, Mary's erstwhile captors, now on the run from justice. They didn't try to keep their identities hidden, either.

THE QUEEN'S AVENGER

They were dining like kings: blood-red juices sluicing through their beards, bones cracking in their teeth, wine splattering from their cups as they clanked them in the air. No doubt, they were celebrating their lucky escape and plotting their next move. Ruthven's gravelly voice grinded at my ears and made my skin crawl.

I could not let them get away. This was my chance, delivered to me by the Almighty, to exact the Queen's punishment on the scoundrels and to show their accomplices that none of them would be safe: they would all be hunted down and brought to justice.

I was only but a humble priest, the Queen's courier disguised as a merchant, unarmed and alone, but God was with me and, as He had, in His unerring wisdom, guided me to this place, His plan must have been for me to deliver His justice right there and then. That was when I remembered Widow Ainsley's mushroom powder. In a guilty man, she had told me, it would awaken his demons. It was time to put it to the test.

I rummaged through my cloak pockets for the pouch. I had been carrying it with me since the day Widow Ainsley gave it to me, knowing that one day I would need it. This was the day.

I summoned the barmaid and requested a jug of their best wine. When she returned with it, I poured myself a cup. It was indeed of prime quality, pungent with rich oaky flavour. It would almost be a shame to contaminate it, but it was to serve a purpose higher than pleasing one's palate. I took a decent pinch of the mushroom powder from my pouch and, as the barmaid seemed distracted by some reveller's unwanted attention, sprinkled it into the jug. I gave it a good swivel, handed her a half-crown and pointed her in the direction of the two Scottish lords.

'Take the wine to my compatriots, with my compliments.'

She grinned widely, her narrow nostrils flaring. 'You'd be the first and last charitable Scot I'll ever run into,' she quipped and, hips swaying, swaggered towards Ruthven and Morton. She set the jug on their table and spoke to them, briefly pointing at me. They both looked up, intrigued. I was hoping they were drunk enough not to get too wary of a stranger's generosity.

I raised my cup to them, making sure that it obscured my eyes.

Dressed in a peddler's garb, my hair and beard unkempt after weeks in the saddle, the chance of my being recognised by either of them was a small one.

Morton's eyes narrowed with suspicion – he'd always been a wily red fox – but Ruthven's pale face crinkled in a big, hearty grin.

Blissfully, the barmaid's wide hips sailed in and moored between me and Morton's glare as she filled their cups. Ruthven grabbed his cup, returned my toast, and gulped it down in one go. He wiped his beard with the back of his hand and nodded to the barmaid for a refill. He drank that too and nudged Morton's cup towards him, encouraging the scowling fox to join him. At last Morton raised his cup.

I breathed relief.

Ruthven's third cupful made it down his gut and that was when he was seized by a powerful fit. His body jolted backwards and knocked Morton's cup out of his hand; it flew across the floor, spilling its contents. He surrendered to a series of bizarre contortions with pink bile foaming from his mouth, his eyes bulging and his fingers gnarling like damp wood scorched by fire.

I had no doubt I was witnessing the old warlock being pulled, tugged and twisted by his many demons as they clung on to his earthly form. Morton tried to grip his comrade's shoulders and shake sense into him, but Ruthven sprang to his feet and, with the strength of the Devil himself, flung Morton across the floor. He then threw himself down to his knees and began to roll his eyes and rave about a blinding blaze of light illuminating his path to Paradise and scores of golden angels coming to take him.

I felt righteous calm spill through me, cold but comforting.

There was no light and no angels waiting for Patrick Ruthven beyond the grave, only the fires of Hell and his own demons coming to claim him.

His body tensed as if pierced with a lance and he collapsed in a puddle of his bile and piss – dead at last.

'Patrick!' Morton's scream slashed the silence that had come down on the tavern like a shroud. He knelt by his comrade's body and gripped his arms, and pulled the wretched warlock out of his own excrement. There was no one to help him. Everyone stared in shock, too frightened to touch the still warm remains of a man possessed by evil spirits.

'Don't stand there! Help me!' Morton shouted, but nobody stirred.

Morton's eyes, wild and shot with blood, darted from face to face. I knew he was looking for me.

I pulled my hood over my brow, turned on my heel and walked out to spend the night under the starry sky, praising the Lord for His timely intervention.

A week later, I arrived in Edinburgh to the wonderful news of the birth of our future king, James VI. Mary was back in control of her own destiny and the destiny of her kingdom. Once again, she had defeated her detractors and retained the love of her people. God was on our side.

PART 4

2nd October 1592, Ratisbon, Bavaria

Gunther sat numb and disbelieving. He pored over and over the last page of Abbot Ninian's confession as if there was still a chance that the dead man could change his mind and alter his words from beyond the grave. Perhaps Gunther had misread something. Perhaps he had misunderstood. But no matter how many times he re-read the Abbot's words, their meaning remained the same: Ninian Winzet had confessed to murder, and by means no less vile than witchcraft.

Gunther pondered his options. Something was telling him that his duty was to notify his elders of this gruesome discovery. Ninian Winzet's body should not have been buried in consecrated ground. It would have to be exhumed and condemned to an unmarked grave outside the town walls, like any other common criminal. His soul would have to wander the earth in the shadows of the night, cursed and alone, until Judgment Day. Except that the Abbot did not deserve such a fate. By Gunther's assessment, Ninian Winzet had been a good, God-fearing man – and Gunther's guardian angel.

Gunther recalled the day he had first arrived at St James's monastery. The fourth son of a Bavarian soldier who had fought on the losing side and fallen on hard times after the plague claimed his wife and three of his four children, Gunther had joined the Order with nothing but the shirt on his back and a pure heart full of good intentions. That didn't seem to be enough for Father Archibald. He had turned Gunther away from the gate – St James's was a Scottish monastery and Gunther was an uneducated Bavarian pauper; he didn't belong here. He was advised to chance his luck as a mercenary in the Emperor's army, or a labourer if the sight of blood wasn't for his eyes. It was Abbot Ninian who had overheard the conversation and taken pity on Gunther. He was the only one who was prepared to give Gunther a chance.

THE QUEEN'S AVENGER

Over the next five years, the Abbot had taught Gunther to read and write and now Gunther's Latin was as good as that of any learned scholar. Two years ago, Gunther had taken his vows. According to Abbot Ninian, God had great things in store for Gunther. The Lord's purpose would be revealed to him in due course. Gunther had armed himself with patience.

Alas two years later, the Abbot was dead and God wasn't showing His hand. Without guidance, Gunther was a sheep lost in the night.

He sat unmoving, his fists pressing against his lips, his eyes unblinking. He knew his duty but he wasn't prepared to do it. He rolled the parchments into a bundle and tied it up. He took the scroll back to the secret compartment in the wall. Gunther Kohlman knew the meaning of gratitude. He would not tarnish the good name of his benefactor.

Something odd struck Gunther as he peered into the vault. At first, he couldn't quite put his finger on it, but soon he realised that it was the scarcity: the cubby-hole seemed half-empty. When he first discovered it, it had been packed tight with the seven rolls of parchment and the leather pouch squeezed between them. The leather pouch was there but the scrolls were fewer than expected. He was holding one in his hand; there ought to be six inside the wall.

He counted them. And, incredulous, counted them again. There were only five. He fumbled through them in the hope that the sixth one might have been pushed to the back of the hollow. He didn't find it there. Gunther's eyes skimmed through the dimly-lit chamber. Had he dropped one of the scrolls? Had he misplaced it somewhere on a shelf? Under the desk? Amongst the dead Abbot's volumes of text—

Then he remembered, and when he did, the blood drained from him and a cold shiver rippled down his spine. Last night, upon detecting the intruder's footsteps on the stairwell, Gunther had left the bundle of papers under the inkhorn on the table, and set off after the spy. In the aftermath of the late-night chase, wary of inviting any more unwanted attention, he had forgotten the papers and didn't return to the tower to lock the study door. Gunther had gone back to his cell to lie low, but the intruder must have crept back into the Abbot's rooms. Found the papers. Took them.

The inkhorn stood in the middle of the table, the trembling flame of the oil lamp illuminating the bareness around it. Gunther's teeth chattered in the sudden, overwhelming draught that penetrated his body from the top of his head and down to his toes. He curled his fingers inside his sleeves. He clenched his chattering teeth, his jaw locking. He had to collect his thoughts.

There was no escaping the fact that the intruder was in possession of one bundle. That meant that the Abbot's confessions contained therein were known to at least one person other than Gunther. The witch's draft had been mentioned in the missing scroll as had Ninian's intention to use it. That didn't bode well for the dead clergyman unless the intruder was prepared to keep the revelations secret. So far, he had done exactly that. His intentions were unclear, but a whole day had gone by without Gunther being confronted about the papers.

On a positive note, the other six scrolls remained safely hidden behind the wall panel. The intruder had not found the compartment. He had certainly been searching for it. With the benefit of hindsight, Gunther could clearly see that the chamber had been thoroughly combed through: the Abbot's volumes had been disturbed and re-arranged on the shelves; the candlestick had been moved and the wax pooled around it had been smeared across the table.

The turmoil in Gunther's head subsided. There was still time to put things right. He had to smoke out the intruder, confront him, maybe plead with him, convince him to surrender the papers, convince him that their disclosure would harm the late Abbot's good name – would in fact tarnish the reputation of the whole Order.

Throughout the day Brother Gunther acted normally. He performed his duties with vigour and joined in all the services with keen dedication. He did everything in his power to lull the intruder into thinking that his misdeed had not been discovered.

THE QUEEN'S AVENGER

After supper, catching the remnants of daylight on the moor, Gunther stole out of the monastery. At first, he hid in the undergrowth and sat watching the delivery shaft through which he had exited to check that he wasn't followed. Once assured, he headed for the moor where he dug up some damp bog peat. He shoved it into a hessian bag, concealed it under his cloak, and slunk back into the monastery, in time for Compline.

When night fell, he headed for the tower, as he had done in the past three days, again adopting a casual, unsuspecting manner. He set the peat in a loose pile by the door of the Abbot's scriptorium, retrieved the next scroll from the wall, and began reading, all the while his ears pricked for any sounds betraying the intruder's arrival.

ANNA LEGAT

XV

Written on this the Nineteenth Day of September in the Year of our Lord 1592

Darnley's penitence did not endure beyond the summer of that year. Hardly a few months had passed since David Rizzio's death when Darnley was back to plotting against the Queen. She was steadfast in her resolve to prevent him from ever acquiring the Crown Matrimonial. The birth of their son had pushed him further down the succession ladder. Darnley was raving.

It was as early as the summer of 1566 when the Queen's spies uncovered his new – wholly insane – intrigue. His contrivance was to sail to the Scilly Isles and from there to launch an attack on England. Accusing Mary of collaboration with the Protestant Lords and the heretic Queen Elizabeth, he had petitioned the Catholic kings on the Continent for their financial and military backing with his foolish enterprise. When Darnley's madness reached the ears of his father, Lord Lennox, he in his turn blamed Mary. He had the audacity to accuse her of offending Henry's honour and humiliating him before the whole country. The only remedy, Lennox claimed, was for the Queen to forthwith grant her husband the Crown Matrimonial and her unconditional obedience. And so, we had come full circle and were back to the starting point of the Lennox ambition to rule Scotland. Darnley himself refused to plead either guilt or innocence, and departed for Glasgow where he was reported to engage in all manner of strenuous physical pursuits, including his now public debauchery and drunkenness.

Back in Edinburgh, the wheels of justice were grinding desperately slowly. No one seemed to be taking seriously the compromised King's orders to hunt down, arrest and punish with death Rizzio's murderers. Everyone knew that the lead conspirators were beyond the reach of the executioner's axe. The lords were safe in exile, if outlawed. Darnley had been publicly

THE QUEEN'S AVENGER

forgiven by Mary so that her reputation and the legitimacy of their son were protected; for now, he stood above the law.

But left behind were the servants and paid retainers – one of them Henry Yair.

I could not let that rabid dog get away with the murder of my old friend, Friar Adam Black. We had known each other since we were young priests when Marie de Guise was Regent. He had been her chaplain. His blood-soaked shirts and the name of his assassin spilling out of his mouth in red-stained foam would for ever be etched in my mind. Yair's mad glare, marked by bloodlust, haunted me by night. The man had no right to live. A defrocked priest, a fanatical Calvinist, and now a murderer, he had to be stopped.

At the end of March I visited Bothwell in his sheriff's office at the castle. I was apprehensive whether he would hear me out, his contempt for Catholics and priests in particular was well known. But he received me immediately, even though his manner was gruff and dismissive.

'What is it Winzet?' He swung his feet onto his cluttered desk and reclined in his chair, eyeing me from under a cocked brow. 'Make it quick.'

Not to test his patience unduly, I relayed to him in sharp detail but without lengthy elaborations the outrages I had witnessed Yair commit in the Queen's supper chamber on the night of Rizzio's slaughter and thereafter his frenzied killing of Friar Black. I swore a testimony to the Friar's last words naming his assassin.

'I already know that,' was Bothwell's curt reply. He stood up and headed for the door.

I had no choice but to leave, disappointed with Bothwell's reaction and despondent that I had failed in my task. I was wrong. Yair was arrested in a matter of hours and by August I watched him being led to the scaffold to be hung, drawn and quartered.

The wretch was unrepenting to the last breath he drew, shouting blasphemy and insults against the Queen and the Holy Father in Rome as the noose was tightened on his neck. Crazed though it was, his bloodshot gaze fell on me and his eyes narrowed with cold lucidity.

'Beware! Adam Black – John Noir – a papist whore and French spy is dead, and I rid the world of him. But the traitors are still walking amongst us! Hiding within the mob! You kill one, another comes in his place. Beware!' And he lifted his bound wrists, his bloodied forefinger trained on me.

Several curious gazes descended upon me. I swiftly drew my hood over my brow and, shoulders hunched, withdrew from the crowd. I could hear the creak of the trapdoor opening on the gallows and the hollow thud of Yair's body dropping, and then the squeak of the gibbet as he kicked and swayed before giving up the ghost. I did not stay to witness the quartering. It would have been too dangerous to draw more attention to myself. There was a Calvinist fanatic on every street corner, ready to step into Yair's shoes.

In October, the Queen and her court came to the town of Jedburgh on the English border to hold a justice ayre. We lodged in a bastle house in the main street. My heart was warmed by the overwhelming love bestowed upon Mary by the residents of the town. She was not only the queen of her kingdom but also the queen of her subjects' hearts.

Alas, a few days after her arrival, Mary fell violently ill. She was overcome by episodes of vomiting so frenzied that she would lose consciousness. Her Marys tended to her day and night, their faces drawn with exhaustion and worry. They wouldn't say it out loud, but it was written in their eyes: they feared their beloved Queen was dying, possibly poisoned by her enemies.

Eleven days into the malady, Darnley rode into Jedburgh. I looked into his eyes and saw anxiety and, for a moment, I believed he was concerned – frightened for Mary. That moment however passed faster than the blink of an eye.

He threw his cloak at me as if I were a manservant and strode into Mary's bedchamber, his sword clanking at his thigh. He sent away her physician Arnault and other attendants, and was left with her alone. My hopes that he was offering her comfort were quickly dashed. Within minutes of an ominous silence that followed Darnley into the room, he began to shout. He was demanding *his*

THE QUEEN'S AVENGER

due: the Crown Matrimonial. He raved about his rights, his status, his superiority. He accused Mary of putting his life in danger, of breaking promises, of lying, of consorting with servants. He had the audacity to tell her she was dying and that it was his turn now to rule Scotland – by right.

Outside the door, I ground my teeth in hopeless fury. I clenched my fists and held back an outpouring of profanities. Given a chance, a moment alone with the vicious invert, I wouldn't have hesitated to cut his throat to stem the flow of vitriol coming out of his mouth, and free my Queen from the hold he had on her. My fingers curled over the pouch strung from my belt. I was tempted. Maybe by the Devil himself – I didn't care – but I was tempted to slip the witch's draft into Darnley's drink. And if he had stayed that night, I would have done so. But I heard him howl, 'So you refuse me, Madam? You'll come to regret it! Either way, you're a dead woman!' and he charged out of the chamber. He snatched his cloak from me and left. He went to Edinburgh to drown his anger in drink and depravity.

We swarmed into Mary's bedchamber, her Marys and I. The expression in her eyes was that of unspeakable horror. Her face had contorted into an odious twist, her lips pulled back from her chattering teeth. She was looking at me. She whispered, the effort deforming her speech, but I understood her every word:

'He'll kill me... Protect my son... Prince James is to succeed me should I—'

She was seized by a powerful convulsion. Her body arched and she collapsed in her bed. Her limbs seemed to contract, her fingers curling, her feet twisting around her ankles, gnarled like diseased branches. We all fell to our knees and prayed. We beseeched the Lord to breathe life back into our Queen, for her sake, the sake of her helpless son, and for the sake of her kingdom. She could neither join us in prayer, nor hear us. She was dumb, and deaf and blind. She remained so for several days.

I suspected Darnley had cast a deadly spell upon her. He had after all threatened her with dying. His mother was an infamous witch – she must have taught him a few tricks. He would pay, I vowed as I knelt in prayer by my Queen's deathbed.

On the third day, Mary's scheming half-brother rushed to Jedburgh. He sat at her side holding her cold hand, rubbing warmth into it. I was almost fooled, but the next morning he ordered the servants to open the windows of her room – a salient announcement of her impending passing. He and Maitland began discussing funeral arrangements, Prince James's coronation and Moray's regency, all in rapid succession. On Sunday night, after I performed the last rites over Mary's cold and unresponsive body, I saw Moray reach for her hand and attempt to remove her emerald ring.

'My Lord!' I gasped, mortified.

He started, glared at me, scowled his displeasure, but then his thieving fingers shifted away from the Queen.

'Leave us alone, preacher,' he growled at me.

I left the room, but stayed by the door like a faithful dog, ready to pounce and sink my teeth into anyone meaning her harm. A short while later, Moray departed. I went inside to check that all of Mary's rings were present and accounted for.

As mourning dresses were being ordered and funeral preparations were in full swing, Mary began to recover. I had no doubt it was the power of prayer and faith that had brought her back from the dead. And her sheer determination not to be defeated by the servants of Satan.

THE QUEEN'S AVENGER

XVI

Written on this the Nineteenth Day of September in the Year of our Lord 1592

Darnley's descent into madness was unremitting. His unmanly leanings had by now become common knowledge at court. Whispers grew bolder that his lunacy was the result of the great pox he had contracted in dens of ill repute which he frequented openly and with scant regard for the Queen's or his own honour. Unsavoury as it was, his madness was also dangerous in the extreme.

Intelligence reports were arriving thick and fast of Darnley's increasingly daring conspiracies against the Queen. He was writing to Philip of Spain, the king of France, the Pope and even to Mary's uncle, the Cardinal of Lorraine, proposing to seize guardianship of the infant Prince, to overthrow – imprison, even execute if need be – Queen Mary, and to establish himself on the Scottish throne. In return for their support, he vowed to reverse the laws establishing the Reformist Church of Scotland and to reinstate Catholicism. Mary, he claimed, had turned away from the true Religion and sold her soul to the Devil. It was all sheer, unrepentant, unbridled madness.

The man had to be restrained; his contrivances stopped.

A month into Mary's recovery, her chief nobles gathered at the castle of Craigmillar on the outskirts of Edinburgh where the Queen was recuperating under the watchful eye of Arnault and under my spiritual guidance. As much as her physical health was significantly improved, her soul was in the throes of deep melancholy. Her husband's betrayal was weighing heavily on her mind, her suspicions and fears eating into her heart. At long last, she had to concede that her husband, the man she had once loved, the father of her child, the King she had made from the clay and dust of his insignificance, had to be brought to heel.

We all sat in the presence hall hung with the Queen's tapestries, a lively fire blazing in the hearth, and hardly any other light in the room. The faces of the Lords were grey and tight with the gravity of the matter at hand. Mary was seated comfortably, her feet covered with a mink blanket, a soft fur-collared cloak hugging her shoulders. She looked pale and weak, her face silently crying for help. But even in despair she held her head high and her back straight.

Maitland opened the meeting and presented the Queen with evidence of her husband's connivances. She winced painfully. A shudder bristled through the fur of her cloak.

'It is undeniable,' she conceded at last. 'What do you propose we do?'

'Your Majesty, you must consolidate your supporters. I realise the idea of forgiving Rizzio's assassins is odious to you, but bear in mind the loathing they carry in their hearts for the King who betrayed them. If you, Your Majesty, were to harness that hatred to your advantage, you'd gain most loyal subjects.'

'You propose we give pardon to Morton and the others?'

'If it pleases Your Majesty, I do.' There was a slight tilting of the old weasel's head as he added, 'And the Earl of Moray agrees with me.'

'Of course, he does... But why isn't he here to offer me his counsel in person?'

'Your Majesty, he rebelled against you, recklessly and unwisely, he admits, when you resolved to marry Darnley. Mindful of that mistake, the Earl wishes to maintain his distance in the matter of the King's fate. However, I have his ear and his pre-approval for whatever may be decided today. He shall stand by you.'

'We will issue the pardons,' Mary said simply. 'Now tell us how we proceed henceforth.'

'I would recommend a divorce petition be drafted without delay,' Maitland began.

At that, Lord Bothwell – reddened in the face and none too pleased with the pardon and the imminent return of his old enemies – stepped in. 'My Queen, you know I always served you faithfully and I always will. I am a man of sword, not words or legal nuance. So let me speak plainly: I don't believe we have time for dithering and for prolonged legal proceedings. Your husband is a dangerous

THE QUEEN'S AVENGER

villain. He has to be restrained now, before he inflicts real harm on you and our wee Prince James—'

'You don't suggest murdering the King!'

'No, not murder, Your Majesty. Not murder, but an execution.'

'On what basis?'

'Treason. Have we not seen evidence enough to know what he is planning? He is preparing to overthrow you. He's reconciled with the prospect of murdering you if that is what it takes to seize the throne. That's treason and treason is punishable by death.'

'No,' Mary spoke without sparing a moment to even contemplate such a possibility. 'That would amount to regicide. Henry isn't a mere subject. He is King.'

'In name only, Your Majesty,' Huntly was quick to point out. 'Your proclamation wasn't approved by Parliament. We could argue that—'

'No! I said, no,' she raised her hand to him. 'There will be no execution. What other options are there?'

'Divorce,' Maitland resumed his earlier thought. 'We will petition the Pope for a divorce.'

'On what grounds?'

'His conniving against your person, for one. We have ample evidence of the same.'

'Divorce is not permitted.'

'There have been divorces granted by the Pope in the past.'

'But not on the grounds of marital disagreement.'

'In that case, there is his madness. The king has lost his mind.'

'I… We do not… We do not believe he means what he professes in his letters.' Mary seemed troubled by the idea. She stumbled over her words, doubt tripping her up and preventing her from facing the possibility of her husband's murderous intentions having been formed by a man in charge of his faculties. Indeed, he had to be insane. The alternative of his cold, calculated wickedness was intolerable.

'Alleging the King's madness would be kinder to him than raising his femininity – his unholy predilections and debauchery with his own sex—' Huntly said bluntly what everyone else was thinking.

'Yes, a divorce, if it can be obtained,' the Queen interrupted, promptly pushing the warped images out of her mind. 'It must not be sought on grounds that would nullify our marriage *ab initio* and prejudice the legitimacy of our son. Do you understand me?'

We all bowed in silent confirmation.

'We will not allow for Prince James to run the risk of bastardy and we will not tolerate anything that would offend our honour.' Colour rose to Mary's cheeks.

'Everything will be done properly and with Parliament's approval,' Maitland said.

'Then prepare the petition. We wish for Father Ninian to present it to the Holy Father in Rome. This counsel is over. We've letters to write.'

THE QUEEN'S AVENGER

XVII

Written on this the Nineteenth Day of September in the Year of our Lord 1592

I knew my mission was condemned to fail the moment I was denied a personal audience with the Pope. Instead, I would be received by Cardinal D'Amico, Pius's right hand in matters of Counter Reformation and a relentless advocate of the newly devised investigative body called the Holy Inquisition.

He saw me in his dimly lit office, panelled in dark mahogany, with its windows blinded by shutters. He was seated at a desk, the paperwork of the Queen's petition with documents evidencing Darnley's insanity piled neatly on one side. I wondered if he had read it. I wondered if the Holy Father had read it.

I wasn't offered a seat so I remained standing, cap in hand, like a church-step beggar. D'Amico regarded me with his suspicious, heavily hooded eyes. I felt uncomfortable under his gaze, as if my life's transgressions would, at any moment and against my will, creep out onto my tongue and announce themselves to the world.

'Father Ninian,' the Cardinal spoke softly. I lowered my gaze rather too evasively, I feared, and made a reverent bow. 'His Holiness has carefully considered Queen Mary's divorce petition.'

'I'm grateful, Your Eminence.' I deepened my bow.

'It wasn't long ago – hardly a year has passed since you sought His Holiness's dispensation for her marriage to Lord Darnley.'

'Alas, the circumstances have changed radically since then.'

'So I see...' the Cardinal slid his bejewelled forefinger across his lower lip. 'You base your petition on the allegation of King Henry's decline into insanity.'

'Indeed, Your Eminency. Sadly, it has been sudden and rapid. The king is no longer in possession of his own mind. His contrivances against Her Majesty are of grave—'

'His Holiness has received communications from King Henry, too,' D'Amico interrupted my submissions. He jolted his head up impatiently. I could sense his annoyance. 'They do not seem like the ravings of a madman.'

'Appearances can be deceptive.'

'But are they just *appearances?*'

'Forgive me, Your Eminence, I fail to understand your meaning.' Another humble bow on my part.

'He claims your Queen to be dubious in her faith and in her loyalty to the Holy Church. He claims she has abandoned the Catholic cause and is consorting with—'

'That's a calumny,' I protested, inflamed at first, but added more calmly, 'and it proves the king's clouded judgment.'

'A judgment that is rooted in facts,' he fixed me with a hard stare and again, overcome by irrational guilt, I felt like crawling under the floorboards. 'His Holiness has always held his daughter, Queen Mary of Scotland, in high regard. She's been enjoying his unwavering – and taxing on his coffers – support since her return to Scotland. He had high hopes for the Catholic queen to reverse the tide of heresy in her kingdom. Alas…' a theatrical sigh flew from the Cardinal's lips, 'alas our sources report the Queen has surrendered to the forces of Reformation—'

'That is a false and malignant accusation by her sick husband consumed by—'

'Did she not acquiesce to the establishment of the Reformist Church of Scotland and the outlawing of Holy Mass? Did she not proclaim that she would make no alterations in the state of religion and no attempt to restore the true faith?'

'She had no choice! Queen Mary is a devoted daughter of Rome, but the Protestants are a powerful force in Scotland. And they are led by a vile and unstoppable man – John Knox. A convert priest and agitator, he wields enormous influence. He's a venomous viper. The only way to pull out his tongue was to act with caution, build alliances and undermine his power base by showing clemency—'

'Clemency to heretics?'

'To keep peace in the land, Your Eminency. To prevent tumult and sedition.'

THE QUEEN'S AVENGER

'Is your Queen's funding of heretic causes intended to appease them?'

'Funding? I don't understand.'

'We have eyes and ears everywhere,' the Cardinal snapped. He picked up a document from the top of the pile on his desk. He'd been keeping it close to hand, clearly intent to use it in evidence against Mary, 'His Holiness had sent your Queen 150,000 crowns in gold to support her in combatting the apostates, but instead she elected to give £10,000 to the so-called Reformed Church of Scotland. Her spirits are flagging and, in that respect, her aggrieved husband is correct.'

'Your Eminence!' I attempted to object.

He raised his hand, silencing me. 'Our agents verify King Henry's allegations. They are not the ravings of a madman. His Holiness has found no verifiable evidence of his insanity. The divorce decree Queen Mary seeks cannot be granted. At least not on grounds of her spouse's madness.'

I lowered my gaze in submission, bitter as it was. I had not been authorised to raise any other grounds. Darnley's sodomy and treasonous plots would go unpunished. I inwardly wept in impotent anger. I bowed and withdrew from D'Amico's presence with my back bent and my head hung low. The same day left for Scotland.

I arrived in Edinburgh on 9th of February. I was empty-handed and despondent, at a loss as to how I would explain to Mary my failure to secure her divorce from Darnley. As it was the holy feast of Sunday, I would only be able to present myself to Her Majesty the next day. I had until then to ponder how to sweeten for her the bitter pill of the Pope's harsh judgment. I locked myself in my chamber at Holyrood Palace to rest and to clear my head in solitude.

I emerged in the evening to find the palace cold and deserted, the Queen and her courtiers conspicuously absent. After some inquiries, I had been informed that Mary was lodging at Kirk o'Field, the Old Provost's House that lay within the enclave of the collegiate church, on a hill overlooking Cowgate. Her husband was there too, back from his self-imposed exile on his father's estates near Glasgow where he had been conspiring against her so licentiously. The latest gossip was that the King had been struck with an outbreak of the great pox so violent that his whole body was weeping with open pustules and his breath was rank as the sulphurous depths of Hell. Mary, as her charitable nature dictated, was devoting herself to caring for her ailing husband, all acrimonies graciously forgiven and forgotten. Perhaps, I mused, she had reconciled with her wayward husband and no longer cared to divorce him. The papal refusal may not matter after all. I departed to bed in somewhat lighter spirits.

I was shaken awake in the dead of the night. It was like the thunder of cannons firing in a battle fought right beneath my window. The floor under my bed seemed to have shifted and with it, my bed. I sat up, disoriented and in a state of high alert, and crawled out of my blankets. Gripping the walls in the darkness, I crept towards the window.

The new moon shed an eerie light over the thin sprinkling of snow that had just begun to fall. In the distance, to the south, a plume of thick smoke had risen and was hanging over the earth like a leaden cloud. Soon the reek of burning sulphur and stirred dust reached my nostrils. There had been an explosion of some kind, I surmised. Within seconds I could hear a commotion on the stairs and in the lobbies, and the clamour of many agitated voices down in the courtyard.

I lit a candle and found my robes. I dressed hurriedly and, with torch in hand, ran outside. Nobody seemed to know what had caused the bizarre clap of bombardment. We all asked questions and stared at each other in confusion and fear. Then we heard someone shout from the pit of the night, 'Fire! Treason!'

It was George Hackett. His ghost-pale face emerged from the dark, his eyes bulging, his lips pulled back in terror.

'What? Where?' We crowded around him, barring his way, demanding answers.

'Kirk o'Field! The King is dead!'

My heart stopped. Wasn't Mary with her husband? At Kirk o'Field? I gripped Hackett's arm, 'What of the Queen?'

THE QUEEN'S AVENGER

He stared at me, at my fingers digging into his arm, and pulled away from me, 'Out of the way, preacher!'

He pushed me so forcefully that I lost my balance and tumbled to the ground. Hackett disappeared inside the gate.

For a few, blurred moments, I sat in the snow, unable to rise, unable to make sense of anything, paralysed in my resolve. My heart was pounding in my chest, my breath rapid.

What of the Queen?

In a matter of minutes, the Earl of Bothwell was out in the courtyard summoning his soldiers and telling us all to return to our quarters and remain there until he, as Sheriff of Edinburgh, had a chance to investigate. Dragged out of bed, he was dishevelled, frantically fastening his belt, his sword clanking against his thigh. Hackett and his men were milling around him in great agitation, screaming treason and murder.

After some commotion, a party of soldiers was assembled and the gate raised open. They ran into the town, their boots pummelling the icy cobbles.

I scrambled back onto my feet and followed Bothwell and his men to Kirk o'Field.

We found the building collapsed into a pile of rubble, smoke and dust drifting higher and higher into the black sky. Scores of onlookers had gathered in the quadrangle, gasping, crying, lamenting and waving lanterns which illuminated the scene of crime in ghastly flashes. A few citizens threw themselves to their knees and began digging through the rubble with their bare hands. It was better than standing idly so I followed suit though the chances of finding anyone alive were remote. My stomach churned and my heart pounded in my chest like a clapper inside a bell.

What of the Queen?

'Here! Found them! Bring the torches!' The call came from the other side of the ruin. My heart sunk into my gut. We all set off into the garden bordering the Flodden Wall. Torches flamed, turning the night into day. We were held back by the sentries who formed a tight circle around two bodies. Both male, I exhaled my relief.

One of the men was curled on his side, facing down. His nightshirt was rolled up to his waist, and his buttocks and thighs exposed shamefully. The other man lay on his back, also in a short nightshirt. His hand had been placed on his groin; it seemed to guard his modesty. I looked at his face. It was the King. The dead King.

What of the Queen?

THE QUEEN'S AVENGER

PART 5

3rd October 1592, Ratisbon, Bavaria

Gunther's attention was snatched away from the parchment by an almost imperceptible creak on the landing outside the door. He froze and held his breath to listen. Silence answered him. The man outside must have been doing exactly the same. Gunther knew he was there, spying on him. This time he was prepared.

Holding the edge of the parchment, he let it roll back into a bundle, the motion barely a whisper under his fingers. He stealthily rose from the chair and tiptoed to the secret compartment in the wall to deposit the scroll inside it. He would not lose this one – he had learnt his lesson. As he closed the panel the palm of his hand lingered on it briefly to muffle the click. The intruder would not have heard it.

The Abbot's confessions safely locked away, Gunther collected the oil lamp from the desk and stole towards the door where he had earlier scattered some bog peat – part of his elaborate plan to catch the thief. Another creak of the floorboard outside assured him that the intruder was still there. The light from the lamp must have filtered through the gap underneath the door, alerting the spy to Gunther's movements inside. He had to act quickly.

Covering his mouth with a damp linen cloth, he sprinkled the peat with the burning oil from the lamp. The peat began to smoulder, producing a swirling cloud of white smoke. Gunther waved it towards the exit and kicked the door open, shouting, 'Fire!'

The smoke thickened and was belched out onto the landing, momentarily encasing the dark figure cowering there. The intruder inhaled the acrid fumes and was seized by a bout of coughing. Disoriented and blinded by the dense smoke, he swiped his arms around him in a frenzy, at the same time trying to feel his way out.

Gunther reached out and gripped the man's scapular with one hand, the other grappling in the smoke for his hood.

'Reveal yourself!' Gunther croaked through the air thick with smoke, now also penetrating through his makeshift facemask and scratching at his windpipe.

The intruder waved his arms like the blades of a windmill on a stormy night.

'Who are you! Give me back what you stole!' Gunther demanded.

A volley of coughs answered him.

Gunther's fingers slid off the man's scapular as the man wriggled and pushed, trying to extricate himself from Gunther's grasp. They struggled, embraced in some strange dance on the narrow landing, until the spy lost his footing and suddenly all that was left in Gunther's hand was a scrap of fabric torn from the other's robes. His opponent was tumbling down the spiral staircase, his scream dying before he hit the ground with a dull thud.

Gunther reeled at the top of the staircase, his bearings impaired by the shock. He gripped the wall and steadied himself. His eyes were stinging, welling up with tears and blurring his vision. The smoke was thinning, the peat burnt out. Gunther gathered his scattered wits together to think. Locking the door to the Abbot's study was a priority. He stomped the remnants of peat into the floorboards to ensure no live flames remained. There had to be no discernible connection between the scriptorium and the dead man at the bottom of the stairs.

The man had to be dead, Gunther reasoned with himself. No one would have survived that fall: twenty feet down the well of the steep, curled staircase.

One tentative step after another, Gunther descended the steps, negotiating the pitch-black guts of the windowless tower like a blind man with his fingertips tracking the line of the wall. He was on tenterhooks, dreading what bloody mess he would find at the bottom.

The body was lying face down with the hood obscuring the head. Gunther squatted next to it and pulled off the hood. He was obliged to turn the body to identify it. He had no lantern upon him, but the moon was dipping in and out of the rain clouds, giving him intermittent flashes of light. He hooked his fingers under the man's shoulder and hip, and gave it a tug. The corpse was heavy, but then Gunther imagined all dead bodies were. He heaved it and it rolled onto its back.

Cornelius's face caught the ghostly moonlight. A trickle of livid-red blood glistened under his nose. His mouth was a mesh of broken teeth and bleeding gums.

'Oh Cornelius, you damn fool!' Gunther cried out.

Curiosity killed the nosy monk, he told himself. He should have kept to his prayers and to mending tattered robes. He had been good at that. But he had decided to follow Gunther in the dead of night, looking for trouble. He had found it. Gunther refused to accept blame for that though guilt was already nibbling at the edges of his conscience. It wasn't a deliberate act, but he had caused another man's death. The guilt's bite was sharp and deep.

Gunther had to move the body away from the tower. He grabbed it by the shoulders and, doubled-up, began dragging it across the quadrangle. Once in the centre, he arranged it in a Christian way: the hem of the tunic pulled down to cover Cornelius's modesty and his hands bound together on his chest. Gunther said a prayer and made the sign of the Cross over Cornelius's skull.

He couldn't bring himself to leave the corpse lying discarded in the courtyard like some broken earthenware jug. It would be senseless to keep vigil over the body until he was found in the morning by his brothers. Questions would be asked and he would struggle to answer them without incriminating himself. Cornelius had to be taken to the chapel and laid there. Gunther couldn't do that alone. He had to alert the others.

He returned to the tower and climbed the stairs to the belfry. There he rolled up his sleeves and pulled on the ropes. The clapper began to sway, reluctant at first, but slowly gaining momentum. At last it hit the dome of the bell. Gunther pulled harder, the sound of the tolling bell silencing his voice of conscience.

Awoken by the bell, the brothers spilled out of the dormitories, torches flaming, and ran towards the corpse sprawled on the lawn. Some fell to their knees and started to pray. Gunther came down from the tower and, taking a detour via the cloisters, joined the others in exclamation of surprise, horror and grief.

Brother Benedict, who in his previous life had served as physician on the battlefield and was particularly adept at amputating limbs, pushed through the throng of panicking monks and squatted by the corpse to examine it. He poked it, felt around the head, prised open its eyelids and peered beneath them in search of the faintest spark of life.

'In God's name, be quiet, the lot of you!' he bellowed and bared his yellow teeth at his brethren. They all fell into a stunned silence, their hands bound on their bellies.

Benedict pulled off his hood and lowered his head, his ear almost touching Cornelius's bloodied lips. Benedict's right hand appeared to rise and fall on the corpse's chest.

'He's alive,' Benedict proclaimed. Gently he lifted the hem of Cornelius's cowl and ran his fingers over his chest, pausing from time to time to press a bit harder into his abdomen. Pink foam bubbled out of Cornelius's nose. 'He's badly bruised. I can feel a few broken ribs.'

'Is his back broken?' Archibald asked.

'I don't know. Roll him onto a cloak – carefully – and carry him to his cell. I may yet be able to put him together again.'

Gunther felt the blood drain from his head and gush down to his feet. He staggered, his legs refusing to support his weight, and he slumped to the ground. He rocked back and forth, and then let himself fall backwards. He spread his arms and legs on the wet grass, the first droplets of morning dew penetrating his robes and giving him goosebumps. Gunther gazed at the sky above. Dawn was breaking in the corners of the cloud-laden firmament. The night was over. Gunther was waking from a very bad dream. He laughed. At first, it was just a chuckle, then a full-bellied hoot.

Cornelius was alive!

'What are you laughing at?' It was Father Archibald's heavily accented voice.

Gunther sprung to his feet. 'I'm sorry. I was... I...'

'You were laughing. Did Brother Cornelius's misfortune provide you with reason to be merry?'

THE QUEEN'S AVENGER

'No! I thought he was dead.' Gunther seemed incapable of stringing together a logical reply.

'And that thought amused you?'

'No! Not that! I'm happy that he's alive.'

'Barely,' Father Archibald gave a heavy sigh.

'I will pray for his recovery.'

'As will we all,' Archibald nodded. He looked sharply at Gunther, 'Were the two of you close?'

Gunther blinked his surprise. 'Me and Brother Cornelius? I hardly knew him.'

'I see…' Archibald narrowed his eyes and pressed his lips into a thin line. 'I wonder what Brother Cornelius was doing out here in the middle of the night. I wonder how he came by his injuries. Any thoughts?'

Gunther sensed blood flushing his cheeks. He rubbed his face trying to conceal his discomfort. 'Father, I… I was asleep. The bell woke me. I don't know. It is strange.'

'Strange, indeed. Someone knows. Someone tolled the bell.'

'It wasn't me.'

'I wonder who.'

'Yes, so do I. Poor Brother Cornelius…'

'His injuries are serious. You've heard Brother Benedict. Cornelius couldn't have acquired such injuries by simply taking a stroll in the garden.'

'No,' Gunther agreed.

'Well, let's hope he wakes up soon and tells us what on earth happened.'

Gunther spent the rest of the day torn between praying for Cornelius's recovery and wishing him dead. His recovery would save Gunther's soul from the eternal fires of Hell. His death would probably save his skin here on earth. And there was still the question of the stolen scroll. Gunther was in no doubt that Cornelius had taken it, but where did he hide it? It was imperative that Gunther recovered it.

A visit to Cornelius's cell after supper confirmed that he was still alive and still unconscious. Brother Benedict had set his broken legs using an assortment of iron pokers and planks of wood. At least, he hadn't amputated them. Apparently, from now on it was all down to Cornelius. He would either live or die of his own accord. Nothing else could be done for him. Nothing, except prayer.

Gunther sat by Cornelius's side and said a whole rosary, dedicating it to the unfortunate monk's recovery. Or as painless a death as possible. When he was finished, he leant forward and whispered, 'Where is the scroll, Cornelius?'

He received no answer, not even a sigh. Cornelius would either take the scroll to his grave or negotiate its return upon awakening. Gunther had an inkling of what Cornelius might want in exchange for the scroll. He had often felt Cornelius's eyes sliding over him like oily mud. A few times he had felt Cornelius's hands straying dangerously close to Gunther's arse. Gunther gave an involuntary shudder.

He took a few minutes to search Cornelius's cell for the scroll, but there were very few places where he could have hidden it. Short of turning him over in his bed to look there, Gunther was condemned to fail.

'You bloody fool,' he growled on his way out. He didn't want to be late for Compline.

Gunther stayed in his cell until after midnight. He wanted to make sure that the whole monastery was asleep before he ventured back to the tower to continue reading the late Abbot's confessions.

It would have been wiser to wait for a few days, bearing in mind Father Archibald's investigation into Cornelius's *accident*, but Gunther couldn't resist. He was drawn to the scrolls like a drunk may be drawn to liquor. His curiosity was stronger than the voice of caution whispering stern warnings into his year.

As the black night took hold of the sky, Gunther crept across the quadrangle on bent knees and climbed the stairs to the Abbot's lodgings in the dark. He really wanted to know whether the Scottish Queen was dead or alive.

XVIII

Written on this the Nineteenth Day of September in the Year of our Lord 1592

'Where, in God's name, is the Queen!' I heard someone shrill above the clamour of heated conversations. To my shock I recognised my own voice.

George Hackett directed his torch at me. I felt the heat of the flame on my face. 'Father Ninian, how comes it that you are here? And why are you calling for the Queen?' he addressed me, his bald forehead puckered under the dome of his helmet.

'Is she… is Her Majesty… Was she with the King?' I stammered, gesturing towards the rubble of Kirk o'Field.

'There's no need for alarm. The Queen is in her bed at Holyrood. Fear not. She's safe and sound.'

'She is…' The tension released my body from its grip. I stumbled a few steps back on legs of wet clay, and nearly fell.

'Indeed. She retired to her apartments at the palace after the masque.'

I didn't ask what masque. I didn't care to know. I was just relieved that my Queen wasn't lying dead, buried under the debris. 'Praise be to the Lord!' I cried.

My anxieties assuaged, I was now able to cast a cold eye over the scene before me. The dead King and his valet were part-naked, their shirts providing scant cover. A fur-lined nightgown and a cloak lay nearby, as if discarded by them or perhaps ripped from their bodies after death, for they no longer had the need for warmth. I noticed strands of silver fur protruding from the King's lips and being snatched, hair by hair, by the wind. It was the same colour as the trimming of the furred nightgown, most probably silver fox. A chair lay on its side, a dagger dropped further down and a length of rope coiled under a tree, next to a broken branch. Most incongruously, a pink velvet slipper lay discarded in the snow a couple of yards away. I noted numerous footprints around the bodies, and a further trail of prints leading away from the pink slipper, but those could well belong to the throng of onlookers.

What I was seeing brought to mind a scene of execution by hanging which had been rapidly and inexplicably abandoned as if the two intended victims had simply decided to curl up on the ground and die of their own accord.

Indeed, there wasn't a single mark on their bodies to indicate they had been thrown out of the house in the explosion or assaulted in any other way. No scorch marks, no bruises, no blood, no limbs appearing broken or mis-aligned with their torsos.

And then there was the chair and the velvet slipper. The king's feet were bare, I noted. If that slipper was his, where was the other one? Maybe he and his valet had fled the house in a hurry? They were only partly dressed as if they had been dragged out of bed against their will, or had escaped in a great panic.

They had left the house before it was blown up – that much was clear. It was evident from their state of dishevelment that they'd had only seconds to think and act before the explosion occurred. Maybe they had been alerted to it at the last minute? Or maybe, they were its authors? Only why would they have blown up an empty house? Did they expect the Queen to be there? Was it an attempt on Her Majesty's life? Was her life also in danger?

Those and many other disjointed thoughts milled inside my head. I had no answers and no clear clues.

'I heard them – the assassins,' a woman started speaking and as she did so the hubbub of voices was extinguished. 'I saw them, too,' she added.

'What did you see, my good woman?' the Sheriff's eyes picked her out from the crowd. He walked towards her, pushing others aside. 'And what is your name?'

'Barbara Mertine, my name.' The woman stepped forward, several lanterns illuminating her features. She had an open, round face, her pale eyebrows bristling in the light. She stood face to face with Bothwell, undeterred by his abrupt manner.

'I live in Blackfriars Wynd, just off Cowgate. I saw them there, my Lord – running they were. From the ruin of Blackfriars monastery, heading up to the High Street. Stealthy they were –

thieves in the night, I thought. I was minded to raise the alarm, but then I see they wear armour-like under their cloaks. Soldiers, I surmised, going after some mischief maker. Only they were very keen not to be discovered.'

'How did you gather that?'

'Some were wearing mules over their boots, just like that one,' Mrs Mertine pointed to the pink slipper. 'How odd, I thought... I counted thirteen of them, all armed.'

'How come no one else saw them?'

'Like I said, they were very careful not to reveal themselves, but I'm a light sleeper. I heard their muffled voices. Footsteps, soft, like a pack of wolves stalking a prey. Nothing escapes me, my Lord. I heard what I heard,' Mrs Mertine held Bothwell's gaze, unwavering.

'We heard him cry for mercy,' another female voice crept from the dark behind the circle of onlookers.

'Come forward,' the Sheriff demanded. 'Tell me what you heard – word by word. Tell me the truth. No scaremongering, mind!'

Three thin figures shuffled to the front. They looked older that the feisty Mrs Mertine, and poorer. Wrapped in threadbare cloaks, their skirts thin and frayed at the hem, the women huddled together, drawing courage from each other to speak out. 'We shelter in that crumbling old cottage,' one of the women pointed vaguely over her head, 'doing no harm to no one. It's abandoned. We made home there for oursel—'

'Tell me what you heard!' Bothwell brimmed with impatience.

'A voice, we heard, my Lord. A young man's voice cry for mercy. A boy's voice... Harrowing it was, like a pin through the heart.'

'What did he say? What exactly?'

'I'll never forget, long as I live,' another of the three women spoke, her eyes rounded with horror, huge as millstones. 'He cried, *Pity me, kinsmen, for the sake of Jesus Christ.* He begged,' she recited. '*For the love of God, have pity on me, like He did on all the world!* tis what we heard, word by word.'

I took keen notice of the King's dying words: *kinsmen*. He was pleading for mercy with his own kin!

'Traitors!' another woman stepped into the circle of light. 'I saw them run away, my Lord. Two eyeblinks after the explosion. I came to the window to see what the almighty noise was, and I heard Mrs Mertine shout after them, *You've been at some evil turn! Stop! Halt there! Call the sentries!* I ran out just as they were going past my door. I even grabbed one of them by his cloak. I asked him to state his name. Asked him what happened, what mischief he'd been up to. He gave me the evil eye and pushed me away. I'd recognise him, my Lord, if I saw him again. Red beard, mad eyes – burning. The cloak, mind, it was silk. Pure silk, slippery to touch. He was no pauper. A man of high birth, and—'

'Your name, madam,' the Sheriff interrupted her account, rather too brusquely for my liking. 'I'll have my men take your statement later.'

'Mary Stirling, my Lord. I live in Blackfriars Wynd, next door to Mrs Mertine here.'

It was at this point that a surgeon arrived to examine the corpses where they lay. More soldiers flooded in from the castle and Bothwell started shouting orders for them to begin a search for the traitors.

THE QUEEN'S AVENGER

XIX

Written on this the Nineteenth Day of September in the Year of our Lord 1592

A lone figure swaying on top of the Flodden Wall caught my eye. It was a man, clad only in his undergarments. He looked drunk, staggering on unsteady feet, his movements unsure. He tottered to the edge of the wall, recoiled, his legs twisting under him, and fell backwards. The moon managed to squeeze through the cloud and briefly lit the stumbling figure. I recognised Thomas Nelson, the King's servant.

In the tumult below, nobody else seemed to have noticed him. The soldiers had scooped the two corpses onto the cloaks found nearby and were carrying them across the quadrangle towards the New Provost's Lodgings. The mob accompanied them, outcries of lamentation and horror stabbing the already disturbed stillness of the night. I climbed the wall towards Nelson.

As I levelled with him, I realised the man was in shock. His nightshirt was singed at the hem, its sleeves torn clear. His face was begrimed, hair dusted with dirt. The expression in his eyes was that of loss and bewilderment. He must have been thrown out of the house in the explosion and rendered unconscious, must have lain there oblivious for a couple of hours while the search went on in the rubble and gardens beneath.

'Nelson!' I squatted next to him and threw my cloak over his trembling body. 'What happened? What did you see? Who did it?' I bombarded him with a barrage of questions. I knew I had limited time to interrogate him. Once Bothwell's men discovered him, he would be taken into custody and out of my reach.

He clapped his hands over his temples and wept. I shook him by the shoulders. 'Calm yourself, man! Talk to me! Is the Queen in danger?''

'I don't— I don't,' he mumbled, then his gaze acquired temporary clarity and it fell on me, manic, despairing, 'Is the King? Is my master—'

'The King is dead. So is Taylor,' I answered as succinctly as the moment dictated. 'Now, talk to me, man. What happened?'

'I was thrown off clear, I think. I can't remember anything afterwards, not until I woke up—'

'And before that? Was it you who set it all up? Was it Darnley?'

'The King?' he stared at me as if I had lost my wits. 'Did you not say he was dead?'

'Yes, found in the garden. Come on, Nelson,' I prodded him without ceremony, 'Speak! Was the King planning to kill Her Majesty? Did it go wrong? Tell me who was in on it?'

'No…no, no. The King knew nothing of it! They heard noises – something going on down in the cellar, footsteps, suppressed voices, men running out towards the gate—'

'They?'

'The King and Taylor. They'd been asleep in the King's bedchamber. I was in the gallery – didn't hear a thing. Taylor woke me up, clasped his hand over my mouth and hissed there were assassins in the house, said we had to get the King safely out, through the top window. There was no going down to the— They, the assassins, were there setting a trap for the King. A number of armed men – we couldn't tell how many. He warned me to be dead silent. I nodded. We grabbed a length of rope and ran to the King's chamber. The plan was to lower him through the window, into the garden and from there to scale the wall and call the sentries. All we had to defend ourselves were our daggers. The King went first, then Taylor. And then…' Nelson gulped and peered at me without comprehension, 'and then, then the bang. I felt myself airborne, a hole punched through my chest. I thought I'd died.'

'Did you see any of the armed men? Did you recognise anyone?' I pressed him.

'No. I didn't see anyone. I was told they were out there, laying a trap downstairs.'

'Didn't the King say who they were? Did he, or Taylor—'

'The King was panicked, out of his mind! He wasn't— One thing he said,' Nelson frowned, remembering. 'He decried a betrayal, that it was a trap, that he'd been lured there under false pretences. There wasn't much time, Father. We were running for our lives!'

THE QUEEN'S AVENGER

'Who was it? Think, Nelson, think! Who brought the King to the lodgings?'

'The Queen,' he blinked at me stupidly.

'The Queen? What are you saying! That the Queen lured him to his death?'

'No, not that, Father. Only that the Queen brought him back from Glasgow. But it wasn't her who suggested Kirk o'Field. She suggested the Craigmillar Castle, but, but the King was forewarned not to do her bidding.'

'Forewarned by whom!'

'The King's good friend, Sir James Balfour.'

James Balfour... The man was known to me. A Catholic of shaky repute after changing sides like a cheap harlot, Protestant to Catholic, and back again, depending on which way the winds blew. He had painted himself as an ardent Catholic and Darnley's staunchest supporter after the Lords of the Congregation rebelled against him and Mary, and lost. Ever since he had been enjoying the King's friendship and patronage. Like most of Darnley's sentiments, it appeared to be a misplaced one.

'James Balfour warned the King against the Queen?' I whispered, the realisation of the subversive plot against Mary beginning to dawn on me.

'Yes, Father. A message came from him just as the Queen arrived in Glasgow to fetch my master back to Edinburgh. Balfour warned the King that Holyrood was unsafe and that any other place recommended by the Queen for his convalescence could be a deadly trap. He offered his brother's lodgings, instead.'

'Kirk o'Field...'

'And now the King is dead! Blown up to—'

'No, not blown up,' I said. 'Smothered with his own cloak. I saw the hairs of its fur collar lodged in the King's mouth. He was suffocated with it.'

A wail, loud and harrowing, escaped the poor servant and he dropped to his knees. We had been discovered. Two of the Sheriff's men were heading towards us.

'Tell them the truth, Thomas. As you told me,' I breathed into his ear before they led him away, out of my reach.

XX

Written on this the Nineteenth Day of September in the Year of our Lord 1592

Upon my return to Holyrood, I found the Queen awake and in a state of high alert. She had been apprised of the news of her husband's death, but it wasn't grief I saw drowning her eyes – it was fear.

She summoned me to her supper room, the same one where only a year earlier we had witnessed David Rizzio's death. Looking at her, I recognised the wariness, the terror and the confusion I had seen earlier in Nelson's eyes. She gripped my arm, her fingers icy, sending a current of dread through my veins.

'Our life is in jeopardy, Father,' she whispered. 'Our son's life is in jeopardy. We're surrounded by enemies. I,' she switched to the more personal, more immediate pronoun, 'I was marked to die tonight. If it wasn't for Sebastien's wedding, the midnight masque and a last-minute change of plans last night I would've been sleeping at Kirk o'Field. I would have died alongside Henry. They want me dead, Ninian! My enemies want me dead. Who are they? I must know who they are! I must avenge Henry, I must protect my child—' her last few words were no more than a rustle in her throat. She was too frightened to utter them out loud.

'I will find them all out, Your Majesty, I will find them out and bring them before you,' I vowed.

'You, Father?' she peered at me, puzzled. In her eyes, I was only a priest, her confessor and spiritual adviser – not a knight of her realm. It wasn't my place to track down the assassins and dispense justice in her name.

I inclined my head reverently and held my tongue.

'Bothwell will carry out an investigation. As Sherriff of Edinburgh. I have every confidence in him.'

'The Earl of Bothwell? A protestant! The man Your Majesty had once put to the horn for planning to abduct you and force you into marriage?' I tried to reason with her.

THE QUEEN'S AVENGER

'That was a false accusation by a madman,' she gave a faint snort of irritation.

'But you acted swiftly to remove him—'

'Only because I didn't have all the facts before me. Do you know how it started? Bothwell and Arran had been fighting over some common wench. It all got out of hand.'

I raised a doubtful eyebrow and said nothing.

She sighed and went on to explain: 'First, they had come to blows, then Arran succumbed to some outlandish fantasies, shrieking of witches and demons, and from there moved on to tales of conspiracy and high treason. Poor, tormented soul! In the end he was convinced he was our husband. Our champion!' Mary flicked her wrist, 'And *voile*! he then deposited the blame at Bothwell's feet.'

'Still, if I may be so presumptuous, Your Majesty, the Earl's reputation precedes him—'

'His lust for women? His inconstant heart? That is of no concern to me. After all, I don't intend to marry him. But these days,' her expression sobered, 'he is the only man I can trust. He's proven himself to me over and over again. He stood by me when all the others, including my own brother, plotted and connived against me, butchered my dear Rizzio, threatened the babe in my womb... Oh, Father, he may be a Protestant but he's my most loyal subject. Besides, he holds the office of the Sheriff of this city. It's his job to catch my husband's murderers.' At that, a lone tear rolled down her cheek. There was more grief loaded into that tear than any lament, any eloquent outcry of despair.

'I understand Your Majesty and the King have reconciled while I was away in Rome?'

'I brought him back to Edinburgh on Maitland's advice – to keep an eye on him. Running loose at Glasgow, totally out of control, he was too much a risk. We both know how... how unruly he could get,' she lowered her gaze and pinched her lips. She was sad, not angry – I could tell. 'At the time, I will be honest with you Father, at the time, what with all the reports of his treachery and connivances against me, I was determined to be rid of him. Should you fail in your mission in Rome, I was minded to have him detained and tried for high treason.'

'My mission has indeed failed,' I confessed. 'The Pope believed the King's ravings in preference to your version of events, Your Majesty.'

She clenched her jaw, a muscle twitching in her cheek. 'So be it. I have no need for it now. And there's no need for a trial, for dredging up the King's delusions. His death has mercifully put an end to his and my torment. But did I wish it upon him? No! No, no no! I want the King's killers caught and executed. There'll be no more pardons, no more forgiveness. Henry was my husband. He was King. We will no longer tolerate disobedience. Treachery. Conspiracies against us. Betrayal! This land, this kingdom of mine runs with blood, lies and greed. We'll put a stop to it. And that's why we need Bothwell. We have no confidence in any other of our lords, not a single one of them. We are alone but for James Hepburn.'

'I understand.'

She rose from her chair and walked towards the window, her black damask skirts rustling in her wake. She spoke with her back to me, 'I have no illusions that Henry was the only intended victim, Father. He tried to warn me of a plot against both of us. A plot to kill us, Father. I should have believed him, listened to him... Instead, I dismissed his warnings on account of his insanity. The great pox had been playing havoc not only with his body but also with his mind. I had no faith in him. So I asked my brother if it was true, knowing that he would deny it.'

'You asked Moray?'

'No, not him. I asked Lord Robert. Henry alleged that Robert had come to Kirk o'Field Friday last to warn him of the conspiracy. I asked Robert in Henry's presence to confirm or deny it, and he denied it. There was so much anger. They drew swords. I had to plead with James to separate them. But I could see it in Robert's eyes – the guilt. I knew he was lying and I let him. And now,' she finished with a heavy sigh.

'It's understandable. Your Majesty chose to believe her own flesh and blood,' I tried to console her.

THE QUEEN'S AVENGER

'And I was deeply suspicious of Henry and his intentions. It was he who chose to lodge at Kirk o'Field. It was at his request that we stayed there. When I first heard the news of the explosion, I was convinced I was meant to die there and, moreover, that Henry was complicit in the scheme. After all, Father, he didn't die in the blast. He was found in the garden, without a mark on his body, so I am told. I still think that perhaps, he just didn't get out in time—'

As much as I had little regard for Henry Darnley, I felt the truth would give her peace. I said, 'No, he wasn't in on the intrigue. I spoke to his servant Nelson. He told me the King had been warned not to follow Your Majesty's lead but to head for Kirk o'Field, supposedly for his own safety, and that Your Majesty's intentions were to hold him prisoner at Craigmillar, or worse.'

'Who? Who warned him?' Lightning flashed through her eyes.

'Sir James Balfour, I was given to understand.'

'Tell Bothwell. He needs to know.' She turned back, rubbing her temples, her expression weary and pained. 'Leave me now. I'm tired. I'm very tired.'

XXI

Written on this the Nineteenth Day of September in the Year of our Lord 1592

I had no intention of telling Bothwell. As much as the Queen had placed all her trust in that man, I had my doubts about his loyalties. I had him as a man who was loyal only to himself. I remembered the counsel he had given the Queen at Craigmillar – there lain his keen interest in having the King executed or, better yet, disposed of by means rather more violent and less legitimate than a straightforward divorce. I also knew of the familiarity between Balfour and Bothwell. They were kinsmen and friends. So, instead of reporting one to the other, I resolved to conduct my own investigation.

I had limited means and no authorisation to ask questions, but then my plan wasn't to interrogate the nobility. They would either lie through their teeth as their instincts dictated or they would have me whipped for my insolence. No, I would speak to the people with their ears close to the ground and their eyes in every nook and cranny of the city of Edinburgh. I would find witnesses and take their accounts of what they had seen and heard. Then, I would build the whole picture and paint it for the Queen.

Over the next few weeks, while the kingdom was in mourning over its dead King and the Sheriff of Edinburgh was occupied with his official inquiries, arresting suspects, torturing them and having them sign their souls away for the tiniest reprieve from pain, I was scouring the back lanes of the city and the servants' quarters of the palace in search of the truth.

Alas, my task wasn't easy. Someone was taking every precaution to cover all the tracks, silence the witnesses and sabotage my inquiries. Someone powerful.

I re-visited Kirk o'Field two weeks after the explosion. The ruin of the Old Provost's House lay flat under the white shroud of snow with scorched shards of rubble jutting out in all directions like fingers of random accusations. I inspected the debris and, finding nothing of interest, headed for the old cottages on the south side. I wished to interview the three pauper women who claimed to have heard the king pleading for his life with *his kinsmen.* Perhaps the women had also heard the assassins' replies, or better yet, seen their faces.

Of the four cottages, only one seemed to be vaguely habitable with its moss-fortified roof and its chimney intact. Wind howled within the other three – in and out of broken windows, through the holes of empty doorways and crumbled walls. I called out and, when no one answered, pushed aside a hessian rug hanging in the doorway, and entered. I found the place empty. A cracked earthenware jug, straw, some kindling and cheap female trinkets lay strewn across the clay floor. A charred but still useable cauldron overturned near the hearth and there abandoned, told me a story of a sudden, rushed departure. The three women were nowhere to be found. They had either run for their lives or been forcibly evicted. They may be languishing in the castle dungeons, or if they had been more fortunate they may have simply been chased out of the city. I would be wasting my time looking for them.

I proceeded to Blackfriars Wynd where I hoped to speak to Mrs Mertine and Mrs Stirling, the two witnesses who had seen the armed men flee from the scene and who claimed they would be able to identify them. As I was admitted inside, I instantly counted myself fortunate to find Mrs Stirling visiting Mrs Mertine. Mrs Stirling was seated on a stool next to the hearth, warming her back against the chimney breast. Mrs Mertine was busy kneading dough. The room was sticky with warmth and fragrant with something hearty and sweet.

'What brings you, Father?' Mrs Mertine inquired politely and offered me a seat.

I didn't want to tower over her and make her nervous so I took the stool and squatted on it, affecting contentment.

'I'm Her Majesty's personal secretary,' I began, making myself sound more important than I was. 'The Queen is stricken with grief, mourning her husband's untimely death.'

'An awful tragedy,' Mrs Stirling nodded her head from side to side, looking like a horse pulling on its halter. 'Second-time widowed and still only twenty-three year of age.'

'She wishes to know the identity of the King's assassins,' I continued. 'I heard you say, Mrs Stirling, that you stood face to face with one of them.'

'Aye,' Mrs Stirling shifted her gaze towards the floor, 'and I gave my account to the bailiff.'

'Would you be so kind as to repeat to me what you said to him?'

Mrs Stirling and Mrs Mertine exchanged furtive looks. I could tell Mrs Stirling was keen to tell her story over and over again, but something was holding her back. She grimaced her discontent.

'Well, Father, I can't tell you anything, much as I'd like to.'

'Oh?'

Mrs Mertine stepped in. Her round, cat-like face was flushed with colour, partly from the warmth, partly, I would warrant, from nervous agitation. 'We said what we had to say to the bailiff. We were told to speak to no one else about it. So, that's the end of that. You don't want to get us into trouble with the law, Father, do you?'

I rose from the uncomfortably low stool. 'I wouldn't dream of it, Mrs Mertine. Good day to you both.'

THE QUEEN'S AVENGER

XXII

Written on this the Nineteenth Day of September in the Year of our Lord 1592

The wall of silence surrounding the King's murder taught me an important lesson: I would have to lie, spy and cheat to get to the truth. The witnesses were wary of speaking to strangers. They had been intimidated by someone who had got to them before me. I had to do something to win their confidence and loosen their tongues.

Two days later, I returned to Blackfriars Wynd. I intended to retrace the footsteps of the men Mrs Mertine and Mrs Stirling had seen that night. The thirteen men seen by Mrs Mertine had approached from the derelict Blackfriars Monastery. Notably, no one had heard or seen them in their approach to the monastery. After the explosion, Mrs Stirling had seen the same men run up Blackfriars Wynd, then split at the top of the road: some heading towards the High Street, the others towards the city wall, where they all vanished. It was blatantly obvious to me that the men, at least some of them, lived locally.

I wandered about the neighbourhood and watched the comings and goings. I made intriguing discoveries about two local residents whom I marked as my potential suspects. One of them was a man known as Black Ormiston. He was Bothwell's bailiff and his close confidante. I often saw them in each other's company. The other discovery was even more curious: Lord Morton's house was in St Mary's Wynd, a street parallel to Blackfriars. The wily fox was not in residence, still in exile where I had left him, in the dingy Newcastle inn, hugging the body of his dead accomplice. However, around noon, I spotted his kinsman, Archibald Douglas, leave the house, and return several hours later, just as the sun melded into the city walls and dusk began to drain colour from the sky.

Archibald Douglas was a bull of a man. He didn't walk: he charged forward with his large head sunken into his shoulders and his red beard bristling like it was on fire. It was then, as I watched him, that I remembered Mrs Stirling's words: *he had a red beard and a mad look in his eye.* I was in no doubt she had been describing Archibald Douglas himself. And Archibald, just like the rest of the Douglas clan, was indeed Henry Darnley's kinsman. They had, at first, worked hand in glove to further Darnley's cause and rid him of David Rizzio. Morton, the head of the clan, had been one of the chief conspirators. But within days Darnley had betrayed them and sided with the Queen when she banished them and had them forfeit their estates. Morton would have never forgiven the perfidy. Once double-crossed, he would seek revenge and he would get it. Even though he was still in exile, his clansmen would do the job for him. And there I had my prime suspects. All I needed was corroboration.

As I stood in a narrow alley linking St Mary's and Blackfriars Wynds, pondering what my next step should be, I saw a servant leave through the back of Douglas's House. He was a man in his prime, square-shouldered and of more than average height. His straw-yellow hair sat flat above his shoulders like a thatch. I had seen the man now and again around Archibald Douglas. He was probably his valet. Since I was in disguise, wearing a simple hooded cloak over a brown tunic, I decided to follow the man. He led me to a busy tavern in Cowan's Close. The place was tightly packed and poorly lit, which suited my purpose well.

After a whole day out in the cold, I was hungry and in need of warming up. I ordered some hot pottage and a jug of ale, and sidled up to the Douglas manservant, who was seated at a battered trestle table, wedged into a cavernous alcove of the main chamber.

After exchanging a few nods and friendly grunts, I asked the barmaid for an extra cup and offered the man some of my ale. He accepted eagerly, his face lifting in an appreciative grin. Introductions followed. I told him my name was Wilfred Ramsey, a wool merchant on business from Inverness. He said he was John Binning.

We spent the rest of the evening chatting companionably about this and that, but nothing too stirring. I certainly didn't want to raise his guard by asking about his master's affairs. By the time I said my goodbyes, John Binning was staring at me with eyes glazed over by too much ale. I, on the other hand, was stone sober and a few coins lighter.

I told him my business in the city would extend a week or two, and that as I was lodging nearby I may see him again soon. He nodded, slurring about *The Stag and Goose* being the best watering hole in town.

I spent three more evenings and a good few more merks at *The Stag and Goose* keeping John Binning's throat moist and his guard low, until at long last I raised the matter of the King's death.

'He had it coming, I hear.'

'Aye, he did. And not a day too early, the wretched papist.'

'And a sodomite,' I said and spat out my disgust.

'Aye, that he was, no doubt,' Binning's spit joined mine on the floor. 'It's nowt but sin and debauchery at the Palace. Sodom and Gomorrah what with the Queen being a French harlot, getting up to all sorts and hardly ever leaving her bed chamber, as Master Knox reports from the pulpit of St Giles every Sunday. A disgrace if you ask me! It's a mystery why the roof hasn't yet caved in on the lot of them.'

I swallowed the insult against Mary and washed it down with ale, or else it would have stuck in my throat and choked me to death. I pressed harder, 'Did you see those placards saying it was the Earl of Bothwell who lit the fuse, with the Queen's blessing?'

'I saw them, aye.'

'I suppose the pair did us all a favour.'

'Ha! You suppose it was them, do you?' Binning's ale-infused eyes rolled in his head and he gave a knowing wink.

'Do you know otherwise?'

Excitement must have rung too loud in my voice for he tilted his large head and gave me a sidelong glance. He took the measure of me as if he had just met me for the first time. I feared I might have lost him. I poured him more ale, and a drop into my own cup. I watched him gulp it down and I breathed with relief when his gaze began to soften.

'I don't know who did it, but I can guess why,' I kept on talking. 'The King was nothing but trouble whichever way you look at it.

I travel a lot and I hear things. The word has it he was plotting to invite the French and the Spaniards to Scotland, and do away with the Reformed Church.' I risked making a statement that could easily land me in gaol, if not on the gallows, but taking that risk was the only way to regain Binning's trust. Judging by his earlier comments, he was a committed Reformist and Knox's disciple.

He rubbed his chin thoughtfully, so I added, 'If the King had it his way, the rivers of Scotland would run with blood. If I knew who lit that fuse, I would consider it an honour to shake their hand.'

'It wasn't the blast that killed him, was it though?' Binning grinned and tapped the side of his nose. I could tell he was itching to boast about it.

'True... It was something else. Only what? I hear there were no marks on the King's body, no tell-tale signs of how he was dispatched, so what was it? Witchcraft?'

'His own fancy gown,' Binning lowered his head and looked at me from under his heavy yellow brows, his voice no more than a whisper. 'He was to die in the blast, but managed to flee – was lowered down from the top window in a chair, like a fair maiden.' A chuckle gurgled in Binning's throat. 'Running for his life, he was. He thought he got away, but we had the house surrounded on the off chance of his escape. He wasn't going to live to tell the tale, we had to make sure of that.

'We sat in wait, watching from a safe distance. I saw the Balfours and Black Ormiston, too, top of Thraples they were milling about like a pack of wolves in the moonlight. But he was ours. God willing, we got our hands on him first.

'My Master had rope at the ready, strung it over a tree branch. Fair is fair, the treacherous bastard deserved to swing. But he fought back and wriggled – a rabbit in a snare...

'Long lad he was, his toes nearly touching the ground. The branch broke off what with all that wriggling. He curled up on the ground, his arse white as the moon, and he cried and whimpered, *Pity me! Pity me!*' Binning mocked the king's boyish falsetto.

I felt an icy cold descend on me despite the proximity of the burning grate.

THE QUEEN'S AVENGER

Now that he'd started, Binning continued without any encouragement on my part, 'While me and three others was dealing with his valet – slippery wretch he was, too – my Master and two others held Darnley to the ground and shoved his velvet gown down his throat. He fought back, spitting out fur, jolting his body – wriggly as an eel. There was lots of life left in the bastard.' Binning paused to reflect. 'But in the end he went still. And his valet had no breath left in him either. Both dead. Fair is fair.'

'Fair is fair,' I echoed.

'Aye!'

We clinked our cups and drank a macabre toast to the King's murder.

'So, who was behind the explosion?' I asked after a while.

'This I don't know. Maybe it was Bothwell as the placards say. Maybe the Queen. All I know is that the gunpowder was ready and waiting in the vaults under the Old Provost's House before Darnley took residency there. The Queen brought him there from Glasgow so I'd say she was in on it. One good deed from the French harlot, eh?' He winked at me and I hid my face in my drink, retched, coughed and ran out of the tavern to throw up in the street.

ANNA LEGAT

XXIII

Written on this the Nineteenth Day of September in the Year of our Lord 1592

I now knew who had killed Darnley, but that knowledge wasn't enough to protect the Queen. Morton's men may have put the noose around the King's neck but they were only henchmen doing someone else's bidding. I had to discover the identity of the authors of the plot – the men at the top of the ladder. I had to know their objective. Was it just to get rid of the wayward King, or were they aiming higher? Before it was too late, I had to find out if Mary's life was also in danger.

By mid-March the streets of Edinburgh were awash with pamphlets proclaiming Bothwell and Balfour as the masterminds of the conspiracy. The murdered King's father, Lord Lennox, had publicly accused them of being his son's chief assassins, and was crying out for justice. As there is no smoke without fire so there's no rumour without a grain of truth at its source.

I knew Bothwell couldn't have lit the fuse in person. I had seen him at the Palace minutes after I heard the explosion. He had been asleep in his bed, next to his wife while the vile act was being committed. James Balfour however instantly rose to the top of my list of suspects. His name kept coming up with obstinate regularity. Thomas Nelson had mentioned it first. The King's valet was adamant that it had been James Balfour who had urged Darnley to lodge at his brother Robert's house at Kirk o'Field. Then, there was John Binning's claim that Balfour's men had gathered on the night of the blast at the foot of Throplows Wynd, *waiting their turn*. It was also rather convenient that the Old Provost's House was owned by Robert Balfour. The Balfours would have had the access, the time and the opportunity to set the scene at their leisure.

Although I was unsure of their motives, I knew James Balfour to be a particularly slippery individual. He was no stranger to murder. In his youth he had turned against the Holy Church and had a hand in the assassination of Cardinal Beaton. He should have swung for it but instead he had been sentenced to the galleys. Now older and wiser, he'd converted back to Catholicism and was parading as the King's best friend and most trusted servant. Little wonder that Darnley had relied on his counsel without questioning it. He must have seen him as a fellow Catholic in a sea swarming with heretics – one of his last few allies.

But I wasn't fooled by Balfour's return into the lap of the Holy Roman Church. For one, I'd never once seen him partake in Mass. Like many of his kind, he was constant to only one god: himself. He was also Bothwell's cousin and his close associate. And that was how the loop had closed, neatly encircling Balfour and Bothwell as the criminal masterminds, just as the anonymous pamphlets asserted. I had to warn the Queen, but I knew she wouldn't believe me without proof. I had to find it.

Although the official investigation was still pending and a reward of £2000 Scot was on offer for anyone with information about the identity of the traitors, nothing much was happening. No leads, no names and all known eyewitnesses cowering in silence. I could no longer rely on Thomas Nelson's testimony. Since his arrest, he had been interrogated under torture until he could no longer tell fact from the fiction he was being fed by his oppressors. John Binning, if confronted, would deny everything he had told me over a jug of ale – I had no illusions about that. I had to dig deeper and closer to sir James Balfour's doorstep. The good Lord soon showed me the way.

As I was invigilating Balfour's house, wondering how to approach the question of unearthing tangible evidence, I recognised one of the servants. He was a man of advanced years – forty-five at the very least. His hair was thin and dull grey, his posture stooped, round-shouldered. The moment I saw him I was sure I knew him from somewhere. Then, it came to me: the man was a regular worshipper at the Holy Mass services I continued to hold in various secret places around the city of Edinburgh. He was one of us.

Two days after my fortuitous discovery, I was saying Mass at a merchant's house in Canongate. Balfour's servant was present. After the service I gestured to him to stay behind. He peered at me guiltily as if he already knew what I was about to ask him. All nerves, he was crumpling his cap in his hands, his eyes nailed to the ground.

'Can I ask your name, son?' I started.

'Andrew. Andrew Ford, Father,' he replied in a voice so small that I had to ask him to repeat it.

'You are Sir James Balfour's servant, are you not?'

'Yes. Yes, I—' again his voice faltered.

I put my hand on his shoulder and drew his gaze out to face me. 'I can sense, my son, that you are battling with your conscience. I can see it. I can tell something pains you. I can sense your suffering. Guilty conscience – it never goes away. Not until you unburden it before God.'

'I been to Confession, Father, during Advent. Second Sunday of Adve—' he tried to extricate himself.

'A lot of time has passed since then,' I countered. 'The King has been murdered in his sleep. Our Catholic Queen is in danger. If there's something you're privy too, it's your time to speak, before it's too late, my son. I'm here to listen.'

'I... I— I, I've a family!' he stammered and gave in to violent sobs.

'The merciful Lord will look after your family. He always does. But you need to do what's right. You don't want to have the Queen's life on your conscience, do you, Andrew?' I clasped his shoulders and pulled him closer to me, pressing my ear to his lips, 'Your master's involvement in the King's murder, Andrew – tell me about it. Whisper it into my ear. No one else need hear us. God already knows, but you need to say it to me.'

'I'm sorry! I'm sorry, Father!' he broke into sobs. 'I didn't know what it was for, Father! I didn't know until it was done, and then I... I was too frightened to speak out!'

'Don't be. Tell me: what is it you're talking about?'

'The gunpowder, Father! The gunpowder, a whole £60 Scots worth of gunpowder my master bought from a merchant in Cowen's Port. We conveyed it in four barrels, in the night. Two carts-full!'

'The gunpowder used to blow up the Old Provost's House?'

'Aye, aye, the same! We stored it in the vaults. Only two days before the King took lodgings there. I... I didn't know what it was

THE QUEEN'S AVENGER

for, Father! I didn't! Not until that night! We were told to pile it up tight after the cook had gone, then the Queen – she left soon after supper. It was only the King and his men left in the house. I still didn't know for certain, but it'd begun to dawn on me that some serious mischief was brewing. Sir James ordered us to go home and say nothing. Only when I heard the blast, when I saw where it'd come from – only then did I know. Oh, forgive me Father for I have sinned!' Andrew Ford threw himself down onto his knees and gripped my hand, trying to kiss it. Hot tears dripped onto my knuckles.

'Get up,' I ordered him. 'You will have to repeat this before the Sheriff, do you understand? Only then will you earn absolution.'

I hurried to the Queen's apartments. She was under heavy guard, protected by her bailiffs but they let me through knowing how close I was to Her Majesty and how displeased she would be if they tried to stop me.

I found her reclined in her bed, sad, melancholy and as drained of colour as the white sheen of her mourning veil. I promptly, if rather chaotically, reported to her all of my findings.

'Your Majesty, you must act with haste! Andrew Ford is in the throes of remorse and he has agreed to testify against his master, but there are no guarantees that he won't be terrorised into changing his tune when Balfour sniffs out his betrayal.'

'We did ask you to tell Bothwell about James Balfour,' she replied, her voice flat, almost disinterested. 'Why didn't you do as we asked? Is there nobody I can trust to do my bidding anymore?'

That stung, but I wasn't going to dwell on my hurt sensitivities. I persevered with my warning: 'My Queen, I fear that the Earl of Bothwell may also be involved in the scheme. I have no faith in his impartiality—'

'James Hepburn is my only loyal lieutenant! The very man I can trust!'

'Alas, he is also Balfour's cousin and ... they have interests in common. They drink and dine together. I daresay, Your Majesty, that they may well have acted in concert. The streets are littered with pamphlets saying just that. Lord Lennox has been making the same accusations against both men. Your Majesty, you can't trust anyone, not until the truth is out. Not anyone, not even Bothwell—'

'What are you saying, Father? That he too has designs on my life? I am doomed! I'd rather be dead already!' She wept. She wept uncontrollably and as I watched her my heart was crumbling away, piece by piece. I had no further words of advice. I had no words of consolation. I stood helpless, useless to my Queen.

Minutes later she stopped. Her composure returned as quickly as it had abandoned her. She jolted her chin upwards, squared her shoulders and spoke with calm authority befitting her royal status, 'Let Lord Lennox have his day in court. He can bring his grievance against Lord Bothwell in front of Parliament. His peers will judge him.'

The day of Bothwell's trial came and went. Lennox had failed to appear in person while Bothwell rode in with his head held high and his many adherents trotting behind him, the naked blades of their swords glistening in the midday sun. The Lords acquitted Bothwell in a matter of seven hours.

The body of Andrew Ford with its skull crushed was found two days later drifting in the Water of Leith, heading for the North Sea. I said a quiet prayer for his family and commended his soul to God.

James Balfour was presented with the governorship of Edinburgh Castle. It appeared that Bothwell was firmly in control of the situation with the small exception of new placards surfacing in the streets of Edinburgh.

They bore a crude image of a mermaid and a hare. The mermaid, symbolic of harlots, was naked to the waist and wore a crown. The hare had been borrowed from the Hepburn coat of arms. The good citizens of Edinburgh were left in no doubt as to who those images represented and what they were meant to convey: the Queen and her first Lieutenant, the untouchable Earl of Bothwell, were being accused of unholy carnal liaisons and, by necessary implication, of murdering her husband.

Whoever it was that had failed to dispose of the Queen in the blast had devised a new plan of destroying her by besmearing her reputation and turning her people against her. And that person couldn't have been Bothwell.

THE QUEEN'S AVENGER

XXIV

Written on this the Nineteenth Day of September in the Year of our Lord 1592

As the Queen departed for Stirling Castle to steal a few happy moments with her son, I focussed on uncovering the identity of the architect of Mary's downfall. I was hellbent on finding him out and thwarting him through any means necessary, even at the expense of my immortal soul.

With the Queen absent from court and Bothwell basking in the glory of his elevation, his wits blunted by his own arrogance, the forces of evil doubled down on their efforts to destroy both of them. The Mermaid and the Hare placards had engulfed Edinburgh like wildfire. They were everywhere – in every street, every home, on everyone's lips. John Knox, was amplifying the calumnies against Mary from the pulpit of the High Kirk, his vitriol seeping into people's eyes and blinding them to the truth. The whole city was ablaze with gossip and outcries of indignation.

At first I had scoured the streets, tearing the abominable pamphlets down wherever I found them, but soon I gave up on the futile task. There were too many of them and those I removed were soon replaced tenfold. I resolved to get to their source.

There were a few printers in the city of Edinburgh. One of them was churning out the hateful pamphlets. I had to find out who that was for they would lead me to their author.

I ventured into the city past the curfew hour, and lay in wait. The night was bright, illuminated by the full moon that squatted fat and blood-bathed upon the rooftops. Voices of the sentries had long faltered in the streets when I heard a patter of footsteps. Three men appeared at the top of the High Street, creeping from house to house, from post to post, appending sheets of paper to doors and windows. They worked in silence, proceeding methodically along the main street and branching out into side alleys. I watched their operation from the shadows, waiting, patient and hopeful that in the end they would lead me to the printer.

I was in luck. As soon as they ran out of pamphlets, they headed for Haymarket to resource more. The printing house was at the back of a respectable house, the owner known to me personally for I had previously used him to publish some of my own polemical texts. His name was John Havis, a man who I believed to be a devout Catholic. Clearly, I was wrong. Master Havis seemed perfectly content to serve many masters.

I waited outside while Havis and the three men concluded their transaction and the men departed laden with more leaflets to distribute around the city. I watched Havis snuff out the candles and as soon as darkness embraced the house, I burst in. Taken by surprise he stood no chance of recognising me. I jumped him from behind and pressed the blade of my dagger to his throat. His veins bulged and I could count the galloping rhythm of his heart under my fingers.

'Take what you want,' he wheezed. 'There's coinage in the clay pot on that shelf,' he tried to whisk his head to one side, but I held it in a tight lock. 'Please, spare my life.'

'I don't want your money,' I hissed into his ear, my voice as toneless as I could muster. 'I want you to tell me who commissioned the pamphlets.'

'I can't,' he attempted to wriggle out of my embrace, but I held firm. 'You've no idea what you're asking me to do! I'm dead if I tell you.'

'You're dead if you don't.'

'I'd rather die swiftly and painlessly – one slash of your dagger – than be gutted and quartered, screaming in agony,' he spoke with calm composure, his choice unequivocally made.

'Tell me and you'll live, you fool! I won't betray your confidence,' I was begging him by then rather than threatening. I was desperate. 'No one will know it was you!'

'I can't! Whoever you are, stop if your own life is worth anything to you. You're playing with fire. Walk away and I will say nothing of this to a living soul.' Now it was he who was threatening me.

'The pamphlets spread vicious lies about our Queen. This is high treason! Tell me who instructed you or it will be your head on the block!'

'I'll tell you this: my client stands on par with the Queen – maybe higher. Walk away. I said more than I should have done. I shan't say another word. Kill me if you must.' He shut his eyes and his body went strangely limp in my arms, as if he had submitted himself to his fate in advance of the lethal stab I was yet to deliver.

I wasn't a cut-throat. He had probably guessed as much. I picked up a poker and struck him over his head. He dropped to the floor with a groan.

XXV

Written on this the Nineteenth Day of September in the Year of our Lord 1592

Even though Havis told me next to nothing, I was in no doubt that the person behind the treasonous conspiracy was someone high up in the ranks of the nobility. I knew it couldn't have been Bothwell, himself under heavy assault from the authors of the pamphlets. I had no choice but to reach to the highest echelons of the Queen's court. I decided to approach her half-brother, Sir Robert Stewart.

I knew Sir Robert to be a man of integrity. He was faithful to the Queen and a good Christian. He had stood by Mary's side when David Rizzio was butchered. That macabre night, when Ruthven burst into her supper chamber howling for blood, Sir Robert had challenged the madman until he was threatened with a pistol aimed at his chest. He had also tried to warn the King about the plot against his life, a warning he'd later retracted, I suspect out of fear for his own life. I had to find a way of appealing to his sense of duty towards his Queen and his brotherly affection for his sister.

I approached him in the privy garden where I'd followed him from the palace forecourt. He was alone, taking a walk amongst the budding shrubbery and blossoming spring trees.

'My Lord, forgive me for disturbing your peace,' I offered him a bow,' but I have an urgent matter to raise with you.'

He turned towards me and squinted against the sun while he took the measure of me,' You are Ninian Winzet, Mary's confessor?'

'Indeed I am, my Lord.'

'What is the matter?'

'Her Majesty's safety – maybe her life.' I took him through my latest discoveries and suspicions. 'I fear, My Lord, that whoever stands behind the King's death is not finished in their mission. I fear for the Queen's life. I will be as blunt as the circumstances dictate: you tried to warn the King of the danger but you later denied it when confronted by the Queen. Am I correct in my assumption that it was because the Earl of Moray was in the room

THE QUEEN'S AVENGER

with you at the time? Because he is the man behind the conspiracy?'

Sir Robert was taken aback by my bluntness. He looked over his shoulder to check if we were alone. His expression was grave when he answered, 'You do realise that what you just said could cost you your life?'

'I will gladly lay my life for the Queen, my Lord,' I looked him straight in the eye. 'My only purpose is to protect Her Majesty from her enemies.'

'How can you protect her?' his eyes skidded over my humble form. 'You're but a priest.'

'Knowledge gives power,' I said. 'The Queen must know who her enemies are. It is the only way she can rally her true supporters and guard herself against danger. I intend to provide her with that knowledge. If you're privy to any schemes, my Lord, if your sister's life is dear to you, I beg you—'

'Very well. Walk with me, act calmly. We may be watched,' he started along the path and I joined him.

A small smile was quivering on his lips as he talked, making him appear as if he were sharing an amusing anecdote with me. What he was saying was as far away from a joke as could be fathomed. 'Yes, you are correct. In January – it was the Epiphany Day, I recall, late in the evening – I was visited by Moray and Maitland. They wished to discuss with me urgent matters of the state, as they put it. Maitland did most of the talking, but I was in no doubt it was all Moray's contrivance. He hated Darnley from the moment that foolish upstart had turned Mary's head.'

'Darnley had ideas well above his station,' I felt compelled to voice my agreement. 'But killing him…'

'He was a dangerous buffoon. After Rizzio's slaughter, as you may well remember, I had no brotherly love left in my heart for him either. But it was much more serious for Moray. Darnley had displaced him as Mary's closest confidante. He had threatened to undo the establishment of the Reformist Church in Scotland. The man was a thorn in Moray's side. He had to be removed.'

'He was a source of anguish for the Queen, too,' I pointed out.

'She wished to rid herself of him and I was sent to Rome to seek papal dispensation for a divorce—'

'Which they knew you didn't get. Word travelled faster than your horses, Ninian. They knew, even before you arrived back from Rome, that there would be no divorce. Or execution. Maitland said that Mary wouldn't stand for it. She was averse to bloodshed. That avenue was a dead end so Moray had another idea: Mary had to be compromised before her people, then overthrown like her mother before her. Moray would take the reins of the government of Scotland as Regent for the young Prince. For that to happen, Darnley would have to die and the blame for his death deposited at Mary's door. According to their scheme, Bothwell would be disposed of at the same time.'

'Bothwell? One of the Confederates? Isn't he of them?'

'He may think that, but they don't see him as such. The man had grown too big for his boots and got too close to Mary. Hot-headed as he is, he would be as easy to manipulate as Darnley before him. They told me he had already agreed to join them, lured by the prospect of becoming the Queen's next husband. He had jumped at the opportunity, they said, ever the rabble-rouser itching for easy gains.'

My breath caught in my throat upon hearing that: there had been whispers about Bothwell's ambitions for the Scottish crown, but no one really took him seriously. He was a wastrel, a man of unsteady heart and a scallywag – a talented and fierce general, perhaps, but he was no king.

'He walked into the trap like a bear into a wasp nest,' Sir Robert continued, ignorant of my shock. 'Not only did they have his backing for Darnley's murder, but he was also prepared to get his hands dirty. He threw himself into the whole wicked enterprise, body and soul. Of course, he didn't know the full story. He didn't know he would be led, blindfolded, to the scaffold.'

'As a scapegoat?'

'Indeed.'

'But he has been acquitted before Parliament,' I pointed out.

'It wasn't the right time to remove him. He is to marry the Queen with what he believes is the Lords' blessing. They signed a bond to that effect over a tankard of beer in Ainsley's Tavern. He thinks they will stand behind him as their new king. He is as much of a fool as Darnley was,' Sir Robert shrugged and gave a small sigh of amusement. 'But he will be tried for regicide – the evidence against him has already been fabricated and those pamphlets – well, they are there to stoke the fires of public condemnation against him and Mary. You see, Ninian, after his first disastrous rising against the Queen, my dear brother James had learned the hard lesson that without turning the people against Mary, he will never subjugate her.'

I detected sadness in Sir Robert's tone, but it was a sadness of acquiescence. He was as much Mary's enemy as was Moray, as were all the others: Morton, Ruthven, Maitland, Balfour...

'But, my Lord, if Her Majesty is implicated in her husband's murder, her life could be in danger. She could be led to the gallows—'

'No, you're wrong!' he raised his voice over my speculations. 'That won't come to pass. I have my brother's word on it. They will not harm Mary. That's the one condition upon which I agreed to stay silent: she will not come to harm. Who do you think saved her from the blast at Kirk o'Field?'

I gestured my ignorance by throwing up my arms.

'Maitland. He whispered into her ear that a masque was being held that night. Mary adores masques. Maitland suggested she stayed in her apartments at the Palace afterwards. They will not harm her.'

'But they will destroy her nonetheless,' I whispered, horrified. 'They will take away her kingdom. My Lord, this cannot be!'

'That's the price for her life,' he replied. 'Scotland is not England. Scots will not be ruled by a woman, but she will be looked after.'

'In captivity? Humiliated?'

'Go home, Father. Nothing you can do here.'

He was right on that account. That same day, Mary was intercepted by Bothwell on her way from Stirling to Edinburgh. She was taken to Dunbar Castle and even though alarm bells rung across the land calling upon the citizens to rise to arms, no one lifted a finger to rescue her. The tragedy of her demise, as devised by her bastard half-brother, was being played out before my eyes, and indeed, there was nothing I could do to save her.

I watched mortified as barely four weeks later, on 15th May, Queen Mary and Bothwell were married according to the Protestant rite in the great hall at Holyrood. She had been bewitched by the scoundrel – a heretic and a practitioner of the black arts, who in his turn had been conned by Moray.

The frenzy of hatred towards the newlyweds was being systematically whipped up by Knox and the omnipresent pamphlets. The people of Scotland were baying for royal blood.

I was denied access to the Queen but, at that point, my intervention would have been untimely. I was too late. The wheels of the murderous conspiracy were turning, crushing its victims as they went. When it finally came to an open confrontation, Bothwell fled the battlefield at Carberry Hill and Mary surrendered to avoid bloodshed. Although Kirkcaldy promised her the Lords' protection from harm, she was brought to Edinburgh a prisoner in all but name, and was paraded in front of the hostile mob like a wild beast in a cage.

Instead of the royal apartments at the Holyrood Palace, she was taken into town. There she was kept under guard, like a common criminal, in the house of the laird of Craigmillar, William Maitland's brother-in-law.

Denied entry to the house, I kept vigil beneath her window throughout the night. I was determined to bear witness should she come to any harm. I would record the name of anyone who entered the house. I would listen for any alarming sounds, cries for help or threats uttered against her. To my relief the night had passed without a single disturbance.

The next day, the window sprung open and Mary's half-naked person appeared. She looked like an apparition escaped from beyond the grave: her breast exposed, her copper hair ablaze, her eyes distorted with an expression bordering on madness.

'Betrayal!' she cried. 'We've been betrayed! Your Queen is being kept prisoner! Your Queen—' she couldn't finish for a pair of gloved hands pulled her back inside and the window was shut.

THE QUEEN'S AVENGER

My gut twisted painfully, squeezing tears out of my eyes. I begged the Lord Almighty to show me the way of saving my ward, but the Almighty was silent.

A man was walking past. He stopped, looked up, chuckled and spat under his feet. 'Wretched woman! She's no queen. She's a whore of Babylon. And a murderess,' he declared and, so relieved in his contempt, proceeded on his way.

Anger possessed my mind. It blinded me to reason. I was driven to do something – to punish that man for the sins of the Lords, whom I could not touch, and for his insults against my Queen. Pulled by the force of that anger, a force I couldn't resist, I followed the man on his way until he and I were alone at the bottom of a blind alley, with only stone walls surrounding us.

The ruffian faced the wall and started urinating, swaying back and forth on softly bent legs. Standing close behind him, I could smell the acrid stench of his sweat and his piss. His oily hair snaked from under his cap and crawled over his dirty collar. He was a repulsive creature.

'Take it back,' I spoke into his ear.

He swivelled on his heels, startled. Limp in his hand hung his phallus, still leaking urine. Repelled though I was, I didn't give him room to tidy himself. My breath was on his face. I repeated, 'Take it back.'

'What in the devil's name is this?' He was tying his breeches hurriedly.

'What you said out there about your Queen,' I jerked my head up towards the high street. 'Take it back.'

He grinned. 'That she is a French harlot and a murdering bitch?'

'Take it back.' My jaws were locked and all I could squeeze between my teeth was that same chant, 'Take it back, I said.'

'Or what, *father?*' He looked me up and down, mockery glinting in his eyes. 'You won't grant me absolution for my sins?' He gave me a push and menacingly placed his hand on a scabbard holding a short, wood-hilted knife. 'Be gone before I skin your scrawny arse.'

Even if I wanted I couldn't move. I stood rooted to the muck under my feet where a trickle of his urine soaked the ground.

I couldn't let this man walk away. 'Take it back.'

'Fuck off!'

He pulled out his knife, but I was quicker. I carried a fine dagger in the sleeve of my cassock for personal protection. Being a Catholic priest, my life was always in danger. I whipped the dagger out ready to stab, as I had practised on many occasions.

And I did it without a thought.

I drove the dagger, hilt-deep, into his chest. He jolted backwards, his shoulders ramming into the wall.

'I said, take it back,' I stabbed again, and again. And each time I repeated the same chant.

His eyes rounded with disbelief or fear, I couldn't tell. But I could see my own face in those stunned eyes. It was contorted with madness. And for a moment, I thought I was seeing Henry Yair. I dropped my dagger and released my hold on the man. He slumped to the ground, into his own piss, dead.

THE QUEEN'S AVENGER

PART 6

4th October 1592, Ratisbon, Bavaria

Gunther recoiled. The scroll fell from his hand and curled up on the floor. The benevolent and mild-tempered Father Ninian had killed a man in anger, and that wasn't the first time. He had done it once before – only by poison, for that was what the witch's draft must have been – not an elixir of divine truth, but plain poison.

Gunther had done it, too. Last night, in the first few minutes of blind panic, he had convinced himself that he had killed Brother Cornelius. He had then done everything he could to cover his tracks. He had behaved like a calculated murderer.

Killing a man was such a swift and irreversible deed: a thrust of a knife, a push, a shot fired at the twitch of a finger on the trigger. One had to live with it, Gunther reasoned. It was a simple act of self-preservation: surviving the here and now, and worrying about his immortal soul later. And yet, God was giving Gunther's soul a second chance. Cornelius was still alive.

Gunther deposited the fifth scroll he had just read in the secret vault, snuffed out the lamp and went back to his cell. The night was still young and he could steal a few hours of sleep before Vigils, but he chose not to. Instead, he dropped down to his knees and started praying. He now desperately wanted Cornelius to live and it wasn't even to save his own soul. It was because Gunther wouldn't be able to live with himself otherwise.

He was blurry-eyed and faint after two days without sleep when he joined the others at Vigils. They all prayed for Brother Cornelius. Benedict gave them an update on his condition – there was no change but there was hope.

Gunther spent the rest of the day pushing himself to the limits in self-imposed penitence. He offered to clean the stables to Brother Anselm, the head groom, and threw himself body and soul into the task. He was halfway through the job by midday and by Vespers he was done: the horses nestled in fresh straw and a pungent mountain of manure was heaped in the yard, ready for use in the monastery vegetable garden. Gunther refused to take a break though his muscles ached and his stomach twisted with hunger. He hurried to the kitchen to lend a hand with the preparations for supper. It was there, while he busied himself peeling potatoes, that Brother Loui told him about Cornelius.

'He's awake. It's a miracle. Praise be to God!'

Gunther took a deep, shaky breath. He wasn't a killer after all. The good Lord had heard his prayers and saved Gunther's soul by raising Cornelius from his deathbed.

'Best news I've heard all day,' he exhaled.

'Indeed. I was by his side when he opened his eyes and spoke to me. He asked me,' Loui raised his brow, bemused, 'what on earth I was doing in his cell. I said, *Praying for your recovery, Brother. Recovery?* asked he, as if he had no idea of what had befallen him. I said, *You've been in an accident. Your legs are broken and a good few of your ribs. We thought we had lost you.*'

'So he can't remember anything?' A spark of hope ignited in the depths of Gunther's gut.

'He couldn't, not at first, but when he tried to get out of bed, he was reminded rather painfully,' Loui grimaced in sympathy. 'I told him we'd found him unconscious in the courtyard and that Brother Benedict had set his bones.'

'They will take a while to heal,' Gunther said. 'Let's hope his memory returns, too.'

'God willing.'

Brother Loui bound his hands and inclined his head piously, mumbling a prayer. He then tossed a few handfuls of buckwheat groats into the boiling pot and gave it a stir. The hollows of his cheeks flushed red from the heat of the fire.

Gunther watched him, unsettled and nervous. His mind was in turmoil, contradicting emotions bouncing within the cavity of his chest. It was a blessing that Cornelius had pulled through, but the unknown of what he remembered and what he may yet come to remember would hang over Gunther's head like the sword of Damocles.

As if hearing Gunther's thoughts, Loui added, 'Mind you, he asked to see Father Archibald to clear his conscience and receive

Holy Communion.'

'He remembered something, then? Something he wished to confess?'

'Who knows? It's between him and the Almighty. Although he sounded confused when I spoke to him, he told me his memories were fuzzy and tangled. I called Brother Benedict to take a look at him – he wanted to be told the moment Cornelius opened his eyes. *If he ever does,* were his exact words. I don't think even Brother Benedict held much hope for poor Cornelius. And neither did I, judging by the state of him, but God works in mysterious ways—'

'When?' Gunther had no desire to listen to Loui's musings about God's ways. 'When was that? When did he wake up?' Perhaps there was still time to talk to Cornelius before anyone else did, to find out how much he remembered and to plead with him to say nothing, whatever the cost.

'Oh, not long after the Chapter room meeting. I went to visit him and there he was – wide awake, but confounded, like I said.'

Six hours. It had been six hours since Cornelius had regained consciousness. He would have seen a few people since then, spoken to them, and received the sacrament of confession from Father Archibald. Both Father Archibald and Brother Benedict would have attempted to interrogate Cornelius about how he had come by his injuries. The only question was, how much he remembered. Gunther had to find out.

'That's done, then,' he gestured towards the bowl of potatoes. 'I'll fetch water to wash them.' He grabbed a pail and hurried out.

The cloisters and dormitories were empty, all brothers busy with their daily chores out at the workshops and in the garden. Gunther left the pail at the entrance and headed for Cornelius's cell. The door was closed. He knocked and received no answer. He entered without invitation.

'Please forgive my intrusion, but I heard the good news, Brother, and couldn't wait to—' he began and stopped dead in his tracks. Cornelius was staring at him with unseeing eyes. His mouth was hanging open, revealing several broken teeth, his lips a greying shade of blue, purple bruising on his swollen – unmoving – face. The man was dead.

Gunther ran.

His sandals padded on the flagstones of the long corridor like the beat of a war drum. If someone heard him – saw him – they would have jumped to the only rational conclusion, that Gunther was running from the scene of his crime, that he had killed Cornelius. In a strange way, it would be justice, belatedly delivered but justice nonetheless. Gunther wasn't prepared to submit to it. Yes, he had pushed Cornelius to his ultimate death, but he didn't mean to kill him. It had been an accident. Cornelius had slipped and fallen. He died from his injuries. He was now silenced for good. Gunther was safe but only for as long as he kept his wits about him.

He burst into the kitchen and collapsed on a stool, breathing in shallow puffs.

Brother Loui eyed him curiously. 'So, where is the water?'

'Oh, the water!' Gunther sprung to his feet. He had forgotten the water. The pail was standing abandoned by the entrance to the dormitories. 'I found a hole in the pail. I need a piece of cloth to mend it.'

'You won't find it in the kitchen,' Loui said, scowling.

'No... I know that. I just wanted to let you know. I'll pop over to the laundry room and see if I can find some oilcloth.'

Gunther left before Loui could question him any further. He cursed himself under his breath for his scattiness. He must not betray himself. No one could know that he had been to see Cornelius. Someone else would have to find the dead man's body. Anyone, but Gunther.

Gradually, his nerves settled. He proceeded with the rest of the day calmly, attending all services dutifully, and joining others in singing thanksgivings to God for sparing Cornelius's life. At sunset, he arrived in the dining hall and wolfed his pottage – his first meal in the last forty-eight hours.

The supper was nearly over when Brother Augustine, who had taken Cornelius's food to his cell, came running back and announced that Brother Cornelius was dead. The celebration of his miraculous recovery had been very short-lived indeed.

THE QUEEN'S AVENGER

Father Archibald rose from his seat and intonated a prayer for Cornelius's soul while contrition and relief duelled for supremacy in Gunther's own soul. He had got away with murder, but he would never forgive himself, never let himself forget. One day, on his deathbed he would have to follow in Father Ninian's footsteps and confess.

After Compline, he allowed himself a few hours of sleep. He could no longer keep his eyes open. At midnight, he crept back to the tower and opened the sixth scroll.

XXVI

Written on this the Twentieth Day of September in the Year of our Lord 1592

I killed a man, and for once it wasn't God's justice I merely delivered here on earth. It was rage – my own rage. A moment of insanity though it was, killing that ruffian has left a black mark on my heart – a mark I won't be able to erase for as long as I live, and beyond. It will follow me to my grave and from there, to Hell. In a way I am looking forward to the day of final reckoning. At long last, I will be relieved of my burden.

Writing about it has given me no reprieve – no peace. My soul remains as tormented as it has been for the past twenty-five years. At night I write my last confession but, without absolution, this brings me no comfort. I have spent the last three days lying prostrate on the church floor, refusing food, hoping the merciful Lord would grant me a swift end. But it wasn't meant to be. Not yet. I am still here, still drawing breath – a penitent sinner languishing in the purgatory of my own making.

That wretched devil did not deserve to die. The others did. I had killed the wrong man, I knew it as soon as it was done, but in that moment I had no head for contrition. I pulled my dagger out of the man's back and wiped the blade on his cloak. I then said a prayer over his corpse and commended his soul to our Father in Heaven.

With my body shaking and my mind feverish, I returned to the High Street and began clamouring at the door of the house where Mary was being kept. I was threatened with arrest by the hagbutters guarding the house, but I refused to budge and shouted even louder, 'I will have access to my Queen! I am Her Majesty's confessor! You've no authority over her immortal soul! I will not go away!'

At last, having caused them sufficient embarrassment, I was let in.

I found Mary in a state of despondency. She seemed bewildered but her earlier hysteria had subsided. She was alone. None of her ladies were present to help her spruce up her dishevelled appearance. A plate of cheese and bread, untouched, and a goblet full of wine stood on a table next to her bed. A chair lay overturned on the floor.

'Your Grace,' I executed a deep bow, averting my eyes from her scantily covered breasts.

'Father Ninian!' she cried and ran to me. She folded herself into my arms like a chick unto the safety of its mother's wings. Her hot tears burned in the small of my neck.

'We've been betrayed! We've been abandoned by everyone we trusted,' she lamented bitterly, her arms still wrapped around me, her trembling body clinging to mine. 'Everyone – our closest allies, our kinsmen and friends! We were told it was safe to return to Edinburgh only to be ambushed along the way. Oh, the perfidious Kirkcaldy! Oh, the treacherous, treacherous Balfour!'

James Balfour, you vicious dog! My own, silent, scream echoed Mary's. I had been right to suspect him and finally he had shown his true colours. The list of his transgressions was growing longer with every new day. He had started by undermining the King's lodgings at Kirk o'Field and luring him into a death trap; now he was setting snares for the Queen and her new husband, his own cousin and friend. Oh, the treacherous Balfour indeed!

'And Lethington... My trusty Lethington!' she cried, projecting her voice towards the door as if intent on pouring her boiling scorn through it and out into the streets of Edinburgh. She pulled away from me and approached the window. Its shutters had been bolted to the wall after her earlier dramatic appearance. Only a glimmer of daylight filtered through them. Mary stood in that narrow shaft of brightness, specs of dust vibrating in her hair and tears swelling in her eyes, eerily reflecting the light.

'Did he harm you, Your Grace?' I cried. I had always known *her Lethington* could not be trusted, but she – she was innocent and pure goodness. She had faith in that treacherous viper posing as her counsellor and honourable statesman. *Damn you, Maitland!* I cursed under my breath.

'He swore he was on my side. He promised his heart wasn't with the rebels, that he only wanted to avoid bloodshed and that it would be avoided if I surrendered myself to the Lords. I believed his word. I trusted him! This morning, he was passing under my window and I called out to him. He affected he didn't hear me and walked on.' Her beautiful face crumpled in anguish.

'He is no friend, Your Majesty. I should've said it earlier, forgive me, but William Lethington was in on the conspiracy to kill the King and he is—' I began to reveal to her the extent of Maitland's betrayal, but couldn't bring myself to finish the sordid tale.

'I know he was… I didn't believe it – I couldn't…' she pressed her fist to her lips to push back a sob.

'Your Grace knew the part he played? When did you find out?'

'Just before Bothwell departed Cranberry Hill he told me about the plot. He gave me his copy of the bond they all signed. It'd be my collateral, he said, something I'd hold over the heads of the traitors – Morton, Balfour, Argyll, Huntly and yes, Maitland, too. I have their names branded in here,' she tapped her chest with her palm, 'even though they took the document away from me. I shan't forget and this time I won't forgive. Except,' she peered anxiously around the confines of her chamber, 'they don't care for my pardon as long as I'm their prisoner. That's all I am, Father, a prisoner, wholly at their mercy. I dare not eat or drink anything for fear of being poisoned,' she gestured towards the untouched food and wine on the table.

'I've been led to believe that they do not intend to… to murder Your Grace,' I mumbled, not fully convinced myself despite Sir Robert's assurances.

'How can I trust anything they say? They are villains without honour. Their promises stand for dust,' she retorted, her gaze as hard as rock. 'Kirkcaldy gave me his word, and then—' She shut her eyes tightly as if trying to squeeze out from her mind the humiliating memories of her capture. 'Then they taunted me, insulted me, paraded me in the streets shouting, *Burn the whore!*' Her voice caught in her throat. She swayed on her feet and pressed her hand against the wall to steady herself.

I approached her and offered her my arm. She leant on me and allowed me to lead her to the bed where she slumped with a heavy groan.

'I am tired, Father,' she whimpered. 'I'm covered with dirt, slime and clay. My clothes are spoiled and torn,' she pressed her hand to her bosom. 'I'm not permitted to receive visitors. My letters, I'm certain, are intercepted by Morton. I don't know what I am being accused of. All I did was what they asked me to do: I married the Lord they'd chosen for my husband. Bothwell showed me the bond – one they all signed in his support, declaring their loyalties to him as their future king: another Scot, another Protestant – one of them!

'I did their bidding, yet they turn against me. Why? They say they have delivered me from the hands of the villain who kidnapped and ravaged me, but it is the same man they had recommended I marry. They accuse him of murdering the King but I've seen evidence of their own guilt – the very crime they accuse him of! And now, they are baying for my head on the block. Why?'

I opened my mouth to answer, but she wouldn't let me. She was consumed by bitterness.

'What have I done to offend them? I did everything they asked… I am their anointed Queen and yet I am in fear for my life. I'm in fear of my own subjects, men who swore their allegiance to me before God. Why are they doing this to me? When will they stop?'

'When you're out of the way and Moray assumes control of government,' I said at last.

'James is behind this whole conspiracy?' she stared at me, incredulous and frightened like a wounded deer no longer in command of its own body, trapped and painfully aware that it has nowhere to flee. 'But his name wasn't on the bond. He wouldn't have— He is my brother! Are you sure? James wasn't even here when Henry was killed. He was away, by his wife's side. Did you know? You didn't! She'd suffered a miscarriage. No, not James!'

'He didn't have to be in Edinburgh to pull the strings. He's careful. He works in the shadows. His name is never mentioned. But he won't rest until you're overthrown and he rules Scotland.'

'These are serious accusations, Father Ninian,' the Queen strung her trembling lips into a tight line. 'You'd better have undeniable proof.'

'Sir Robert Stewart is my proof, Your Grace,' I said and relayed to her everything her brother had told me.

XXVII

Written on this the Twentieth Day of September in the Year of our Lord 1592

Mary didn't believe me. Not at first. Although she wept bitterly, remnants of hope clung to her heart. Rescue would come, she kept saying. I dared not ask from whom: her wayward husband who'd fled from the battlefield in her moment of need, or her ambitious bastard half-brother who had orchestrated her downfall.

On Monday evening, she was transferred to the Holyrood Palace and reunited with her beloved Marys. I followed her; we would not be separated. I had vowed never to leave her side. They would have to prise me away from her with hot irons.

We sat down to supper in the same chamber where Rizzio had been slaughtered. I offered to taste her food in case it had been poisoned. Morton, who hovered behind her chair like grim death, gave a contemptuous snort, 'If we wanted her dead, we would've resorted to a sword, or an axe. Poison is a woman's weapon.' His eyes narrowed and he inclined his large head towards me, adding menacingly upon reflection, 'Woman's and a canny priest's.'

A chill rippled down my backbone. Had he recognised me from the tavern in Newcastle? I evaded his eyes and affected preoccupation with the content of the Queen's plate.

'Shall I taste it nevertheless?' I asked.

Her shocked gaze left the audacious old brigand, and she gave me a curt nod. I picked a morsel of meat from her plate and tipped some of her wine into my goblet.

'Make haste,' Morton shifted his bulky form uncomfortably. 'The horses are ready and waiting. We have some distance to cover tonight.'

Mary's eyes brightened, 'We're off to Stirling? I can't wait to see my dear son!'

Morton grunted a non-committal response and departed to oversee the preparation for the journey. Immediately after the supper, we were instructed to mount horses despite the Queen's protests of ill health and demands for a litter.

At Leith, we realised that Stirling Castle wasn't our destination. We were heading due north. To investigate, I cantered ahead to the front of our convoy led by the new Lord Ruthven, the son of the man I had sent to the Devil a year earlier. I approached with stealth, unsure of his intentions. Whatever the spawn of Patrick Ruthven was contriving couldn't have boded well for the Queen. I pulled my horse's reins to steer it into line behind Ruthven's stallion, my manoeuvres shielded by the starless night.

'Are you certain? Who would dare mount a rescue? They'd sure as hell be doomed to fail,' Ruthven was talking to his comrade whose wide shoulders enhanced by his furred collar made him look like a bear on horseback. 'Surely not Bothwell. The last I heard of the devil was that he'd sailed to Orkney.'

'No, not Bothwell. My man says it's the Hamiltons,' I recognised Lord Lindsay's deep voice.

'Damn them!'

'We'd better pick up pace. I've posted armed guards by the crossing, but they won't hold if the Hamiltons come in large numbers.'

I didn't listen to the rest of their war counsel. I turned around and spurred my horse into a gallop. I reached the Queen and conveyed to her the good news of a potential rescue mission.

'We must delay our progress and give them a chance to catch up,' she said, her eyes sparkling in the black night with their own inner light. She tugged her horse's reins violently and groaned with exaggerated discomfort.

'I wish to dismount. My horse has a limp—'

She barely settled her horse to stand still when Ruthven appeared and whipped it into a jittery trot. 'Keep up!' he bellowed. Several soldiers arrived with him and grouped into a tight formation at the rear of our convoy. A mouse wouldn't slip through it.

Hours later, after an exhausting horseback journey at breakneck speed, we stood on the bank of Loch Leven. The sun was beginning to rise over its dead-still, bleak waters. The black square tower of Lochleven Castle rose from an island in the middle of the lake.

Three boats appeared from the vapours of the morning mist, heading our way. Mary was to become an unwilling houseguest of Sir William Douglas, Morton's cousin and his successor in title. He was also Moray's half-brother on his mother Margaret Erskine's side. The castle was well fortified and accessible only by boat. We couldn't have landed in a more hostile environment than that.

I stole a furtive glance at my Queen. She looked white, all colour bleached from her face. Her jaw hung slack and her eyes appeared to have fallen into the back of her head. She swayed on her feet and tried to step backwards, but her body failed and she swooned into my arms. With the help of two of her escort I carried her to one of the boats. She remained unconscious throughout the lake crossing.

I sat by her side, deep in thought, the splash of the oars stirring the lake and scattering my wits. No other sounds disturbed our passage as if the world, mortified at the injustice, stood still and held its breath.

I was glad she had fallen unconscious. At least, she didn't have to contemplate the hopelessness of her situation. The prospects of rescue from this remote fortress were less than negligible. Raising an army in her name was just a fantasy as her reputation lay in tatters. She was already defeated. The only reasonable hope I could harbour was that she lived, and even that became increasingly unlikely.

She was carried, roughly and without regard for her status or her delicate condition, by two soldiers: one hooked his arms under her armpits, the other held her legs by the ankles. It was an undignified image that would never leave my mind: my beloved Queen manhandled by a pair of louts like a drunken wench.

Only she wasn't drunk – she was dying.

Her condition failed to improve despite the efforts of her physician and her devoted ladies. She hovered between life and death for weeks. We feared the worst. In the brief moment of her regaining her lucidity a month into her illness, I heard her deathbed confession and administered to her the Last Rites.

Towards the end of July she was seized by agonising cramps. She howled in pain, sweat drenching her gown and her bedsheets. Blood appeared. First, a small quantity seeped through the linen, colouring it bright red – a warning sign of more to come; then, she started to haemorrhage. I was dispatched from her bedchamber. The physician was called. As I took post by the closed door, I watched, bewildered, as maidservants hurried in and out, carrying bloodied sheets and bowls of crimson-stained water that splattered out onto the flagstones at their feet. Mary had suffered a double miscarriage. Bothwell, the babes' father, wasn't there to share in her grief.

The miscarriage was only one of many painful episodes in the long line of misfortunes that had already, or were yet, to befall the Queen. She was still incapacitated in her bed, too weak to walk and scarcely able to speak when Lindsay marched into her chamber and thrust a bundle of papers in her face.

'We require Your Grace to sign these,' he growled in his bearish baritone. He had brought a quill and an inkpot with him and set them on the bureau by the window.

'What are they?' she inquired in a voice so faint that I, sitting right next to her, could barely hear.

'Your abdication and the establishment of regency in favour of Lord James Stewart during your son's minority,' he replied, his tone blunt and matter-of-fact.

'What a preposterous idea!' she shook her head; her fingers curled over her bedsheets, her knuckles turning white. 'Why should I even contemplate it? You are supposed to be protecting me. Instead, you are holding me against my will and conspiring to steal my crown. You have no authority to—'

'There's a warrant for your imprisonment,' he cut in without much ceremony. 'I have every authority.'

'A warrant? Who issued it? On what grounds?' Despite her illness, Mary raised herself on her elbow and faced Lindsay eye to eye.

'The warrant was signed by nine of the Lords of this realm.'
'Names! Give me their names!'
'The earls of Glencairn, Home, Morton—'
'Morton! But of course! The murderer of the King!'
'But it is you, Madam, who must answer for your part in the King's death.'

'I?!' she cried, her face a picture of innocence despoiled. 'I've ordered a full enquiry into the matter, demanded the murderers to be brought to justice, and you have the audacity to point a finger at me! Get out!'

'Our enquiries led us to you, Madam.'

'Then take me before Parliament. Let me hear your accusations, and let me answer them in public view.' Her tone was now measured. There was an implicit threat in it. 'I have evidence of your conspiracy and I wish to put it before my people.'

'The enquiries are complete. The warrant is out. You are to resign your crown in favour of your son. Sign the papers!' His hand crossed to the hilt of his sword and he lurched menacingly towards the Queen.

I jumped to my feet and charged forward to block his way. He barred me with one sweep of his arm, his elbow slamming into my jaw and sending me to the floor. 'Stay out of it, preacher,' he snarled.

'I shall not sign away my God-given rights,' Mary threw the papers at his feet.

'Then I will be compelled to cut your throat, however loathsome such act would seem to me. Don't force my hand!'

'Add regicide to your crimes, sire. Do your worst.' She slumped back onto her bed and fixed him with an unwavering eye. Her body may have been weak but her spirit could still move mountains. At that moment, I admired her – worshipped her.

'I'll be back and when I return you will sign the letters,' Lindsay turned on his heel, sent me a cursory glance of utter contempt and, stepping over my person sprawled on the floor, stomped out of the chamber.

As soon as he was gone, I scrambled to my feet and rushed to Mary's side. She stared at me, her features seized by fear. 'They will kill me, Father,' she whispered. 'If I don't sign,' she gestured towards the papers scattered at the foot of her bed, 'I will be dead and buried at the bottom of this cursed loch.'

I feared she was right. I knelt before her, 'Your Grace, you will always be Queen of Scots – they will never take that away from you. Even if you sign the cursed letters. They aren't worth the paper they are written on. You will be signing under duress and as such the act of abdication will be invalid in law. They won't be able to hold it against you.'

'So that is your counsel, Father – for me to abdicate?'

'To save your life, Your Majesty, yes, this is my advice,' I hung my head low, somewhat embarrassed by my own words.

She sat silent for a long while considering the import of my counsel. Tears welled in her eyes and rolled down her cheeks. Soon, they dried and her eyes regained clarity. At last she spoke, 'We shall do as you suggest. Perhaps, once it's done, we will be free to go and, once we're at liberty, we will rally our army and take back what's been stolen from us.'

Within the next two weeks, the Queen was queen no longer, her son was crowned King of Scotland and Regent Moray was on his way to Lochleven Castle to decide her fate. From now on, Mary would be fighting not just for her kingdom but also for her life.

XXVIII

Written on this the Twentieth Day of September in the Year of our Lord 1592

Mary Stewart was born to be queen and, although her body was ailing and she was kept under lock and key like a wild beast, her spirit remained undefeated and her natural charm had soon gained her a valuable sympathiser – her gaoler's brother, George.

He was a young man with a head full of notions of chivalry and adventure. He had fallen under Mary's spell like a love-stricken minstrel. But he wasn't just a hapless admirer. Possessed of a brave heart and quick wit, he was prepared to disobey his elders and sacrifice his fortune in service to the Queen. He arranged for Mary's correspondence to be smuggled in and out of the castle, under Sir William's nose. Mary was able to send for help to her uncle, the Duke of Guise, as well as to Philip of Spain and her cousin Elizabeth, Queen of England.

After a long time of creeping in the shadows, her evil half-brother, the Earl of Moray, returned to the scene of carnage he had set months earlier in order to assume control of the realm. He visited Mary at her Lochleven prison, temporarily raising her hopes for release from captivity. She had relinquished to him everything he desired and no longer posed a threat to his authority. At least that was how she presented it to him when they met face to face.

She put on the most impressive performance of sisterly devotion as, holding her nose, she welcomed him with open arms and kissed his flushed cheeks, loudly praising the merciful Lord for bringing her dear brother back to her.

He wasn't convinced. If anyone was impervious to Mary's charms, it was her own brother, a man who owed her not only allegiance but also, love. He glared at her sternly and, standing with his legs wide apart and his thumbs hooked over his belt like a father chastising his prodigal child, he began hectoring her about the fatal error of her ways.

THE QUEEN'S AVENGER

In his foul speech filled with resentment and loathing, his ego floated to the surface like dung. He had the audacity to accuse Mary – his Queen – of disobedience and pointed out that her wilful failure to abide by his superior judgment was the sole cause of her fall from grace. He threw in her face her *childish choices unbecoming of a queen*, choices he perceived as purposefully designed to vex and undermine him: her choice of religion, of husbands and of advisers she had put above him. It was her fault, her fault alone, he claimed, that she had ended up burying some of those closest to her.

I watched Mary's face transform from joyous to shocked, to aggrieved, to furious. I feared she may lose her composure, a luxury she could not afford. If she lashed out at the ungrateful bastard, there was no telling what he would do. He was the one holding all the trumps in this showdown of power.

She must have realised it too for instead of scolding him for his impudence she hid her face in her hands and wept. 'God knows I am innocent of any crimes. None of what I did was borne out of pride or self-indulgence, but with the best interests of my kingdom and my subjects at heart—'

'Your subjects don't see it the same way, Madam,' he snapped, unmoved by her tears. 'Innocent though you may be before God, your reputation is in tatters. It's how the world sees you that matters. Tongues are wagging and gossip spreads as fast and wide as flood waters. And you've been judged an adulteress. A murderess—'

'I am innocent! As God is my witness!'

Her cry shook me to the core.

'That may well be,' he responded, his voice cold and flat, 'but that's not how you're perceived.'

'Then let me go free, James,' she grabbed his hand, 'Let me go before Parliament and let me present my case. That's all I ask for. You can take the burden of government away from me. You can undo my mistakes. I don't deny I made them. But, please, I beg you,' she raised his hand to her lips to kiss it, but he brusquely pulled it away. 'Please let me go! Let me clear my name!'

'No.'

'You cannot hold me prisoner!' Anger flashed in her eyes. 'I'm your Queen!'

'You have resigned your crown, I should remind you,' his lips curled back from his teeth.

'But I am still your sister—' Mary's tone softened to a whimper.

'And as your brother, I must keep you safe. If I let you go, the crowds in the streets will tear your flesh from the bone. You are hated in your own kingdom. For what you did and for what you are believed to have done. It's my duty to keep you safe as the King's mother. You're comfortable here, wanting nothing.'

'I am a prisoner! I am held against my will!'

He fixed her with a gaze flaring with menace, 'Get used to it. Should you try to run, I will catch you and this time you won't escape the executioner's axe.'

That was the brother's parting words to his queen-sister. He left and took with him the very last shred of hope she may have been clinging to.

It came as little surprise when, just hours later, Mary fell ill again. Her body swelled and her skin parched and turned yellow. Once again, she was looking Death in the eye.

I was convinced she had been poisoned on Moray's instructions. He would not get away with it, I made a solemn oath before God, and then I prayed fervently and constantly for the miracle of Mary's recovery.

My prayers were answered. She fought back and, with the Lord's blessing, regained her physical strength. Soon her mental resolve returned. She wouldn't give in to Death and she certainly wouldn't give in to her inferior – her subject, at that.

Within the tight circle of her loyal servants, which included myself, George Douglas and Mary Seton, we began to plan her escape. We were under no illusion that Moray and his cronies would ever let her go free. In truth, we were certain that if she stayed on the island her body would at some point float to the surface of the loch and rumours would be spread across the land that, gripped with guilt for her husband's murder, she had thrown herself to her death from the castle tower.

THE QUEEN'S AVENGER

Indeed, the news reaching us from Edinburgh reinforced our beliefs. Leslie wrote to report that the Regent had raided his sister's coffers as if she were dead already and acquired all of her priceless jewels – those belonging to the Crown as well as her personal treasures.

Mary was inconsolable. If she had any hope of Bothwell dashing to her rescue, that hope was snuffed out when we learned about his capture and imprisonment by the Danish King Fredrick on the grounds of some unresolved matter of honour. A Bothwell-led counterattack against Moray was as likely as snow in August. In fact, Bothwell's stronghold, Dunbar Castle, had fallen into the Regent's hands, thus extinguishing the last bastion of pro-Marian opposition to his rule. By the end of that year, Moray's appointment to regency was cemented in law by Parliament.

A month or so later, on a morning shackled with ice which no fires could thaw, a letter arrived from Leslie. It had been smuggled by a brave washerwoman, concealed in the hem of Mary's chemise.

The Queen read it with bated breath, her hand pressed to her bosom. I kept guard by the door to make sure no one burst in on us, as such raids had become increasingly frequent. I watched her lips lose definition as blood drained from her face replaced by what seemed like frost rising all the way to her eyes. I knew the news wasn't good.

'Parliament has spoken,' Mary said at last. 'My kidnappers have been excused from any wrongdoing. I stand accused of having been privy to my husband's murder. They are baying for my head on the block.'

'Is there no one? Has nobody spoken for you, Your Grace?'

'Who's left to speak for me? Those last few men loyal to me have run to save themselves. Any witnesses to the Lords' crimes have been tracked down and executed. It's Moray's word against mine, and he has the floor. I'm trapped here, gagged.' She tossed the letter into the fire.

'Will he be satisfied at last?'

'No. My dearest brother will want me dead to ensure my silence.'

We were in no doubt that Mary had to run to save her life. There was no time to spare for any more deliberations. Her first attempt at breaking out of Lochleven was unsuccessful – she had been recognised by the hired boatman, and returned to the island. The boatman had kept quiet about it, but there was no telling for how long. A drunken boasting at a public house was all it would take to alert Mary's captors to her plans. Suspicions were already rife amongst the locals in nearby villages. Word had it that Mary's escape had been prophesised by a well-respected wizard, the laird of Markyston.

The Queen's most ardent ally was George Douglas. His young uncorrupted heart had instantly recognised true virtue. Alas, he had been banned from the island amongst rumours of his over-familiarity with the prisoner and suspicions that he may be plotting her escape. Which he was. It seemed like Mary had run out of lifelines.

But George wouldn't be defeated. He concocted a new plan of escape. He engaged the services of his younger cousin, Willy Douglas, a lad of small posture, thirteen years of age and with hardly a whisker on his chin, but cunning beyond his years.

The plan was to carry out a masquerade during which Mary would be able to flee the island disguised as one of her chambermaids. Willy took charge of organising a May-Day pageant, appointing himself to play the part of Abbot of Unreason.

An abbot, how auspicious! Even today I smile at the memory.

Every person, from the Queen herself to the lowliest oyster boy assembled in the quadrangle. The weather itself conspired with us: the sky was cloudless and the sun wrapped the revellers in a warm, self-indulgent numbness.

Willy entered wearing crimson robes with ermine trimmings – on loan from Mary – and a bishopric hat made of felt. Too big for Willy's head, it was leaning onto his ear, making his head appear lopsided. He affected intoxication, staggering from side to side and mumbling blessings spiced with lewd curses. That evoked immediate merriment amongst the crowd. Rotten food and handfuls of mud were slung, affectionately, at the youngster, and he sought shelter under ladies' skirts. From there, he provided more bawdy entertainment by screaming obscenities, wafting their petticoats and making noises of fornication. Some of the ladies joined in the spectacle. They gasped and rolled their eyes, putting on a show of gratification. Willy dived in and out of billowing skirts, licked his fingers and smacked his lips to suggest ideas that I, as a priest, wasn't allowed to appreciate, but even I could not suppress a smile.

Ale and wine were served by the barrel load. Drink loosened tongues and inhibitions. Sentries abandoned their stations and chased after wenches to have their way with them in stables and behind storerooms.

The festivities continued throughout the day, laughter, mischief and general jolliness. By sunset, the excess of drink and debauchery had sent most into a daze. Mary professed extreme exhaustion and departed to her room where she discarded her mantle and slipped into her servant's skirts. So disguised, she marched unchallenged across the courtyard in front of the bibulous guards. Without blinking an eye or a single twitch of a muscle, she strolled out of the castle via its main gate.

I was already there, waiting. Just as she had left for her apartments, I had skulked casually to the shore to sink all but one of the boats in order to prevent pursuit.

I could barely recognise her dressed in her maid's simple garments with her hair tucked under a bonnet and a hood obscuring her face. She affected a limp and hunched her shoulders as if she expected a whip to land on her back at any moment. The queen had always been a keen actress, and good at it. Only the twinkle of mischief in her eye, and her height, betrayed who she was.

She stepped into the boat and curled into a ball, pulling her cape over her head. Willy and I cradled her between us to shield her with our bodies in case of shots being fired. We rowed as if the hounds of Hell were after us.

George was waiting at the other side of the loch with horses stolen from his father's stables. Mary mounted a fearsome black stallion and, to the cheering of peasants who recognised their Queen by the flame of her red hair, galloped to freedom, heading for England and the hospitality of her cousin Elizabeth.

PART 7

5th October 1592, Ratisbon, Bavaria

'Help me carry the body to the infirmary,' Brother Benedict asked Gunther after all the others had left the cell. They had seen enough gore for one day.

'Why?' Gunther frowned his bafflement at the medic.

'Because you're young and strong, and I can't do it on my own.' Benedict rolled his bulging pale eyes. Gunther always found them unsettling. They were like insect eyes, without eyelids.

'No. I mean, why the infirmary? Shouldn't we be taking him to the chapel?'

'That will come later. First, I wish to examine the corpse.'

Gunther crossed himself, appalled by the very idea. 'But Cornelius's earthly remains must—'

'I'm not proposing to eat them,' Benedict cut him short. He spread his cowl on the floor. 'You grab the shoulders. I'll take the legs.'

They heaved the body from the bed. It was heavier than Gunther remembered despite Benedict holding the legs. Cornelius was a chunky man, with dense bones and a stomach bloated by too much beer. They placed it gently on the cowl, as if Cornelius could still feel pain, and lifted it in unison. Benedict led the way while Gunther walked behind, forced to look at the body along the way.

Someone had mercifully closed Cornelius's eyes. The look of horror Gunther had seen in them earlier was now extinguished. The body became animated as they transported it across the courtyard. Its motions made Gunther retch. He had to resist the temptation to drop it and run.

'Let's put him here,' Benedict jerked his head towards a trestle table, the only space in the infirmary free of medical equipment and apothecary potions. 'On three.'

They hoisted the body onto the table. It wobbled precariously threatening to roll off. Benedict placed his hand flat on its abdomen to steady it. Gunther retched again and this time his breakfast came into his mouth.

'Get out! Empty your stomach outside!' Benedict thrust his finger towards the door.

Gunther ran out and allowed the rest of his morning meal to spill out of him in waves of violent nausea. He wiped his mouth and took a few deep breaths of fresh air. Curiosity forced him to go back into the infirmary to watch the autopsy.

'Haven't you had enough?' Benedict sent him a cursory glance.

Gunther shrugged.

'In that case, help me undress him.'

As they pulled the shirt and undergarments from the body, it began to feel more like an object of interest than their brethren's earthly remains, even more so when Benedict started making observations.

'See these?' he pointed to three purpling bruises across the chest. He pressed into them. 'Broken ribs. I can feel them move.'

Gunther swallowed guilt.

'This here,' Benedict tugged at Cornelius's lower right leg, 'was a nasty break. The bone went through the skin. I set it back and it was beginning to heal over. The broken bones didn't worry me. He might have limped a bit and suffered from bad rheumatism in his old age, but he would have lived, I thought. One thing I didn't know was what had gone on in there,' he tapped Cornelius's skull. 'If he'd taken a fall, which was the most likely occurrence going by his injuries, how severely had his brain been shaken? That was an area of interest for me. If it was bad and there was internal bleeding, he would die.'

'So, that's what it was?' Gunther asked. 'The bleed on the brain after the battering it took in the fall? That was the cause of death.'

'No, I don't think so,' Benedict wagged his thick-knuckled finger. 'Of course, I intend to open the cranium and have a look, but in my opinion Brother Cornelius didn't die from a bleed on the brain. He was murdered.' Again, those unnatural bug-eyes rolled in Benedict's head and rounded on Gunther.

Gunther shrunk under that glare. Did Benedict know what had happened in the tower? Had Cornelius spoken to him before dying? Had he told him? And if he had, how much did Cornelius remember?

'It was an accident—' Gunther began to explain.

'Nonsense!' Benedict interrupted him. 'It was deliberate. Someone smothered him. See these finger imprints,' he pointed to three elongated red marks on the right side of Cornelius's mouth. 'They weren't here yesterday. They weren't here when I spoke to him after he came round. They appeared post-mortem. Someone pressed their hand to his mouth and nose, and held it until Cornelius ran out of breath. Murder, plain and simple.'

'I see,' Gunther's mind was in complete meltdown. He didn't kill Cornelius, but someone did. Why? Was his death in any way connected to the stolen scroll? But if so, then why had nobody come for Gunther?

'I'll report my findings to Father Archibald.'

'Will the Authorities have to be notified?'

'I doubt it. Archibald will want to conduct the investigation behind the closed doors of the monastery. One should always take care of one's own dirty laundry. Unless, of course, it is established that the killer came from outside.'

'Yes, absolutely,' Gunther mumbled, half-heartedly.

'Now, would you like to watch me open the skull? It may be interesting what we may find out about the original—'

'No! Sorry, Brother. I've no stomach for this.'

Gunther fled the infirmary. His brain was on fire. He ran for the well, pulled up a bucket of ice-cold water and tipped it over his head. It sharpened his senses. His thoughts coalesced at last. He had to compose himself to act normally. Steady, no one was after him.

He decided to make one last effort to find the missing scroll and thus put his mind at ease that he had not been exposed. He headed for Cornelius's cell. He had searched it already but he hadn't had a chance to check the bed. It was the most likely hiding place.

He entered the chamber to find Brother Loui squatting on the floor, a birch-twig broom in hand. He was sweeping straw and rushes into a hessian bag. The bedding was gone, the wooden frame of the bed squatting over a piss pot. Bar the crucifix on the wall, the bed pallet and a hassock, the cell was empty.

'Brother Gunther, come to help?' Loui presented his slightly askew smile. 'I'm almost done here.'

'What did you do with the bedding?'

'The straw stuffing was damp and it smelt of mildew. I burnt it. The fire is still going by the storeroom. I have this to add to it,' he hoisted the hessian bag with the sweepings.

'I'll take it there for you. I'm going that way anyway,' Gunther offered.

He hurried towards the outbuildings in the hope that he could still retrieve what was left of the bedding and what was potentially hiding inside it.

When he arrived, he knew he was too late. Damp as the straw may have been, the fire had devoured it rapidly. There was nothing left. Gunther emptied the hessian bag into the flames. They burst into life. He sat by the fire and mused. Perhaps Cornelius had hidden the scroll in the straw of his bedding and perhaps it had just been destroyed. If he had told someone about it and they had found it, wouldn't they be confronting Gunther about the rest of the Abbot's writings? Unless Cornelius had kept Gunther's identity to himself. He had always wanted something from Gunther, always tormenting him with his unmanly advances. The scroll was the leverage Cornelius had against him. Maybe he had decided to keep that trump card close to his chest.

The rest of the day passing uneventfully confirmed Gunther's speculations. He was not under suspicion.

At midnight, he headed for the tower to peruse the last bundle of letters left behind by Abbot Ninian. After that he would have to decide what to do with them.

XXIX

Written on this the Twenty-first Day of September in the Year of our Lord 1592

I didn't trust the heretic English Queen, but Mary believed she was her last resort. They were *sisters,* Mary insisted, and sisters took care of each other. In any event, what could be worse that the nest of vipers Mary had left behind in Scotland? I had no answer to that, at least not at the time. Mary fantasised of meeting her *sister* face to face, conveying to her what had really happened, denouncing her rapacious half-brother as a traitor and usurper, and securing Elizabeth's military support in restoring her to the throne of Scotland.

Her hopes were dashed when Elizabeth refused to meet her in person.

I guess she couldn't bring herself to look Mary in the eye. Instead, she used her courtiers to lie and make promises on her behalf that she didn't intend to keep. Mary was sorely offended. She demanded safe passage to France to seek backing from her brother-in-law, King Charles, and her cousin Henry, the Duke of Guise. That was the last thing the imposter queen would consent to. She knew how tenuous her hold on the English crown was. She knew it would only take a small spark for the fires of a common uprising of all good Catholics in England to erupt and consume her alive. So, she had Mary moved to the fortress of Bolton, as far away as possible from the Scottish border to prevent any attempt of rescue from the pro-Marian faction active in Scotland. It was even further away from London to preclude the rallying of English Catholics around their true Queen. Mary became Elizabeth's hostage in all but name.

Bolton was a forlorn and isolated place in the depths of North Riding in Yorkshire. Bleak and unfurnished, draughty and swarming with vermin, it wasn't an abode fit for a queen, not even for a queen's dog. The veneer of Elizabeth's hospitality began to wear thin. The pretence of Mary being her guest was exposed for what it really was: an act of betrayal. Elizabeth was preparing the ground for getting rid of her rival and the only legitimate heir to the English throne.

The bastard Queen of England was no better than the bastard Regent of Scotland. They both wanted to destroy Mary, only their methods were different: he resorted to rebellion, theft and violence while she relied on much subtler but equally callous, and ultimately lethal, ways of disposing of her rival. Elizabeth decided to put Mary on trial.

Mary's emissary to the English Queen, Lord Herries arrived from London in July. He had been negotiating with the English the ways of resolving the deadlock over Mary's release. He was in high spirits. He requested an immediate audience with the Queen. He had good news to share with her.

He was still in his riding gear, mud wet on his boots and cloak, when Mary received him in her presence chamber. He bowed to her, 'Your Grace, Queen Elizabeth sends her sisterly love to you.'

Mary tilted her head in a tentative nod of acknowledgement. 'What of our return to Scotland? Is she going to assist us or not?'

'She assured me personally that her wish is to restore you to the throne of Scotland.'

'Then why doesn't she? We have asked for her help over and over again! Our pleas fall on deaf ears!' Mary could hardly control her exasperation.

'It is because accusations of regicide have been made against Your Majesty – allegations of Your Majesty's complicity in the murder of King Henry.'

'And she believes them?!'

'She does not, but her hands are tied. The accusations are made by Your Grace's brother, the Regent. She is obliged to give them due consideration.'

'They are all lies and he's an usurper.'

'She knows that but her Lords – some of her Lords don't. She must ensure she has their loyalty. Justice must be seen to be done, the rule of law must be seen to be obeyed by everyone, even the Queen.'

'So, she will put us on trial? We are her equal – no, we're more than that, we're her superior – not her subject. Her laws don't apply to us and we will not submit to her idea of *justice*. We've heard it all before. You have failed in your mission, my Lord.' Mary rose from her seat abruptly, her eyes as bright and brisk as lightning in a storm, her breast heaving.

'There'll be no trial, no judges, no executioners. Please hear me out. Your Grace, please!' Herries jumped to his feet, distraught. 'She proposes to call a conference to give you an opportunity to present the evidence you've been offering to her personally. Your Majesty will be able to clear your name to a commission of her highest-born nobles who will stand in her place and stead as if they were the sovereign. This way they will be satisfied that she upholds the laws of this land and that she abides by them. But her mind is already made up. Whatever the outcome of the conference, she promises to restore you to the Scottish throne. She gave me her word.'

Mary turned around, 'And her conditions?'

'If the Scottish lords bring reliable evidence of your guilt—'

'My guilt?' her eyes flashed again, but she reined herself in. 'Continue, Lord Herries.'

'Then you will pardon them for their rebellion and imprisonment of your person.'

Mary said nothing but pressed her lips into a thin line and her hands into tight fists. I could tell she was barely containing her outrage. She had sworn she would never forgive the traitors, and never forget. Yet now, when her freedom was at stake, she was forced to compromise her principles.

'If they produce no proof and you're exonerated, you will return to Scotland as their sovereign with Queen Elizabeth's full support provided you cut your ties with France, abandon Mass and renounce your claim to the English throne—'

'My claim derives from God. I'm the great granddaughter of Henry Tudor. I cannot renounce what is mine by blood!'

'You only need to hold back during her lifetime, and the lifetime of her children, if she has any, Your Majesty. The chances of that ever coming to fruition are slim. She is older than you, past her childbearing age—'

'Yes, I know, I know,' Mary waved her arm, annoyed. 'I'm in no position to negotiate, am I.'

'Your Majesty, she assured me that the conference was just a formality to silence any discontent amongst her nobles, but, no matter the outcome, she will do everything in her power to return you to the throne of Scotland.'

Mary thought for a short while. She looked at me, briefly, almost furtively, and I knew she could read doubt and warning in my eyes. I don't think she wished to hear my arguments. She wanted to cling on to hope, to her only chance of regaining freedom, however improbable it was.

'So be it,' she said at last.

The conference was set up to take place at York. Mary's representatives comprised myself, my old patron John Leslie, now Bishop of Ross, and three Scottish nobles still loyal to Mary: Livingston, Boyd and of course, Herries.

We arrived at York in late Autumn. I took lodgings in town. They were clean and tidy, situated above a tavern where I was fed adequately, although the spirits they served weren't half as good as the Scottish malt. The people of Yorkshire were friendly towards me and I soon discovered that many Yorkshiremen remained faithful to Rome and keen to hear Holy Mass. I felt almost at home there and relieved to have left behind the oppressive drabness of Bolton Castle. Hope was beginning to take root in my heart for a fair outcome to the legal process that had every potential of clearing my Queen's good name.

I spent many hours at my escritoire and burnt oil well into the night drafting submissions on Queen Mary's behalf. I put my legal training to the best possible use and was looking forward to the hearing.

Alas, my high spirits plummeted to the bottom of my gut when one evening I descended to the tap-room for supper and a pint of ale, and discovered Moray and Maitland seated at the table in the company of Ralph Sadler, the Earl of Sussex, and Thomas

Howard, the Duke of Norfolk. Those were the two English lords who had been appointed by their Queen to adjudicate the accusations against Mary. They were supposed to be independent and unbiased and yet there they were, making merry and fraternising with Mary's accusers.

I edged closer towards their table, and sat behind them facing away, my ears tuned into their conversation.

'Her hand is available in marriage, her divorce from Bothwell a mere formality,' Maitland was saying. He was clearly referring to Mary. Was he offering her in marriage to Thomas Howard?

'It would be the greatest honour of my life,' Norfolk replied, verifying my speculations. 'However, it would be prudent to tease out Queen Elizabeth's mind on the marriage?'

'Isn't it your Queen's dream to bring our kingdoms together, united in the Protestant faith? The only person that stands in her way is Mary and her papist ways, not to mention her blood links with France. For as long as she eludes our control, she will remain a threat to Elizabeth. But we can bring her to heel. She can be controlled by a Protestant husband who also happens to be a loyal subject of Queen Elizabeth,' Maitland reasoned, his voice as smooth as poison laced with liquid honey.

'It is something worth exploring,' Norfolk replied.

'With great caution,' added Sussex. 'Elizabeth will not tolerate any challenges to her authority.'

'Mary will not be gladly restrained,' Moray said, his voice tense with agitation. 'I warrant that she won't submit and she will never renounce her claim to the English throne. There are still many in Scotland and a good number of Catholics here in England who will follow her all the way to Hell. They believe in her. She's still their queen. The best way is to discredit her by showing her as guilty of murder and adultery.'

'Not without proof. Elizabeth is reluctant to pass judgment on her without seeing compelling evidence of Mary's crimes, and frankly, so are we,' Sadler folded his arms across his chest. I saw it from the corner of my eye.

'We have proof – letters, love sonnets written in her own hand. Instructions, in writing, given to Bothwell personally,' Moray sounded triumphant.

'Instructions?'

'Her blessing to get on with the killing of the King, to rid her of her husband so that she'd be free to marry his murderer.'

'You have that in writing?'

'Indeed. Lord Morton's men found a silver casket amongst Bothwell's belongings after he fled to Orkney. Mary's letters were discovered in the casket. They prove her complicity unequivocally. If they are to be taken at face value,' Maitland said.

'Is there doubt as to their authenticity?' Sadler asked.

'None,' replied Moray.

'Well,' Maitland rubbed his beard, thoughtfully, 'only Mary can say whether she wrote them.'

'She'll lie to save herself,' Moray growled.

'I know her hand,' Maitland countered, 'tidy, Roman letter formation. She was taught calligraphy in France, under her Italian tutor. It isn't that easy to replicate. Those letters – some of them at least… Let's just say, not all of them are what they purport to be. And Morton sat on them for a year before releasing them. There will be doubt—'

Moray gripped Maitland's neck and hissed, 'Only if you raise it, William.'

'I'm just proposing a better option – a union with England, the Protestant faith supreme across these isles. It's cleaner that way. Neater. Less blood spilt,' Maitland spoke softly, but there was steel in his tone. He had his own vision of the future and it didn't align with that of the Scottish Regent. I was glad to hear discord creeping in between them.

'We'll need something to fall back on should your dream of union fail to come true,' Moray spoke through his teeth.

'Let's not jump ahead of the game,' Norfolk intervened, his tone conciliatory. 'I'm obliged to report the existence of the letters to Elizabeth.'

'Good!' Moray set his tankard on the table with a triumphant thud. 'That will sway her to put Mary's head on the block before it's too late.'

'I rather hope it'll convince her to wash her hands of Mary and leave her to me,' Norfolk replied, and one of them chuckled.

I didn't wait to hear the rest of the conversation. I climbed to my lodgings upstairs and threw my submissions into the grate. The fire devoured them swifty. They were useless. The battle for Mary's kingdom – and for her life – wouldn't be concluded in the courtroom. It was being fought behind closed doors with the weapons of calumny, forgery and treason. I packed my saddlebags and galloped back to Bolton.

THE QUEEN'S AVENGER

XXX

Written on this the Twenty-first Day of September in the Year of our Lord 1592

Mary acted swiftly. On the same day I reported my discoveries to her, she wrote to Elizabeth demanding an opportunity to peruse all the evidence provided by Moray and to present her own case in person, not through her commissioners. It would be her word against her brother's as they stood eye to eye and made a solemn oath on the Holy Bible.

While waiting for Elizabeth's response, the Queen and I spent many days collating our evidence. There was one document Mary Seton had managed to smuggle into Lochleven Castle when she was allowed to join the Queen there. That document had survived our escape from Scotland and the undignified search of our persons carried out by the English. It was a bond for the murder of David Rizzio which Darnley had surrendered to Mary when he confessed the conspiracy to her, thus betraying his accomplices, Moray, Maitland and Morton amongst them. This gave them a motive to kill the King in revenge for his betrayal.

Unfortunately, I pointed out to the Queen, the bond was also compromising for her. Darnley had signed it too and his hands were covered with her beloved Rizzio's blood. She had a reason to want him dead.

We debated this matter for a long time and in the end agreed that the bond would be submitted in evidence. In mitigation, Mary would raise the pardon she had granted to Rizzio's assassins, including the King. She would have forgiven him anyway. It was evident from the bond that he had been duped into signing it by promises of the Crown Matrimonial made to him by none other than Moray.

Mary had also seen a much more compromising bond, that for the murder of her husband. It had been entrusted to her by Bothwell before he fled. As much as Bothwell was a signatory to it so were the other Lords – the same Lords who had now been throwing accusations of Mary's complicity in the crime. Alas, that document had been forcibly removed from her after her surrender at Carberry Hill. As soon as Mary was permitted to testify in her defence, she would swear to its content and expose the real killers of her husband, the very men who would be standing across the floor from her in court, accusing her of murder.

She would also declare that those were the same men who had encouraged Bothwell to ravage the Queen and take her dead husband's place with or without her consent. Another bond to that effect had been signed by those swindlers at Ainsley Tavern. We didn't have it, but again Bothwell had told Mary about it and given her the names of the signatories. Mary had committed them to memory. They were not hard to memorise because, again, they were the same men as those who had firstly dangled the Scottish Crown before Darnley to seduce him into their murderous intrigues.

I coached Mary through her depositions. She practised for hours on end. Her performance was polished and believable, primarily because it was God's own truth. Hope returned to her heart.

Three weeks later a reply arrived from Elizabeth. In it, she informed Mary that the conference had been moved to Westminster and would recommence imminently. She again declined to see Mary and went on to say that it would be unnecessary for her to appear at the hearing. Mary could however make her representations in writing, answer accusations through her commissioners or in person to Elizabeth's Lords dispatched to Bolton for Mary's *convenience*. In essence, Mary would remain incarcerated and under guard at Bolton Castle while Moray would be free to flash forgeries and fling false accusation against her with impunity at Westminster.

'I'm damned. This is a death warrant,' Mary passed me the letter and dropped her hands to her sides. Her head fell backwards onto the back of her chair and she gazed at the ceiling vacantly.

I read the letter, my heart pounding furiously. 'It's a travesty of justice!' My voice shook with anger. 'Her nobles enjoy greater rights and freedoms than you, Your Grace, her equal. This isn't a rule of law – it's a rule of lawlessness.'

THE QUEEN'S AVENGER

'She wants me dead, doesn't she?'

'Indeed. She's looking for an excuse to kill you and she won't let the truth stand in her way,' I had to agree with Mary no matter how much saying it would hurt her.

'At least, death will liberate me,' she spoke with unnerving calm. 'I cannot bear this confinement for much longer, Father. It's killing me day by hopeless day.'

'If I may, Your Majesty has put undeserved trust in the heretic Queen. She has never been Your Majesty's friend. She never intended to be Your Majesty's saviour. Quite to the contrary.'

'I realise that now. I will withdraw my commissioners from the conference. It's a farce. I am a woman condemned. All I have left is prayer.'

'Prayer will give you peace, Your Majesty, by all means, but not all is lost,' I said, my mind already made up. I went on to apprise her of my plan: 'She wants you dead because she fears you, and she fears you because you only need to say a word and legions of Catholics here and in Scotland will rise against her. You have diehard supporters on these isles and on the Continent, Your Grace, but they need a divine sign – a voice in the desert to unite them. They need God's blessing to spur them.'

'They won't act because I can't give it to them,' she peered at me, her eyes moist with tears. 'I'm a prisoner, prevented from leaving this God-forsaken hovel and under constant surveillance. My visitors are searched, my correspondence intercepted, my seal violated, my letters stolen. I am cut off from the world.'

My chest contracted painfully when I spoke next, 'Your Majesty, I vowed to stay by your side to the bitter end, but I feel I can only be of service to you if I leave. If you appoint me your emissary, I will take your case to Rome, to France and Spain. I will petition all the faithful princes of Europe on your behalf. I will knock on every door until rescue is mounted and your freedom and Crown are restored to you.' I knelt before her and hung my head, awaiting her decision.

She rose from her chair, approached me and placed her hands on my head, 'Go with my blessing, Father Ninian. Save me, or avenge me.'

XXXI

Written on this the Twenty-first Day of September in the Year of our Lord 1592

When the spectacle of Elizabeth's *conference* was over, having achieved no resolution either way, I was finally permitted to depart, alongside Mary's other commissioners.

It was at Tutbury Castle, on an unforgivingly cold February day that I said farewell to my Queen. I would never see her again other than in my dreams, and nightmares.

She saw me to the castle gate, as far as the sentinels would allow her to go. Her mink-trimmed hood framed her face tenderly; her cloak clung to her. I envied her cloak the intimacy, wishing I could touch her and feel her closeness, and take that ephemeral bit of her with me for safekeeping. Tears glistened in her eyes.

'Can we have privacy to say goodbye?' she asked George Talbot, her new gaoler. The Earl had accompanied her from her apartments, reluctant to let her out of sight, as if anxious that she and I would at the last moment swap places. He took a sharp intake of breath to reply but thought better of it and stepped away.

Mary approached me, cupped my head between her hands and kissed my forehead. Even now, twenty-three years later, that kiss lingers on my skin, warm and meant from the heart. 'You've been like a father to me.'

'I tried my best. All those years ago, I promised your mother to watch out for you, Your Grace. I'll never stop trying.'

'You are my only hope.' She removed one of her rings – a gold enamel band with four bright emeralds set in the shape of the Cross. She passed it to me. 'Take this as a token of my faith in you and a seal of my authority. It was a gift from my uncle. Henri will know it. He will commend you to King Charles.'

I had letters for Henri de Guise, her cousin in France, sewn flat into the lining of my cloak, together with letters to her son in Scotland, to her ambassador in London, the Holy Father and several Catholic princes of Europe. I also had her petition to the

Scottish Parliament for a mandate to start divorce proceedings from Bothwell.

I took the ring and slipped it into the pouch with Widow Ainsley's draft that I carried tied to my belt alongside my rosary. I knelt before her.

'God's speed, Father.'

I heard her skirts swish as she turned and walked away. I couldn't see anything. My eyes were blinded with tears.

I spent the whole of that year – the year of Our Lord 1569 – delivering Queen Mary's letters across the Continent. I was always treated with courtesy, but it was laced with cold indifference. It appeared to me increasingly that saving my Queen wasn't a straightforward mission of asking others for help. I had to work on many fronts and build alliances. That would take time.

One of the first objectives was to restore Mary's good name which had been left in ruins after the campaign of defamation run by Buchanan in Scotland and Walsingham in England. Together with John Leslie I co-wrote *A Defence of the Honour of Marie, Queen of Scotland* and took it to Bohemia to have it published anonymously. Word had soon spread to France and from there to England.

In May, I returned to Scotland to deliver Mary's petition for divorce. I was confronted with a kingdom plunged into discord and desolation, a kingdom held with an iron fist by the self-appointed *Regent:* Moray. He ruled by means of fear, coercion and blackmail. The air was thick with despair.

I submitted the Queen's petition but could find no way of penetrating the wall surrounding her beloved son, James. In any event, the prince was still a young child, incapable of reading his mother's words for himself. I would have to entrust the letter to someone of his immediate circle, but I could trust none of them. They were all the worst of religious deviants and Moray's lackeys.

I had almost resigned myself to failure and was packing my trunk to leave Scotland the following day when Maitland appeared at my lodgings.

'Sire!' I barely recognised him. The man was a shadow of himself: painfully thin and drawn, grey of complexion.

'Ninian, I need your help,' he slumped in a chair, his palm pressed into his chest as he recovered his breath. 'I need you to put me in good stead with Mary.'

'My Lord, I don't believe we're on the same side,' my tone was icy. I hadn't invited him to sit down. I regarded him with suspicion. My eyes shifted nervously to the door he had left open behind him to check if he had come alone.

'I understand your lack of confidence in me. It wasn't long ago when we stood opposite each other, fervent adversaries in York, me backing the brother against his sister, you—'

'Me backing the true monarch – the Queen of all Scots, you – an imposter,' I retorted angrily.

'Indeed. You were on the side of righteousness and I was wrong. I can see it now. My heart is heavy with regret.'

'Too late. You have committed treason, my Lord. That cannot be undone or forgiven.' I wasn't afraid. He didn't scare me. I was looking at a broken man, already condemned in his own mind.

'I will answer for that before God Almighty, but it isn't too late for the Queen. It isn't too late to stop Moray. He has his eye on the throne and he'll stop at nothing. Mary isn't safe and neither is King James. She is wanted for the murder of Darnley.'

'How? She wasn't found guilty at Westminster.'

'Westminster is far away. This is Scotland. She was proclaimed guilty by the Regent's recent decree. There is no shortage of cut-throats waiting for her to cross back over the border—' he started to cough, blood-laced spittle flying from his mouth.

I poured a cup of watered-down wine from a pitcher and handed it to him. For a second I was tempted to drop a pinch of widow Ainsley's powder into it, but decided against it. I was curious to hear what he had to say.

He drank the wine and continued, his voice rough and dry like a scab. 'King James is only a bairn, defenceless in his cradle. I wish to protect both the Queen and her son. Help me do that. Help me mend the error of my ways before I'm dead and can do no more.'

'How?' I asked.

THE QUEEN'S AVENGER

'I will vote for the annulment of Mary's marriage to Bothwell. I will canvass for other Lords, sympathetic to Mary, to do the same. We'll start preparing the ground for her safe return.'

'As Queen?'

'As Queen-regent. She will have to marry once the annulment is through. Duke of Norfolk, a high-born English noble. That will appease the English Queen, I should hope. It will bring our two kingdoms close together, strong and united against foreign intrusion. I'll take care of the negotiations, but I need your help in establishing channels of communication with Mary.'

'How do I know you won't betray her again? You changed sides often enough. You made false declarations. How do I know this isn't a trap to lure her back here—'

'My solemn word,' he wheezed. 'I swear it on the Holy Book. I am standing over my grave, looking into the mouth of Hell, Ninian. All I wish to do before I die is to make amends and to atone for my sins. To save my soul.' His expression was humble, his eyes, dimmed with illness, pleading with me.

'If there is the slightest chance,' I began. He smiled. He knew I couldn't say no. I wasn't awash with offers of help from any other quarter. 'I will write to the Queen.'

'Thank you. God bless,' he rose from his chair with a groan.

I bit into my lip, venting my anger. I didn't need his god's blessing and I still despised the man. But I couldn't exact the Queen's revenge on him. This wasn't the right time, but the right time might yet come.

'Please wait, my Lord,' I stopped him. He turned, trained his eyes on mine, hope flickering in them as if he was expecting an absolution.

I had something else in mind. I untied Widow Ainsley's pouch and picked some of the witch's draft – no more than three pinches. I wrapped it in a piece of cloth and gave it to him.

He turned it in his hands, baffled. 'What is it? A medication? I don't believe I can be cured—'

'No, sire, I don't wish to cure you, but I can help you. When you're truly ready to face your demons here on earth, before you die, sprinkle it into your wine and drink it.'

He thanked me for it and left.

I am glad I trusted him to be his own judge. He remained loyal to the Marian cause until his dying breath. Hunted by Moray, he took refuge at Edinburgh Castle held by Kirkcaldy on behalf of the Queen. When four years later the castle fell to the English and he was taken to Leith to face a traitor's death by hanging and quartering, Maitland died at long last on his own terms. Word has it that he committed suicide after the old Roman fashion – by poison.

I have no doubt that it was Widow Ainsley's draft. It conjured his demons – for there was no room for angels in his corrupt heart – and they confronted him with the extent of his depravity.

I had warned him. He knew what to expect. I respect his courage. In the end he faced his evildoings, his betrayal of his Queen and of the true Religion. I could ask for no more.

Perhaps, in a small way, his contrition on earth would help him after death. Yes, he risked dying by taking the draft but he may have saved his immortal soul, and I helped him with that.

THE QUEEN'S AVENGER

XXXII

Written on this the Twenty-first Day of September in the Year of our Lord 1592

Buoyant and reinvigorated after my meeting with Maitland, I remained in Scotland for the rest of that year. I carried messages, approached prospective allies and was slowly building a network of pro-Marian support across the land. Alas, Moray and his henchmen were equally vigorous in untangling that network through intimidation and bribery. He had Parliament in his pocket. At a congress of Scottish Lords, the majority proclaimed that Mary was forever banned from returning to Scotland. The dissenting minority was being persecuted, terrorised, often divested of their titles, estates and even liberty. Many went into exile. It had become apparent to me that with Moray at the helm of government, the Marians would be ultimately divided and annihilated. Moray was like the head of Hydra that had to be cut off and buried deep under a rock, so that the monster could at long last be defeated.

I wasn't the only one who had come to that conclusion. I was spending Christmas of 1569 at John Hamilton's house. He was an unwavering Catholic, Archbishop of St Andrew's, and an ardent supporter of Mary.

It was after the Christmas Day supper that the conversation veered towards the desperate state of affairs in Scottish politics, and in particular the Regent's reign of terror.

'He has now disposed of all his detractors but those few hiding in exile,' Hamilton observed with a shake of his head. 'All witnesses to Darnley's killing have been tortured to provide false testimony, and then promptly executed.'

'John Hay attempted to tell the truth from the scaffold, remember Uncle?' James of Bothwellhaugh, the Archbishop's nephew, recalled.

'Indeed, he did. He decried the assassins and the whole plot, implicated Balfour, Maitland, Morton and Moray, but to what end? He lost his head nonetheless. They hacked off his limbs and posted them on town gates, paraded them in the streets to baying crowds. But not a dent in Moray's reputation. The bastard is indestructible. And mark my words, he's already plotting to seize the throne.'

'That's what William Lethington believes too,' I added, referring briefly to the conversation I'd had with Maitland in July.

'Moray has to be stopped,' the Archbishop said, 'but it won't be easy. We don't command sufficient numbers to confront him on the battlefield. The French and the Spanish are slow to act. How do we rid ourselves of him?'

'He's been clamouring for the Queen's death ever since she fled from his clutches and landed in England,' I said, resolved to speak plainly. 'He provided false testimony against her at Westminster, before God. His objective is to have her executed by order of the English Queen. I have heard that from his own mouth. There is only one solution to his crimes. He has to die.'

'An execution?' Archbishop Hamilton clasped his hands together, mortified of what he already knew had to be done. Nonetheless, he spoke without betraying acquiescence. 'Moray has wiped out every last shred of evidence of his wrongdoings. He has disposed of witnesses and had most of his fellow traitors killed or subjugated to his will. We will find nothing against him. No one will speak out.'

'I do not mean an execution, Your Eminence. I'm talking about an assassination. For the greater good of this kingdom and God's glory, for the restoration of Queen Mary on the Scottish throne and the true Religion amongst her people. The fire of devotion ignited in my breast, the memory of my Queen's words, *save or avenge me,* rung in my ears. The time for revenge was upon us. 'It's the only way.'

In January we received news that Moray was at Linlithgow, visiting one of his many mistresses. Within minutes, James Bothwellhaugh and I were on horseback, heading for my hometown whence from I had been ejected twenty years earlier by the servant of the Devil, Dean Kinlochy and his partisans.

THE QUEEN'S AVENGER

When we arrived, my heart contracted at the sight of my beloved church of St Michael's, now reduced to a cold, empty shell, and of the beautiful loch shackled in ice, like the rest of the town.

We took residence at Archbishop Hamilton's house conveniently situated on the south side of the high street. We spent three days watching the Regent's routines. He was reckless. Every morning, he would ride at his leisure and without escort through the main road to his mistress' house and would return in the late afternoon, heading back for the safety of Linlithgow Palace. On the fourth day of our surveillance, Moray would not reach his apartments.

We had two hand pistols. Their range was limited as was the visibility just as dusk had begun to set in. We had to abandon the safety of the house and come close to the street. By good providence, the chambermaid had hung out some laundry that morning and it was drying, spread on the bushes and on the rope strung between the door and an apple tree. The white sheets of bed linen, smelling of lime and vinegar, provided excellent cover. Despite the biting northerly wind, the sheets remained still, rigid with frost.

Our horses were saddled and waiting at the back of the house. We loaded our pistols and took position behind the laundry line. We waited. Moray was unexpectedly late that afternoon. The greyness of the cloud-laden sky had descended on the town, bleaching out its colours and blurring shapes. My hands lay frozen on the trigger. Bothwellhaugh was blowing warm air onto his frost-bitten fingers.

At last we heard the unhurried clatter of hooves on the cobbles. A single rider appeared at the top of the street and was heading towards us, his fur-lined long cloak wrapped tightly around his shoulders. Although his head was drawn into his chest and his beard thick and unkempt, obscured his features, I recognised Moray at first glance. There was something in those quick, flashing eyes, black as the bottom of the loch, that I would never mistake for anyone else's.

Those eyes brought back memories of the sacking of my church of St Michael's and the sacrilege committed there by the Protestant rabble while Moray, Morton and Maitland looked on, jesting and laughing. Once again, I stood hiding in the bushes and watched this vile man, this monster, a heretic Lord parading his unholy person before me with impunity.

Twenty years ago, I could do nothing, but that day, the 23rd of January in the year of Our Lord 1570, I was in charge. I aimed my pistol at his head, at the spot between his black eyes, and pulled the trigger. My pistol failed to discharge.

I looked towards Bothwellhaugh. His face was contorted with panic, fear, horror – I didn't care to know what. My eye caught his pistol shaking in his hand, his wrist loose. He was incapable of firing it.

'Shoot!' I shouted.

My scream attracted Moray's attention. I saw him pull on the reins of his horse and scowl, staring right at us but not seeing us behind the sheets. Panic set in his eyes and he kicked his horse's flanks. I had no time to think. I wrestled the pistol out of Bothwellhaugh's hand, aimed and fired.

Moray doubled up in his saddle, dropped the reins and clutched his stomach. His horse reared and made a few fitful sidesteps, thus dislodging the rider. Moray fell onto his side. A hollow groan was pushed out of his lungs as he hit the icy ground. But he wasn't dead yet.

He heaved himself onto his knees, managed to rise to his feet and staggered a few paces forward. I unsheathed my dagger ready to pounce at him and finish the job with a thrust into his back, like with that random man I had killed in Edinburgh's blind alley.

I didn't have to repeat myself. Moray spat blood and plunged to the ground, face down. The traitor was dead.

I seized Bothwellhaugh by the collar of his cloak and forced him to his feet. He was muttering something incomprehensibly. I dragged him to the back of the house and helped him mount his horse. I slapped its back and it took off, Bothwellhaugh's figure wobbling in the saddle. I mounted my horse and followed him.

I felt as light as a feather, free as a bird. The cold air was bursting in my lungs, pumping up my chest. On the town's border snow began to fall, covering our horses' hoofprints.

My Queen's nemesis was no more. God was on our side.

THE QUEEN'S AVENGER

XXXIII

Written on this the Twenty-first Day of September in the Year of our Lord 1592

In the year of our Lord 1579 I received a letter from Leslie in which he outlined his latest scheme to free Mary and restore her to the Scottish throne. It would be done jointly with her son James who would soon be assuming personal rule of Scotland.

I was an old man by then, exhausted and disillusioned with all our previous failed attempts. A couple of years earlier I had retired from public life and assumed the position of abbot at St James's monastery here in Ratisbon. I had devoted myself to writing theological texts and educating a new generation of priests who one day would return to Scotland proudly brandishing the standard of Catholicism.

At first, I folded Leslie's letter and secreted it between the pages of my Bible. What he was suggesting was an audacious plan involving the kidnap of young James, his removal to the Continent with a view of converting him to Catholicism and marrying him to a Spanish princess. He was also planning a full-blown invasion of England by the Spanish and French forces with the objective to topple Elizabeth and establish Mary on the English throne. The scheme, in true Leslie fashion, was foolhardy, and I had no conviction in its success. And yet, in the days that followed, my conscience would not let me rest. My promise to Mary remained unfulfilled and I still had one more letter to deliver on her behalf, arguably the most important of her letters: the letter to her son.

He had now come of age and would be able to read his mother's words on his own and judge the truth of them for himself. The least I could do was to hand Mary's letter to the conspirators for delivery to the young King. And that, I hoped, would bring closure to the other unfinished business I had with the last of the Scottish traitors: Morton.

The Queen's letter, should James finally come to read it, would give him his mother's first-hand testimony about Morton's role in the murder of Lord Darnley – James's father.

I wrote back to Leslie to accept the invitation and the next day I was on my way to Joinville, the seat of the de Guises.

Four of us were present at the meeting: John Leslie, now as frail in body as me but, unlike me, possessed of a sharp mind and a passion I had long squandered; Henri, Duke of Guise and Mary's first cousin, a zealous advocate of Counter-Reformation; and Esmé Stuart, Count of Aubigny. All our hopes rested on Esmé.

He was a handsome man, in the prime of his years. He was eloquent of speech, charming of demeanour and possessed of intelligent eyes that radiated strength of conviction. He was young King James's cousin on his father's side and it would be through his agency that Leslie's scheme was to be realised. He would travel to Scotland to formally congratulate the King on his assumption of government. From there, he would ingratiate himself into the King's favours and plant the seed of Catholic thought in the young man's mind. He would mould him to his will and once his influence was firmly established, he would lead King James into the arms of his mother and the Holy Church. Listening to Esmé, I was in little doubt that if anyone could succeed at this, it would be him.

'I have letters from Philip of Spain and from the Holy Father promising their backing for our enterprise,' Henri said. 'Once we have James safely out of the country, the invasion will commence.'

'God willing, we'll have Queen Mary rule both Scotland and England,' Leslie raised his gaze to Heaven and bound his hands, pleadingly.

'She is the only legitimate heir,' I added.

'And there is the papal blessing for any faithful Catholic to remove the usurper queen from the English throne,' Leslie said. He was referring to Pope Pius's Bull *Regnans in Excelsis* in which he had excommunicated Elizabeth. She was a heretic, a bastard and blasphemer fashioning herself as the new Virgin Mary. Alas, although the Bull had been promulgated ten years earlier, Elizabeth remained unchallenged as an English sovereign. She was an insult to God and every honest Christian.

THE QUEEN'S AVENGER

'Pope Gregory will be reinforcing her excommunication soon. He intends to issue a communique stating that anyone disposing of the imposter English Queen will be doing God's service and gaining merits with our Father in Heaven,' Henri said.

'That should mobilise many a good man across the British Isles. Many will take up arms, and gladly,' Leslie enthused, his eyes bright with elation.

'It will also make the Protestants in Scotland wary of a counter-reformist backlash. They are in charge now, with the Earl of Morton at the helm as Regent. They will close ranks around King James. It will be nigh impossible to get through them,' I pointed out.

'Leave that trifling detail to me, Father Ninian,' Esmé flashed me a self-assured grin. 'James and I are dear cousins. I'll find a way to sneak behind the old brute's back. He's no match for our blood kinship.'

'I have every confidence in you, my Lord,' I smiled, reassured. I resolved that this was the right moment to hand him Mary's letter together with her emerald ring. 'I will be obliged if you could personally deliver to King James his mother's letter written in her own hand, with this token of its authenticity. I have carried this letter for ten years, waiting for an opportunity like this. It will be of great interest to the King to learn directly from his mother what really happened to his father and who was responsible for his death. Some of the murderers are dead, and good riddance to them, but a few are still walking this earth with impunity, Morton amongst them.'

'The Queen accuses Morton in person?' Esmé snatched the letter from my hand and immersed himself in its content. He read several, most explicit sections out loud for the benefit of Leslie and Henri. I further elucidated on the confession of the Douglas complicity that I had obtained from John Binning, Archibald Douglas's servant, and the revelations imparted to me by Sir Robert Stewart, the Queen's brother.

'So Morton was art and part of the King's father's murder? That's interesting,' Henri pressed his forefinger to his lips contemplating the import of this. 'We could rid the King of the old dog, give him an excuse to dismiss him and pave the way for Esmé…'

'We could do better than that,' I suggested. 'We could have his head set up on a spike. The King will not stand for the murderer of his father to live and enjoy the fruits of his heinous crime. It's a matter of honour. Morton must die.'

'If only we had a copy of that bond Morton signed!' Henri blew out his cheeks in frustration. 'We would need nothing else. It would be impossible for him to refute Mary's accusations. Alas—'

'My Lords!' I exclaimed, a realisation dawning on me, 'There is someone who may have a copy of that bond and who has fallen out of favour with Morton. I warrant he would enjoy stabbing Morton in the back. A vile character in his own right, but he may be persuaded to testify against his former comrade. Double-dealing is something he's rather familiar with. He lives in exile, hankering to regain his lost title in Scotland.'

'Who do you have in mind, Ninian?' Leslie looked puzzled.

'Balfour. Sir James Balfour.'

The next day I was on my way to the Low Countries to meet with Balfour. He resided in an unassuming tenement overlooking the murky waters of a canal. My stomach turned and I had to swallow back bile when I stood face to face with the man who betrayed his own kin Bothwell, and the Queen herself, and lured her into captivity; the same man who had filled the vaults of Kirk o'Field with gunpowder, minded to dispatch the Queen's second husband to Kingdom come. He was a man without scruples and without conscience, once a Catholic, then a Protestant, now professing the old religion again.

I explained to him the purpose of my visit. We sat in his parlour. He dwelt on the matter for a long time, with me hanging on tenterhooks, looking out of the window at the wind tearing into the treetops and the raindrops crashing against the surface of the waterway, waiting.

'I may have kept a copy of the bond,' he uttered at long last.

'Will you produce it?'

'That will depend, Father.'

THE QUEEN'S AVENGER

'What are your terms?'

'I will require a written assurance of immunity from prosecution for my part in the—' he pursed his lips thoughtfully, '... *unfortunate enterprise*. My signature is on that bond, too.'

'I understand. This I am authorised to confer upon you on behalf of the Duc de Guise and his royal backers.'

'With all due respect, Father, your word means nothing to me. I want assurances in writing direct from your masters.'

'And you will have them,' I ground my teeth. 'Please name your price.'

'All in good time,' he gave me a mysterious look, his brow cocked and his lips pinched. 'We can discuss the details over supper. I trust you'll join me?'

I nearly choked sharing a meal with the traitor, but it had to be done. He drove a hard bargain and in the end we agreed on the price, including his immunity, unmolested return to Scotland and the restoration of his Scottish estates.

Two days later I was again on the road, back to Joinville, carrying Balfour's conditions. They were all met without quarrel and finally in the winter of the year of our Lord 1580, James Balfour travelled to Edinburgh for a pre-arranged audience with King James.

Two weeks later Morton was denounced for his part in Darnley's murder and imprisoned in Edinburgh Castle to await trial. I returned to Ratisbon to await the final outcome. There was nothing else I could do except pray for his slow and painful death, and beyond that – his eternal condemnation. I was looking forward to our paths crossing again.

In May the following year, I received a letter from Esmé informing me of Morton's imminent trial and the widely anticipated guilty verdict. James Douglas, the Earl of Morton, was already a damned man. Esmé suggested that I should start making travel arrangements if I wished to witness the spectacle of the traitor's execution. I was unable to resist.

On 2nd June in the year of our Lord 1581 I had a front row seat before a guillotine set up in the Grassmarket in Edinburgh for the public execution of the former Earl of Morton: a murderer, a traitor and an all-round scoundrel. My heart drummed triumphantly in my chest.

He was led onto the platform with his hands bound, like a common criminal. His appearance was dishevelled, bruised, broken – his once large frame shrunken to a shivering lump of bone and sinew. His face was ploughed with exhaustion, his eyes infused with fear. I drank the vision of his final defeat with relish, becoming intoxicated on it, almost airborne.

In his last heartbeat on this earth, just before he put his head down on the block, his eye caught mine. I smiled. He squinted, a trace of recognition laced with disbelief and helpless fury fleetingly crossing his face.

He remembered me – the man from a Newcastle tavern who had offered him and his comrade Ruthven a pitcher of ale spiced with the witch's draft. Ruthven's violent death must have flashed before his eyes for he recoiled and a tremor rippled through his body.

'I will see you in Hell,' I mouthed to him, still smiling.

And now, eleven years later, Ruthven, Moray, Maitland and Morton, the four Lords of the Congregation, are all dead. But so is Mary, Queen of Scots, my ward entrusted into my care by her mother at birth. She died a martyr's death.

I couldn't save her.

But I did manage to achieve the next best thing – I have avenged her.

Everything I did was to protect the God-anointed Queen of Scots against harm and the true religion against the scourge of heresy. I kept my word and I kept my Faith. It may have all been at the expense of my immortal soul, but now, standing over my grave, I can say with unwavering certainly that I would not have done anything differently, save perhaps for that one man I killed in the blind alley of Edinburgh in a moment of madness. For that, the merciful Lord will be my judge. I commend my soul to Him.

THE QUEEN'S AVENGER

PART 8

7th October 1592, Ratisbon, Bavaria

Gunther paced the chamber, contemplating his next step. His gaze wandered to the bundle of parchment filled with Father Ninian's shaky handwriting, the words undulating towards the end like disentangled wool. This was the last of the Abbot's confessions, and probably the most damning. He had died soon after he wrote it, on the same day in fact, as if, his conscience unburdened, he had finally allowed himself to let go of the past. Was there any point in raking through his sins post mortem? How would that benefit anyone?

No, Gunther shook his head, he wouldn't expose Father Ninian's transgressions. It was now between Father Ninian and the Almighty as to how the dead man's immortal soul would fare in his afterlife. But here on earth —

'So this is where you found them.'

He had not heard Father Archibald and Brother Florian enter. Gunther jumped to his feet, the chair falling behind him with a clap. On an impulse, he swiped the parchments from the desk, the loose sheets coiling in his hand. He pressed the scroll to his chest.

Father Archibald reached his hand out to him, palm out, 'I'll have this.' He pulled the scroll out of Gunther's fist, brought it closer to the light and started reading.

Gunther stared at him in silence, his heart pounding in his temples, his mind in retreat.

Brother Florian picked the chair up from the floor and sat in it, his eyes trained on Gunther. He was Father Archibald's right-hand man. He used to be a soldier, like Brother Benedict and like Gunther's father. Now he was responsible for maintaining order at the monastery and keeping the brothers safe. It was likely that Father Archibald had tasked him with finding Cornelius's killer. Instead, Florian had found Gunther.

'I didn't kill Cornelius,' Gunther protested. 'It was an accident. We struggled. He fell. But someone else – someone else smothered him.'

'I know,' Florian raised his shoulders and took in a deep breath. He blew it out slowly, his gaze gliding over the shelves and the walls behind Gunther, as if Gunther was invisible. 'You don't need to concern yourself with Cornelius. Whatever quarrel you had with him is of no interest to me now that Cornelius is with the Lord. Accidents happen.'

'But he was...' Gunther searched for the right word. 'Murdered.'

'I'm looking into it. Brother Benedict reports his findings to me, as should you.'

'Cornelius had one of these scrolls,' Gunther gestured towards the parchment in Father Archibald's hand. 'He stole it. I fear – maybe – someone killed him for it.'

'It's a possibility, yes,' Florian nodded thoughtfully. He approached Gunther and stood face to face with him, his acrid breath hitting Gunther's nostrils as he asked, 'Where is the rest of them?'

'In here,' Gunther jolted his head towards the wall. There was little point in denying any knowledge of them. 'There's a vault concealed behind the panel.'

'Well, let's get them out.'

Gunther nodded and pressed his finger against the catch hidden in the panel. It sprang open. He started removing the bundles of parchment and handing them one by one to Brother Florian who laid them on the desk. When he wasn't looking, Gunther closed his fingers around the leather pouch containing Widow Ainsley's powder. He slipped it into his sleeve. He didn't know why he did it. It was perhaps to salvage what was left of Father Ninian's reputation. Secreting a witch's draft in his belongings – a dangerous, soul-corrupting poison; a weapon the late Abbot had used at least twice in his lifetime – didn't look good for him.

'Is that all?' Florian inquired.

'That's all I found.'

'You read all of them?'

'All except the one written in Scots.'

Florian, who like Gunther was a Bavarian and couldn't read Scots, shuffled the bundles around until he came across the foreign document. 'Father Archibald will be able to decipher it.' He pushed it towards Archibald who was still deeply engrossed in the Abbot's confessions written in Latin. Gunther observed Archibald's features tighten and his face flush crimson. He clearly wasn't comfortable with what he was reading.

'Why didn't you bring them to me when you found them? Didn't you regard them important enough to report their existence?' Florian continued to question Gunther. His voice was non-threatening, almost friendly, but it had an undertone which Gunther found deeply intimidating.

'I... I, I was going to—' Gunther stammered and blushed. 'At first, I didn't know what they were, then I became caught up in them. And then I thought it might be better to leave them where they were.'

'It wasn't your decision to make,' Father Archibald averted his eyes from the parchment and looked at Gunther sternly.

'I'm sorry, Father.'

'So, Cornelius found you out and stole one of the scrolls. Just the one?'

'Yes.'

'Is there anyone else who knows about them? Anyone you may have mentioned them to?'

'No, Father. I wanted to read them first for myself before deciding what to do about them. I was curious.'

'Curiosity, huh? I suppose it was easy to give in to temptation as long as no one found you out? But God knows everything. He sees it all, Brother Gunther. You can't hide from Him.'

'I'm sorry. I was weak and stupid.'

'Never mind, we'll take care of this matter. Go to your cell. Talk to no one about it. And next time, my boy, leave decision-making to your elders.'

'Father,' Gunther bowed his head and scuttled out of the chamber.

The following week passed uneventfully with Gunther devoting himself to prayer, penitence and his daily chores. He had begun to think that the entire affair of Abbot Ninian's deathbed confessions had been consigned to the past when he was summoned to Father Archibald's office.

'In two weeks' time I am expected in Rome to receive my appointment as the next Abbot of St James's from Pope Clement.' Father Archibald propped his elbows on the desk, bound his hands under his chin and fixed Gunther with narrowed eyes.

Gunther writhed under that glare, uncertain what to say and wondering what Father Archibald really meant and how it may relate to the scrolls.

'Brother Florian is coming with me. I would like you to accompany us.'

'Me?' was the only uttering Gunther was able to make.

'Yes, you, Brother. You're a smart young man. Who knows, your future may lie in the Holy City. And besides I don't believe I have a choice,' Archibald pushed himself away from the desk and dropped his shoulders. 'I'm taking Ninian's confessions to Rome. You, as it happens, were the first clergyman to receive the late Abbot's confession, *receive* in a manner of speech, of course,' he steepled his fingers and raised his eyebrows in a commanding fashion. 'I've determined that your presence will be required when we surrender the letters to the Holy Father. We are leaving tomorrow after Mass.'

They were travelling on horseback. Father Archibald, Brother Florian and Gunther were strong and fit, and all three were experienced riders. Gunther's father, God rest his soul, had taught him to ride without a saddle when he was barely ten. At the time, his father had been a groom tending to twelve purebreds at Baron von Lintzberg's stables, and Gunther was his ostler boy.

It was mid-October: cold but dry, the tracks were firm under the horses' hooves, and the forest canopies, opulent with hues of rusty-red and gold, hung illuminated by the low-lying sun. They would cover some twenty kilometres a day, and stop for supper and rest at sideroad inns. On the fourth day however, they continued past an inviting looking travellers' lodge after sunset. There wouldn't be another one for some ten hours on horseback. Gunther was puzzled but it wasn't his place to question his elders' decision. Perhaps they knew of a place to shelter for the night further down the track.

They ventured deep into the forest. Trees had long begun blending into one another, swallowing the track before their eyes. The last few burning smudges of the red sun were fading in the treetops.

'We'll rest here for the night,' Brother Florian pulled at his horse's reins and led the way off the beaten track, his horse sidestepping gingerly down a steep slope. Gunther and Father Archibald followed, Gunther growing increasingly baffled by the choice of their night respite. The area was heavily wooded with wild beasts roaming about, hunting under the cover of darkness.

They stopped at the foot of the slope and unsaddled their horses. After the extended journey of the day, the creatures looked worn out, their heads drooping, sweat rising from their flanks.

'You remember that stream we crossed a third of a league or so up the road?' Florian pointed north. Indeed, Gunther recalled going over a brisk watercourse that was tumbling over its pebble-tiled bed. He'd been mindful for his horse not to twist its narrow ankles on the slippery surface of green rocks. He nodded.

'Let the horses rest, Gunther. Go on foot and fetch some water. We'll set a camp fire and get the supper ready.'

Fatigued though he was, as well as bruised from the four days spent in the saddle, Gunther didn't question his superior's strange order. He slung their three cowhide water sacks over his shoulder and headed north-east, determined to circumvent the steep gradient. He was hoping to find a flat route to the lower-lying part of the stream.

The night was falling fast behind him. He would have to quicken his pace if he wanted to find his way back to the camp. He was still mulling over the bizarre decision to press on into the depths of the forest instead of stopping at an inn, having their horses tended to properly and enjoying a warm bed at night when his ears pricked up to the murmur of running water.

By his reckoning he was nowhere near the stream, having covered some three hundred yards and still being slightly off course, at the bottom of the hill. Nevertheless, there seemed to be water nearby and he may not have to tread all that way uphill after all.

He followed the murmuring sound and was soon standing over a pool fed by a small waterfall cascading down the hill. Pleased with his good luck, Gunther filled the sacks and set off back to the camp.

Although the dark was now firmly set under the canopy of trees, Gunther spotted a light in the distance, firstly only a faint flicker but as he approached he could tell that it was the campfire. It was blazing fiercely. Two figures, the narrower, slightly stooped silhouette of Father Archibald and the broader, taller bulk of Brother Florian, stood close to the fire, feeding it with more fuel.

Gunther was just about to call out to them that he was back when he realised that what his companions were throwing into the flames weren't logs but scrolls of parchment.

They were burning Abbot Ninian's confessions.

Gunther dropped the water sacks on the ground and crept towards the camp. He squatted in the bushes.

'The boy has to die, Florian,' Father Archibald was saying.

'He's kept the secret so far,' Brother Florian sounded doubtful. 'Perhaps we can trust him?'

'I can't take that chance. The reputation of the old Abbot and our Scottish Monastery is at stake here. Witchcraft, murder, assassination – we'd never recover if this came out. Pope Clement, I have it on good authority, is already in two minds whether to continue funding our Order in Ratisbon. He thinks the Scottish counter-reformation cause is lost. I can't afford to give him information that will prove him right. We'll be disbanded. It won't happen. Not while I am in charge.' Father Archibald sucked air through his teeth noisily and threw another scroll into the fire.

'We could swear young Gunther to secrecy. Explain to him how important it is. He's a clever boy – he'll understand.'

'Cornelius was a clever man and look what he did – he couldn't wait to tell me about the scroll and what was in it. I simply cannot

THE QUEEN'S AVENGER

leave that one last loose end. Gunther is the only witness. I know you have a soft spot for the boy, what with you two being countrymen and your loyalties to his father, a fellow soldier, but don't forget your allegiance is to the Order.'

'I'll make it quick and painless.'

'And I will commend his soul to the Lord. We will all keep him in our prayers at the monastery. We'll say he was mauled by a bear. We were too late to save him.'

Gunther slumped on the ground, his heart ramming in his chest. They were planning to kill him. They had destroyed Ninian's letters. They didn't have the slightest intention of taking them to the Holy Father. Gunther was next to die. He couldn't comprehend why! Why hadn't they left him be? Why hadn't they let him keep the confessions secreted in the wall of the Abbot's scriptorium? That was precisely what he had intended to do in the first place: keep them away from prying eyes. He wanted nothing more than to preserve Abbot Ninian's good name!

He had to think fast. The first idea that sprang to his mind was to run. But they had led him into a trap. He was alone and on foot in a deep forest. He would soon become disoriented. They had horses and weapons. Brother Florian's long dagger flashed under his belt. A pair of pistols protruded from his saddlebags. Gunther stood little change of getting away alive.

His second thought travelled to the leather pouch tied to his belt. It was the very pouch he had concealed from Archibald and Florian – it was the pouch with the witch's draft. That was the only weapon Gunther had and it would have to do.

He crawled on his elbows and knees away from the fire, towards the spot where he had earlier dropped the waterbags. He pulled the stopper from one of them and emptied the pouch into it. He steadied his breath and put on a relaxed and unsuspecting expression. He rose to his feet, the poisoned sack hanging across his chest, with the other two over his shoulder, and walked to face his companions.

Father Archibald startled when he heard Gunther step on a dry twig that snapped under his foot. 'Oh, it's you, Brother Gunther! That was quick. We didn't expect you for a couple of hours yet.'

'I was lucky. I came across a pool. The water as clear as crystal. It tastes of berries.' He relieved himself of the two sacks on his shoulder and opened the poisoned one. 'It even smells of wild fruit. Shall I pour you some?'

'Come to think of it, I'm parched,' Brother Florian said and sheathed his dagger which he had taken out when Gunther appeared.

'No wonder,' Gunther smiled and passed the sack to Florian, 'After so many hours in the saddle without a break.'

Florian took a few deep swigs and, wiping his mouth, passed the sack back to Gunther, 'Good. Indeed, very good.'

'Oh, I've already had my fill at the pool. You, Father?' Gunther offered the sack to Archibald who accepted it and drank greedily, his throat making gulping noises.

Keeping one eye on Florian and his dagger, Gunther sat and waited. He remembered from the Abbot's account that it shouldn't be long before the Devil's potion took effect but, then again, even a split second would be long enough for Florian to cut Gunther's throat. A quick and painless death, as he had promised.

And it was quick. Florian's eyes bulged and he emitted a howl that wasn't quite human. It tore through the darkness like the talon of a wild beast. 'NOOO!'

'Brother Florian?' Archibald gawped at him, alarmed. 'Are you—'

He couldn't finish. Florian sprang into the air and, unsheathing his dagger mid-flight, flung himself at Archibald and knocked him to the ground. Landing astride him, he sliced the poor man's throat and began to stab his chest, repeatedly and manically, as he grunted and howled, and wept.

For a moment, Gunther was spellbound. He was looking at a man possessed by the Devil, doing Devil's work, his agility and inhuman strength taking Gunther's breath away. He should be crawling away to safety but he was paralysed with shock.

When there was not a dry spot left on Archibald's breast and neck, Florian's attention turned to Gunther. His mad eyes narrowed and his blood-stained teeth flashed as he shrilled and pounced at him.

THE QUEEN'S AVENGER

Florian's dagger caught Gunther's armpit and pierced his skin, before Gunther recovered his wits. He rolled onto his other shoulder, Florian's dagger wedged into the log upon which Gunther had been sitting seconds earlier. Gunther tore himself away from his shirt that was trapped under the knife and threw a punch at Florian's temple. That stunned him and he fell flat on his face, his hand however was still wrapped around the hilt of his dagger. He tried to pull it out but Gunther was upon him. And he had the advantage of being the only man standing. He grabbed a burning log from the fire and swung it at Florian back.

His cloak caught fire. Florian released his hold on the dagger and rolled onto his back to put out the flames. That was Gunther's chance. He seized the dagger and stabbed repeatedly at Florian's chest. When he was sure the man was dead, he collapsed to his knees and gave in to sobs.

He sat there weeping until dawn. The fire had died. His horse had managed to loosen its reins and came over and nudged him on the side of his head with its wet nose.

Gunther stirred. He wiped his face and looked around at the scene of the bloody carnage in the stark light of the new day. His hands had blood caked on them. A heavy, sticky stein weighed on his cowl. No one would believe him that Florian had gone mad, killed Father Archibald and tried to kill him too. There was no return to the monastery for Gunther. He had to disappear.

He went into the woods to collect logs and dry moss. He then restarted the fire until it was burning fiercely. After saying a prayer over the two bodies, he pulled them onto the pyre, Father Archibald first, and after his corpse was well engulfed by the flames, Brother Florian. He watched their flesh wrinkle and peel off the bone, their teeth emerging in two ghastly grins.

When it was done, he poured what was left of the poisoned water onto the dying flames. He dug a shallow hole in the soft, root-free soil and tossed the bones into it. He covered it with moss and white ashes. Hopefully, they would nourish a new life into being in the spring.

Gunther said a short prayer over the grave. *Requiescat in pace.* He had nothing else to add. He wasn't good with speeches and didn't believe he owed his two brethren any apologies.

He saddled the horses, mounted his and pulled the other two behind him, heading up the hill back to the track. He would sell them and then his plan was to join the Emperor's army. He now knew for certain that he did have the stomach for killing.

THE QUEEN'S AVENGER

AUTHOR'S NOTE

History is written by victors. Mary Stewart is one of history's most famous losers. Little survives of what she had to say for herself, in her own words. The notorious Casket Letters attributed to her are almost certainly forgeries by her contemporaries eager to destroy her reputation. They are difficult to verify as historians are dealing with translations of originals which no longer exist (or never existed in the first place).

There may be some hope yet in getting to the truth. I was intrigued to learn that lately Mary's coded letters had been deciphered using modern AI technologies. We may soon be able to hear from the Queen of Scots herself, in the first person. Until then, our take on her life, her rule and her legacy are subject to speculation based on unreliable and scarce primary sources.

Mary lived in the turbulent era of the Reformation and the religious wars that engulfed not only Scotland but the whole of Europe. Her defeat by the Protestant English queen, Elizabeth I, is symbolic of the suppression of Catholicsm in the British Isles and the ultimate triumph of Protestantism.

I wanted to convey Mary's story from the under-represented perspective of a defeated Catholic queen as that version of history would have been buried under layers of the victorious propaganda of her time. This led me to deploy one of her most loyal supporters in the role of her avenger.

Ninian Winzet was indeed a historical figure, but he most definitely did not commit any of the deeds I attribute to him in my book. However, I do hope that I was able to capture the extent of his righteous despair and frustration that could plausibly have led the best of men to take such drastic measures as the fictional Ninian had in my version of Mary's story.

I am indebted to several historians who painstakingly and with the greatest respect for the available primary sources explored Mary's life and the circumstances of her rise and ultimate fall. I would like to acknowledge Alison Weir (*Mary, Queen of Scots and the Murder of Lord Darnley*), Antonia Fraser (*Mary, Queen of Scots)*, John Guy (*My Life is My Own, The Life of Mary Queen of Scots*), Graham Roderick (*An Accidental Tragedy, The Life of Mary, Queen of Scots)* and Jane Wormald *(Mary, Queen of Scots)*.

My heartfelt thanks go to my husband Steve, my first reader and kind but honest critic, to my fellow writer Tim Stretton for his insightful editorial advice, and to Richard Foreman at Sharpe Books for taking the risk of publishing Mary's story told from this rather unorthodox perspective.

Finally, thank you, dear Reader, for choosing this book and for your support. I hope you enjoyed this story of betrayal, treason and revenge. If you did, please leave a review or write to me at annalegat.author@yahoo.com. I would love to hear from you.